CURRENT RIVER REDEMPTION

To Carol & Dick

by

CAROL JUNE STOVER

Carol June Stover

PublishAmerica
Baltimore

First printing

ISBN: 1-4137-3227-5
PUBLISHED BY PUBLISHAMERICA, LLLP
www.publishamerica.com
Baltimore

Printed in the United States of America

DEDICATION

I would like to dedicate this book to my husband, Frank T. Stover, for his encouragement and loving support in writing my first novel.

Acknowledgments

Thanks to my parents Lowell and Louise Gibbs and brother John Gibbs for their encouragement and to my grandmother, the late Ora Adams, who enthralled me with stories about growing up in rural Arkansas as the granddaughter of pioneer preachers. Thanks to my first readers for their patience, insights, and support: Judy Stover, Frances Stover, Dr. Lea Queener, Frances Penn. A very special thanks to Dr. Ray Granade, Director of Library Services, Ouachita Baptist Univ., Arkadelphia, AR, for not only meticulously reading my first draft, but for his input on authenticating the era, times, and religious backdrop of this novel.

Thanks to all who granted interviews and/or helped me research this book:
Ms. Kathy Buchanan, Corning Library, Corning, AR
Mrs. Ann Blankenship Carroll, Granddaughter of L. F. Blankenship, author, *Directory of Randolph County, 1910*
Ms. Pat Conley, Secretary /Clerk, Success Town Hall, Success, AR
Mr. Neil Dahlstrom, Archivist, John Deer & Company, Moline, IL
Mr. Jimmie Brooks, Mayor, Maynard, AR
Ms. Bea Hearn, Recorder/Treasurer, City Clerk, Maynard City Hall, Maynard, AR
Ms. Margaret Johnson, Historical Research Center, Univ. of Arkansas for Medical Sciences Library, Little Rock, AR
Ms. Shirley Manuel, Tuckerman Library, Tuckerman, AR
Mr. Bruce McCalley and Mr. Jay Klehfoth, Model T Ford historians, mtfca.com
Pastor Butler W. Smith, Mount Pleasant Baptist Church, Pitman, AR
Mr. Scot Stout for his transcription: *Current River Baptist Association* by Leroy Carson Tedford.

Directory of Randolph County Arkansas, L. F. Blankenship, 1910

"Such is the land we are speaking of. We do not ask you to take our word for these things. But we do ask you to come and if you could look over our land – a land that is warmed by the sun and kissed by the dew – a land that is nearly as perfect as could be desired by man –a land where famine comes not and pestilence is but a phantasm of a dream. Seeing is believing, and could you but once overlook this fair land of ours, you would exclaim: "The half has never been told.""

CHAPTER 1
REDEMPTION

Amazing Grace, how sweet the sound,
That saved a wretch like me.
I was lost but now I'm found,
Was blind but now I see.

Hot rays of sunshine beat down on Amy Blackwell as she wades into the cold rushing water. She played on these dirt-packed shores years ago, but there'll be no frolicking today.

She expected God's everlasting love to calm her, but her hands tremble and her knees shake like willow branches. *Be sweet, now—set an example. Everyone's watching.* Once again, she tries to relax, but nothing works, and she twists her hanky around and around almost into a knot. Pastor Holloway Blackwell, her very own grandfather, stands hip deep ahead impatiently beckoning, so Amy edges her bare feet along the river's rocky bottom. She had pinned her new dress tight between her legs, but its hem floats about like fish nipping at her knees the farther she wades. *Never mind your skirt now.*

Finally, when she's at her grandfather's side, the last stanza of *Amazing Grace* fades. The Pastor raises his praying hand toward the Almighty, bows his head, and solemnly begins, "Blessed Jesus…" His rhythmical praying concludes, and the Pastor intones the all-important question.

Amy has been ready for weeks, but cricket-chirps ring loud in her ears, and her head spins around. She feels strangely removed, like she's up in a pine tree looking down on the scene, certainly not smack-dab in the middle.

"Do you, Amy?" he repeats, flashing a broad smile at the worshipers gathered on shore and, then, growling in her ear through clenched teeth, "Straighten out, girl."

A rib-nudge prods Amy's affirmation at last. She snaps back into the scene.

The Pastor squeezes the handkerchief tight over her nose and lowers her until the cool river water laps over her face. Amy's slender body feels light as a feather leaning back on his arm, helpless as a newborn, solemn but silly. *This is the moment. Now Grandpa will lift me from the water and rejoice by my side for all to see.*

But, the bony hands lower Amy deeper into the depths than she expected, pinching her flesh grabbing hold. She winces in pain and her mouth flies wide open as Current River rages inside, pushing her tongue deep down into her throat. Amy springs upright at once with spastic coughs that gush forth like geysers, dousing her grandfather with green river spew.

The Pastor's face drips with the phlegm-laden water. He winks and blinks droplets trickling down from his brow, stone faced and too befuddled to speak. There's no smile, no "Praise God" for Amy. No sweet rejoicing in front of his flock. He nudges Amy toward Deacon Fitzgerald standing on shore and smiles warmly at Luella Somes wading in next to be saved. She'll, no doubt, execute her baptism perfectly and emerge fresh-faced with excitement.

Amy sloshes to shore. *Act like you haven't been such a disgrace. Hide it, just like always.* Wet corkscrew ringlets spring up all around her face, so she gives them an embarrassed pat with one hand and starts repeating John 3:16 over and over, *"...whosoever believeth in him should not perish, but have everlasting life."*

It took Amy months, even years, of contemplating salvation before this day. Years of sitting on the rock-hard pew right up front. Years of hearing her grandfather's call soar around the church rafters like angel wings, golden tones concluding each sermon. Word rolled after word, dripping like warm salve onto the lost souls of sinners. Up the aisle they'd float weeping, propelled by the Pastor's heartfelt invitations to come forward, falling into his waiting arms and vowing to seal their salvation beneath Current River's flow at the very next baptism. Today was to be Amy's turn, but not now. Salvation will surely elude her after such a catastrophe, and God will surely see through her ploy—not that she had ill intentions.

For years, Amy ached to believe as her grandfather urged, but, even as a child, she worried about the smallest of points. "How could Noah's ark *really* float on the water—crammed full of animals two by two?" Or, she'd persist, "How could a few tiny fish *really* feed multitudes?" The Bible stories defied her childish but clearheaded logic. Hoping that things might come clear with repeating, she even tried winning over her classmates at school, sitting them down on the brick steps like her Grandpa would gather a flock.

Amy's little Methodist friends wouldn't listen. Becky Wright had drawled, "My Papa says your Grandpa's just a hard-shell old preacher." The others sat there smug and unmoved as well.

Amy didn't know what "hard-shell" meant, so after awhile she had stopped explaining, blaming herself for the failing, for surely her grandfather had done all that *he* could. It was her fault alone that she couldn't figure things out or persuade. *How come things are so easy for him? How come my understanding flip-flops back and forth?* She was desperate to get things right and be baptized along with the others—it was the least she owed her Grandpa after all he had done for her and little sister Effie. After all, hadn't he taken them in?

Even *more* was at stake than repaying her grandfather's kindness, for, as her Grandma Gert reminded her daily, "Un-baptized, you'll suffer eternal damnation, young lady." She'd shake her finger almost touching her nose, "No decent young man will have you, an unsaved heathen. Never ever!" Despite the membership benefits, especially snagging a beau, Gert's urgings didn't bear fruit.

Amy struggled with the predicament for ages it seemed, until, finally, she had the solution one day. She rethought redemption, reasoning, *I don't have faith now, but maybe I'll see the light down the road—just like Grandpa does clearly.* It made perfect sense. She'd *grow* into God's grace, but she'd keep the pact a secret between her and the Lord. If the plan didn't work or things got worse at home, she'd just run away, but that seemed so scary. *"No,"* Amy figured, *"this is a much better plan: baptism now, understanding later."*

Still, Amy hoped for a sign of God's approval—any sign would do—like a visit from an angel, or a burning bush or something. However, as baptism day approached, no sign appeared one way or the other; so she took this as a sign, of sorts, too. She marked the date carefully in her Bible: Saturday, *April 5, 1917–My Current River Redemption.*

Amy sloshes toward shore. Even with nerves jangling, she marvels at the river's mesmerizing beauty—not that the river doesn't have dark stories to tell. Take Sister Ethel's dunking last spring. Blinded by the green water's thick silt, she'd walked out the wrong direction, stepped into a hole, and was lost before God or anyone else could save her. Then, there was old Brother Luke who cried "Hallelujah" to excess, his heart gave out, and he sank to the river's bottom on that lovely fall morn. Of course, there's always the dreaded spring flooding. But Amy wasn't thinking of such distractions today. Indeed, she'd waded into the river with hopes high for salvation, or at least one step toward redemption—whichever God chose. That was before gagging. Now it's all ruined.

Wading out is agonizingly slow. The water weighs down her legs, and she wobbles like a high wire walker with nothing to grab hold of. She scolds herself, *Better not slow down Grandpa's service.* At last, she reaches the shore and dries her face with the towel that Deacon Fitzgerald extends. Little sister Effie and Grandma Gert stand there singing "Gracious Savior" along with the others, Gert's loud alto prevailing. Amy nudges in beside thirteen-year-old Effie who stifles a giggle.

Amy'd love to go hide by the trees, but that won't do. There are three more to baptize, and she always helps out at the end. Today is no different, newly baptized, or not. A thought flashes through her mind, *After such a disgrace, I'll have no choice but to leave.* She shivers at the notion and then realizes, *But what about Effie?* So, Amy stays put in her dripping wet dress, singing along while she plots a new getaway, this one dragging Effie along.

Amy and Effie are first to reach the wagon after their Grandpa's service. Their arms are loaded down with damp towels and hymnals. Grandma Gert lags behind and the Pastor holds court with his deacons walking along.

Effie blurts out, "Good golly, Amy! Why did you spit river water all over Grandpa? I'll bet you really *get it* back home!"

"I nearly drowned!" Amy whispers, still embarrassed.

"Aw, pshaw. Just a little water, that's all, Amy. Weren't nothin'."

"It *wasn't anything,*" Amy whispers frantically as their grandfather approaches, "Do you want Grandpa to hear you talking like a farm hand?"

"Hush up, Amy. I talk just fine," Effie mocks back.

Amy shifts into the bright sunlight at the back of the wagon until they all climb aboard. Grandpa Blackwell sits tall on the bench, paying no mind to his wet Preacher's garb, and Grandma Gert perches alongside him, a commanding presence as always.

The metal-rimmed wheels churn up gravel chunks on the road, and the sisters are lulled by the "clop clop" of the horse's hooves. In no time, Effie's head drops onto Amy's soft lap, and it stays there all the way home and rounding the bend heading up to their house. The sassy horses pull hard to reach the cool of their barn, and Amy's thoughts race ahead, *Grandpa didn't say one word the whole ride home. Maybe it wasn't such a transgression. Maybe he won't be so cross.*

The Pastor halts the wagon by the gravel path that leads up to the house. He unhitches the horses and quickly heads up with his wife following closely behind.

Amy nudges Effie off of her lap, climbs out of the wagon, and points her groggy sister up the path, too. Then, Amy heads for the wash tubs in back. She's half finished rinsing sandy towels under pump water when she spots her grandfather walking across the lawn toward her. She freezes in place.

Holloway Blackwell is a lean, six-foot-tall, good-looking man of 65 years with a wide, square jaw and craggy, dry lines etched up to his cheek bones that makes him all the more handsome. He combs his wavy, gray hair back on both sides—a full head and still nice and thick. His presence makes men stand up straighter, wives smile warmly and young daughters run up in delight. Most church leaders around Pitman are called "Brother" so and so, but Holloway Blackwell inspires "Pastor" out of respect, just like at big city churches. Nonetheless, the man is oblivious to his charisma, remaining focused on his true mission—bringing sinners to Christ. No place is too destitute for him to pursue a lost soul or to tromp out the devil.

Just like his father before, the legendary Pastor J. B. Blackwell who hacked through Tennessee woods into Arkansas, Holloway Blackwell's mission is devout. He heard God's call at the age of six years, and, by the age of ten, he stood at the pulpit next to J. B. winning converts with his cute little prayers. Yes, he spends his life serving the Lord, reaping the blessings and enjoying the challenges—but *nothing* is quite as challenging as his young granddaughter Amy. In the Pastor's view, she's turning out to be just like her absent father, Buck—independent, doubting, and even harder to persuade. Or maybe, it's just that women and even girls seem to confuse him.

Amy lowers her head as her grandfather approaches. He has changed into work clothes and stands peering down.

"Today is a very special day for you, Amy," the Pastor intones.

"Yes sir," Amy nods.

Her Grandpa is wearing his most solemn look—the look she first saw when she and Effie arrived in Pitman on that cold winter day, when the Pastor instructed, "Now, girls, you must be brave. Your Mama's with our Lord up in heaven, and she wants you to be 'sunbeams,' bright shining sunbeams for God here on earth."

Little six-year-old Amy nodded back then, "Yes, Grandpa. I'll be a sunbeam."

"Good girl," he had smiled, patting her head, beaming the broad smile that washed her in warmth, a feeling she never forgot and (though she hates to admit it) she has never stopped craving.

At first, six-year-old Amy was so excited about her mission that she held her head a little bit higher, minded her grandparents better, and was much nicer to Effie. She tried so hard to please her mother in heaven, not to mention her grandfather on earth—and she definitely wanted to please *him*. Just walking along the streets of Pitman with him was exciting. Townsfolk strolled over so friendly, and they'd bend down to Amy, tickling under her chin, "How pretty you are, Miss Amy," and she'd proudly reply, "I'm a sunbeam for God!" Her Grandpa beamed with approval, thrilling her like nothing else could—except if her daddy returned.

However, as years wore on, the task of being so good was impossible to bear, and Amy began to wonder what "good" meant anyway. Her Grandpa's religion enfolded her like a tight linen shroud until she couldn't gasp fresh air or ever feel worthy. So, eventually, Amy evolved a new way to survive, replacing his tight shroud with a non-thinking blankness. It wasn't perfect, but it worked most of the time.

Amy stands next to the washtubs longing to explain, "About this morning down at Current River, Grandpa, it wasn't a folly. You grabbed me so tight." Yet, her tongue is still as her blank shroud enfolds, and she nods the dutiful nod that confirms, "Yes, I'm still a sunbeam."

The Pastor pats her on the head and gazes deep into her eyes—until his own eyes fill with that all-too-familiar glow.

"Must I?" Amy asks.

"It'll put things right with God for today," he replies.

He marches Amy swiftly around back of the house, swings the door open, and closes it firmly behind as she descends down the old wooden steps.

Amy weeps alone in the fruit cellar's blackness.

The Pastor locks the fruit cellar door and saunters around to the front of his prim little house. Its black shingle roof runs crisp along the white wooden clapboards and wide windows gleam upstairs and down. It looks so cozy and snug from the outside, somehow—a fine refuge for his old age. He maintains the place in apple-pie order with his exemplary carpentry skills, consigning Grandma Gert to her kitchen and garden, a magnificent patch that consumes the back yard. Come summer, he'll count row upon row of her fine corn towering above vines hanging heavy with fat red tomatoes. His mouth will water for the bounty that'll grace his dinner platters clear though August— maybe even September.

His wife starts all plants from seed, and everything the woman harvests is bigger, brighter and juicier than anyone else's around. Year after year, her fuzzy green okra sways in the breeze, and her bright orange carrots, sweet onions, starchy white potatoes, and fat turnips burrow deep in the Arkansas soil. What's more, Gert's lush patch of lilies runs the full length of the smokehouse, displaying lovely white funnels ready for church weddings or funerals. Their fragrant white blooms are the envy of neighbors. Gert never hesitates to brag, "The Lord watches over my lilies. They're quite divine." None of them doubt it, not even the Pastor.

The Pastor mounts the wide wooden steps and strides swiftly across the front porch. The spindle screen door snaps hard on its spring, the old porch swing vibrates, and a pillow tumbles onto the floor. "That screen door could wake the dead," he mutters, mentally adding the repair to his list and tossing the pillow back up onto the swing. He heads for the solitude of the front parlor he commands as his study, the one place he can sit in peace these days, sunlight streaming in through the window, God's blessed rays.

For eight months of the year, Pastor Blackwell teaches in Pitman's one room brick schoolhouse, and the term has just ended. It's a noble calling, a true mark of status in these parts. Nonetheless, he prefers his ministry work with a passion. Pleasant Hill Church ordained him in 1884, just as they had his late father twenty years before. Year in and year out, he leads Sunday services, holds prayer meetings, sponsors revivals under big tents in town, and feasts at countless church suppers, causing his wife, Gert, to whine, "Can't you rest a little this week, Pastor? Even the Lord rested up on the seventh day!"

His answer is always the same, "Misses, you know good and well that Pleasant Hill can't afford paying me four Sundays a month. I must go about adding more time." So, he travels dirt roads to Mud Creek, Siloam, and Poyner on alternate weeks and even up to churches in Union, Missouri.

Holloway Blackwell's father was self-taught, but he insisted on his son taking more schooling. Accordingly, Holloway went to common school, but he also poured through books hour after hour at home. He even sat faithfully alongside his father as men of law, politicians, and even scoundrels stopped by for counsel, all preferring the Pastor's calm mediation to the Arkansas court's heartless bureaucracy. The lessons that young Holloway learned far exceeded any that a school could provide. Furthermore, it's acknowledged that he, just like his father before, has the sharpest mind in all of Randolph County—not to mention the best library around. His books cram inside Arkansas pine hutches that he built by himself. Christian brothers seek out solace in the room packed with knowledge that they'll never possess, showing up on the Pastor's doorstep year round. He prays with them over their sins and, these days, he prays hard again that the nation prevails in the horrid war just declared. Grief and commiseration are his constant companions, and, on a very good day, there's some joy.

The Pastor sits down in his favorite chair behind his desk, its brown leather worn like a soft, rippley glove. It's the time of day that he customarily reads his Bible and prays, but today something troubles his soul, so he stares out the window and muses, "Amy's baptism didn't go right, and she didn't have that newly-saved sparkle." Also, he just noted out there in the yard that her blank look persists. He has seen it so often in Amy's eyes—that nothingness where joy should be dancing. It's no secret that she questioned the scriptures from the time she was little, but he thought that was all settled.

He can still picture little curly-headed Amy sitting wide-eyed on her pew, awestruck by his calls for sinners to come up and repent. She heard them so often that she could have, no doubt, recited them herself, but she never marched up the aisle. He'd ask her why not, and she was truthful about doubts that stifled her faith like water dousing a flame. The Pastor listened as her childhood questions turn into teenage debate that made her Sunday school teachers sputter and the entire class laugh. Still, Amy remained unmoved and unsaved, planted on her pew like a cold Arkansas rock.

Thinking it over now, he's pretty sure what had troubled Amy the most—yes, that must be it, for, the older she grew, she kept asking the very same question: "Grandpa, why can't my nice friends get into heaven—why only Baptists believing like your Pleasant Hill flock?" *Why couldn't she see it?* He was determined to get through, but he always lacked the patience for Amy that he had in his pulpit.

Ironically, the Pastor remembers questioning the same thing when he was

16

young, too. In fact, he used nearly the same words as Amy, and he can still feel his cheek stinging with his father's reply. Right after that, he saw the light and ran up the aisle to answer God's call. The Pastor realizes something else, too, thinking it odd that, after all of these years, he'd just notice—Amy has the same glazed-over look that her father had growing up. Indeed, try as he might, the Pastor never saved young Buck's soul, a fact that still turns him inside out with regret. *It's not too late to win over Amy. I'll not make the same mistakes that I made with my son.*

Amy shivers on her crate praying for grace in the root cellar. The moist air hangs thick with potato and turnip, and the dirt floor chills her feet through her shoes. Grandpa calls it "deep prayer," just like his father before, but it feels more like penance. She dares not refuse. Ironically, it was just inches from the cellar door that she first questioned the faith—soon after she and Effie moved in with their grandfather.

The incident started out like an exciting adventure. They were playing rag dolls on the porch one Saturday morning, their favorite pastime. Grandpa was hitching up the wagon for his weekly trek into town, and Grandma Gert called out, "Don't forget, Pastor—get me a chicken to fry up for supper." He waived six-year-old Amy and four-year-old Effie down off the porch, and they quickly scrambled into the wagon for their first ride to Hamm's General Store.

"Look at all the food. Can we pick out something, Grandpa?" the little girls begged when they arrived. Scarce tins of peaches sat beside bins of unpolished rice, rolled oats and salt. School notebooks and pencils spilled over onto black ribbed cotton hose and apparel shipped down from St. Louis. Feed sacks and wooden barrels were stacked two deep around on the floor, and the girls rolled their eyes at the bounty, enjoying aromas of smoked hams mixed with ginger cookies and peppermint drops. There wasn't anything like this where they lived before their mama's accident. "What can we have, Grandpa?" they begged, once again.

"I'm just here for these few things today, girls," he replied, measuring out lard from the hogshead barrel and flour into a can on the counter. Then, this being their first time to the store, he relented. "All right, choose a cinnamon stick apiece from the jar next to the scale—only one!"

Amy and Effie trotted up front, happy as two little larks.

"Them coffee beans just came in today, Pastor Blackwell, nice and fresh," Mr. Hamm flashed his engaging gap-tooth grin. The two chatted on a bit about crops, the weather, and news from St. Louis. Then, the Pastor headed out toward the wagon, the sisters skipping behind. The next stop was not far down the road at Mr. Cobb's old weathered brown house. The Pastor hitched up the wagon and disappeared inside, reappearing moments later bobbing up and down at the waist, calling out all the way back to the wagon, "Thank you, Brother Cobb, thank you so much." He now clutched a large burlap bag that gyrated wildly from side to side.

Effie and Amy asked, giggling from the back of the wagon, "What's that in the sack, Grandpa?"

"It's just a chicken," the Pastor drawled, hoisting up the wriggling bag like it was nothing that special at all.

Once home, Amy and Effie resumed playing dolls on the front porch when, without warning, a loud screech pierced the afternoon air. The girls leaped down and raced around back just in time to see their Grandpa, bloody axe in hand, standing transfixed by a headless chicken running wildly about the yard. Around and around it silently sprinted, amid Grandma Gert's tomato vines and out again through the corn. Finally, the poor headless foul dropped dead next to the okra.

"You killed the little chicken!" Amy yelled.

Effie stood wailing next to her big sister, "You killed him dead, Grandpa!"

The Pastor twirled around, his first impulse to laugh at the girls' clueless horror. Then, realizing their deep distress, he knelt down to explain, "You see, Brother Cobb gave this chicken to me for his church tithing. It's his way to contribute."

"You killed it! Now he has no head!" Amy cried.

"Well, Brother Cobb intended it for food, and the Good Lord says that's all right," the Pastor tried reasoning.

"The Lord says it's all right to kill chickens like that?" Amy sniffled.

The Pastor offered, "Yes, it's all right because God provides them for our sustenance."

"But if they're dead, then they can't lay any eggs and hatch little baby chicks! Not if they're dead with no head!" Amy protested.

Little Effie wasn't buying it either. "That's right," she sobbed, "no little baby chickies." Huge tears ran down her sweet face, gluing her long blonde curls to her wet apple cheeks.

The Pastor thought fast, "It's truly all right, girls. It says in the Bible...." He paused again, wishing he'd wrung the creature's skinny neck before it let out that screech. His patience was gone. He stood up shaking his head and muttering as he stormed over to the okra patch, "Tiny-tot sermons are best left to the Sunday school teachers." He snatched the dead chicken up by its gangly neck, scooped its googley-eyed head up in his other hand, and marched into the house with his kill, leaving the girls all alone in the yard.

Amy and Effie sniffled all the way back around to the front porch. Amy tried to remember how her mama used to comfort little Effie, but nothing came to mind, so she thought up, "Grandpa knows all about God, Effie. I guess it's all right." However, the seeds of her doubt were already sown, and, now that she's almost grown, they still thrive, even fester.

Amy can't stop shivering in the smelly dank root cellar. She should be praying, but the religious contradictions pester instead, nagging doubts that she desperately tries pushing aside. "Anyway," she whispers, "why dwell on them now? For better or worse, my baptism is over." Now another issue pops into her head—not nearly as weighty as redemption, and, in fact, she feels ashamed attaching much importance to it at all. But, after all, Grandma Gert had brought the matter up herself months ago, *Now that I'm a proper church member, I wonder, will Grandma Gert permit me a beau?*

Most of the other girls at church her age have a special boy friend, all except for Amy. She never wanted one, either, until that nice looking fellow showed up at church several months back. She'll never forget it. She was busily collecting hymnals off of the pews after services. Just as she reached the last pew, the books shifted in her arms, and one hit the floor. Bending down to retrieve it, several more crashed down, and Amy gasped, "Oh, no!" most annoyed with herself. She was crouching on the old wooden floor retrieving the books when a young man walked over and offered, "May I help you, Miss?" Amy looked up into the bluest eyes and friendly smile that she had ever seen in her life. Her heart definitely stopped for a minute, she later recalled.

Amy nodded as the stranger crouched down to help gather books, too. When they completed the task, they stood up in unison—embarrassingly close. Amy's face flushed, but the tall stranger didn't step back, not one inch. He kept right on smiling and looking down into her eyes. He was about to speak when someone called out from the door, "Ready to go, now." Amy recognized the caller, but he hardly ever showed up on Sunday and was, pretty much, a stranger to her. The young man half whispered before rushing off, "Hope to meet again someday, Miss. I'm Ernest Lee." Amy stood there dumbfounded as he disappeared down the aisle and out the church door.

After that, Amy couldn't get the young man out of her mind, and she prayed for weeks and weeks that he'd return to Pleasant Hill Baptist church. In fact, she'd almost given up hope when she saw him walk into last month's Sunday service and sit down in the very last row. Amy thought he looked at her sitting up front, but she couldn't be sure, so, after the last hymn, she peeked around to spot where he was. He looked right back, giving a friendly smile before rising to walk out with his friend.

Just the thought of the fellow named "Ernest Lee" wards off the root cellar's chill. Amy's mind starts to drift, *We're sitting in rockers in front of a fireplace, peacefully rocking, looking into each others eyes, holding hands, and now Ernest Lee is standing alongside me, very close, stroking my hair, and now ....*

Grandpa Blackwell bangs hard on the root cellar door. It has been precisely one hour, and deep prayer time is over. He assures Amy as she exits the cellar, "You'll be stronger for it, girl."

"Yes, sir," she whispers in passing, head bowed, wondering if she'll have to serve more time later.

Amy enters the house through the kitchen and climbs the steep stairs to the bedrooms. She shares the tiny room at the top with Effie. It's one of three rooms upstairs. Grandma Gert and Grandpa have the bigger room in front overlooking the church and the other was their father's growing up that they now call the "spare bedroom" and use it for sewing and storage.

Amy enters the bedroom, closes the door, and carefully raises her white cotton dress up over her head so the stitches won't pull. She made the dress herself just a few weeks ago. Sewing quiets her mind and brings back fond memories of sitting alongside her mother, little fingers playing with scraps like she was sewing, too. She hangs her new dress in the chiffarobe and reaches in for the other—a blue day dress with a well-worn apron that ties in the back.

Effie clamors up the stairs and into the room, chattering on as usual, oblivious to Amy's quiet reflection. She flops down on her skinny bed that sits parallel next to Amy's.

Amy isn't jealous of her younger sister—that would be sinful, however, she can't help but note how Effie's blonde curls spill so pretty over her shoulders, how her bright blue eyes shine and how they're rimmed with gorgeous dark lashes. And, Effie's voice is soft like a breeze, and, when she wants to, she can be a real little lady. Amy imagines that her own voice must sound harsh by comparison. Yes, Effie has beauty and charm, making Amy despise her own homely plainness. However, her little sister does have one trait that Amy finds most annoying—Effie talks all the time.

Effie pesters, "What took you so long coming in?"

"Root cellar."

"Oh, golly," Effie winces, and then just as fast, she brightens, "Can I have your new dress some day? Can I?"

"Probably. You get everything I hand down, don't you, Effie?"

Amy worked hard on the dress, stitching it together from a handmade pattern that she cut out of feed sacks. Months ago, she rode with Grandpa to the general store making sure that he didn't buy feed in the ugly brown muslin sacks. She begged him to choose the pretty sacks with the rosebud pattern she wanted and three just alike, enough for a dress and hair ribbon to match. After what seemed like ages, the feed sacks were finally empty, but they had a foul, mealy smell. So, Amy washed them in sweet brook water and dried them nice and flat in the sun. To her, the bright fabric is as pretty as any Mr. Hamm has in his store. Her pretty new dress will, no doubt, be Effie's some day.

"Are you wearing your new dress to the Church picnic tomorrow?" Effie pesters.

"Maybe," Amy says, though she really hasn't thought much about it. She truly forgot. The same people always show up and they'll ask the same questions, "What will you do now that you've finished up school, Miss Amy? What will you do in the fall?" She knows what is expected—Grandpa made it clear. "You'll be a big help to me now," he had said, expecting her to stay home in Pitman. Who else will help keep his church records on those paper charts?

Amy truly admires her grandfather's better traits—he's such an upstanding citizen, so honest and godly. Nonetheless, she hates toiling over his church work, no matter how noble the cause, and then there are the family chores, too. Even with such a small barnyard, they keep workhorses, a few cows, laying hens, and an occasional goat, their care and feeding falling mostly to Amy. Not to mention that, Grandma Gert has her digging in the hot garden these days, never admitting that she's any help, but enjoying the fruits of her toil, nonetheless.

"Amy, haul these turnips over to the root cellar," Grandma Gert orders each harvest. Amy heaps the fat purple and white tubers into the wooden wheelbarrow that Grandpa built from a bicycle wheel and scrap lumber stored in the barn. The wheel wobbles all the way up the hill, and Amy struggles to reach the dreaded root cellar before it tips to one side. Then, Grandma Gert calls her for afternoon chores, until its time to help out with their evening meal.

Year round, Effie is no help with the outside chores. With Grandma Gert's blessing, she begs off from laborious tasks, with a preference for working indoors. No amount of begging can move Effie out of the house and into the garden or barn. Sometimes, Amy leans on the end of her hoe, dreaming of being on her own and teaching school like her Grandpa one day.

Grandma Gert shouts such dreams right out of her head, "Get busy, young lady. That hoe won't dig dirt by itself!"

Effie sprawls out on her bed, persisting with unending questions, "When will you know if you're going to the picnic tomorrow, Amy." Then, she sits up wide-eyed at the thought, "Who'll I be with if you don't come?"

Amy reassures, "Don't worry, you'll find plenty of others to play with—anyway, Grandpa will make sure that I'm over there, just like always."

Now Effie wants to know, "What was it like under the river water, Amy? Could you see any fish?"

"Of course not," Amy scoffs.

"Well, are you good and baptized? I mean, do you feel happy inside like they say? Are you saved?" Effie persists.

"I'm as saved as I'll ever be," Amy says, not answering exactly, nor explaining her homemade plan of salvation. Besides, she doesn't know yet if her baptism "took."

"Were you a sinner, Amy?"

"Yes, I guess I was," Amy frowns.

"How did you know it?" Effie asks.

"I'm not sure. The Bible says evil lurks in our hearts—like that time when we threw acorns at old Mrs. Isay years back. That was a sin."

Effie is puzzled, "Golly, we didn't know it was wrong at the time. So, why was it a sin?"

"Why do I have to have all the answers, you pesky pest?" Amy chides.

"Because you're the oldest," Effie's brow furrows.

"I may be the oldest, but I don't have answers all of the time, Eff." Amy hopes her sister will move off of the serious subjects.

Effie goes right along, "Do you think our Daddy's up in heaven with Mama?"

"Whatever made you bring that up now?" Amy pauses. Now she feels guilty. She shouldn't be so impatient with Effie, especially remembering what her mama had asked just before she had died, "Always look after your little sister, Amy. I'm counting on you."

22

Amy puts her hand on Effie's shoulder, "Daddy will come back some day. I'm sure that he will."

"How do you know?" Effie squinches up her nose.

"I just have the feeling," Amy replies, knowing full well that it's not the whole story. She remembers what happened the day before he left, and it comes back to haunt her—wondering if *she* was the reason. Not that she was so disobedient, but, still, maybe what she did, drove him away. She can still smell the spring rain and the ground soft with brown mud, the kind she loved to squish between her six-year-old toes. He forbade her to walk in the muck, but, playing in it was so much fun that she disregarded her father's instruction. He was very cross and sent her to bed that night without supper. She always wondered later, did that make him leave the next morning? Now that she's older, she realizes it didn't. But maybe it was something else that she did—something forgotten a long time ago. The thought has troubled her for years. Her daddy had assured her that he'd come back for them both, but he never returned. Now, Amy wonders if he ever will. Still, she reasons, *Why dash Effie's hope all to bits?*

Amy blurts out, "Eff, what if we lit out from here and tried to find Daddy some day?"

"Where would we go?" Effie says, eyes bugging out.

"It was just an idea," Amy backs off. *The idea of leaving feels so good inside, but it's foolish to think I can drag Effie along.* She drops the thought from her mind. "Now let's scoot—I've got to get dressed and do my chores, Eff. We'll talk more tonight."

Amy pulls her blue cotton dress down over her homespun slip. She walks over to the pine chest and stares into the streaked mirror hanging above. Amy groans.

"What's the matter?" Effie rolls over on her bed.

"I wish I looked like those newspaper ladies—those St. Louis ladies at Liberty Teas with their pretty hairstyles and feather trimmed hats."

"Me too!" drawls Effie.

"And, oh, their daughters all decked out in those wide-collared dresses with matching hair bows. I'd cherish one of those fine dresses," Amy closes her eyes, trying to imagine.

Folks tell Amy that she's pretty as a picture herself, and they mean it sincerely, but Amy knows better. She pokes her face closer up to the mirror. *Look at me. Plain looking with mousy brown curls around my face and straggly curls hanging down in back. No wonder I don't have a beau.*

Effie says softly, "I think you look mighty pretty, Amy."

Amy pats a wayward curl. "Thanks, Eff," she whispers, smiling weakly on her way out the door. She descends down the stairs slowly and tiptoes on the last step by the parlor, walking by quickly before the Pastor looks up.

Effie feels lonelier than ever as Amy disappears out the door. At thirteen, she's almost finished with common school but has no true friends at all. The older her big sister gets, the lonelier Effie feels. They used to spend time together, chattering on about this and that, or playing house at the oak tree alongside the brook. They'd pretend that its root nooks were magical rooms, and that patches of moss were fluffy green rugs. Flat heads of Queen Ann's Lace became pretty round tables with acorns for little seats all around. Every day they'd recreate the rooms, making new furniture from the brook side debris. Little Effie would say, "Let's play like Mama's alive and that Daddy came back, and we're all living together."

"Oh yes, and let's play like it's time to set Mama's dinner table," Amy pretended back.

Effie also remembers that dreadful day down at the brook after they'd lived there barely two years—she was six and Amy was eight. They had just romped out through the kitchen door after lunch, heading to the brook to play house, when Grandma Gert handed each one a bucket, instructing, "Fetch me some fresh brook water, girls—and behave down there, or I'll have the ghosts come to get y'all."

The girls never knew what to make of such silly threats, "That's just Grandma Gert's way of kidding, I suppose," Amy would say.

Effie complained all the way down the hill, "Our chores never end. This bucket's so heavy," and on and on.

Reaching the brook, they soon forgot all about Grandma Gert's water, and hours went by. They were so engrossed with their tree rooms that they barely heard steps on the other side of the brook—someone walking down to fill their own bucket from the babbling stream. It was poor widow Isay, the recluse that lived on the hillside above. Neighbors checked on her in bad weather and brought food, but they respected her quiet ways back in the woods. Amy and Effie had never laid eyes on her before.

"Amy, look at that sorry sight," Effie pointed toward the hunched over old woman. Mrs. Isay's scraggly gray hair was tied up with cloth strips in long braids on top of her head, her dress was a mass of patches sewn over worn holes, and her skin was pale as chalk dust.

"A ghost, a ghost, a ghost," Amy and Effie chanted. Pretty soon they picked up acorns and tossed them in the old woman's direction, making up a silly ghost song all the while: "Creepy, Creepy-Booo, Booo, Booo. It's a Ghost, Ghost-Wooo, Wooo, Wooo." The acorns splashed in the water, startling the poor old woman as she turned away back into the woods and started up the hill. Just when their giddy chant grew the loudest, a menacing shadow fell between the girls as their grandfather approached from behind. He had witnessed their shameful display and there was no mistaking his anger.

Brow furrowed and speaking in harsh, measured tones, Pastor Blackwell had asked, "Amy, Effie. What does the Golden Rule teach us?"

"Do unto others as you would have them do unto you, Grandpa," the girls had mumbled in unison.

"Right," he growled with lips stretched tight over his teeth. "Now get up that hill to your room. The very idea of throwing acorns at anyone, especially that poor, lonely old woman." Then he warned sternly, "If I ever see this sinful behavior again, you'll pray in the root cellar every day for a week."

Lying on their beds, staring up at the ceiling that night, little Effie had whispered, "Was Mrs. Isay the ghost that Grandma Gert sent to scare us, Amy?"

"Of course not. No such thing," Amy had whispered back.

"Well, she sure did look like one. We were only funning her. Was that truly a sin, Amy?"

"There's no such word as *'funnin,'* Effie! Anyway, even if it was fun for us, if it's not fun for all, then it's not right with God, I guess. It probably says so in the Bible somewhere. We'll have to do better next time," Amy had nodded.

The very next Sunday, all during his sermon, "Kindness and Charitable Acts," Pastor Blackwell glared directly down from his pulpit at his granddaughters perched on the first pew.

His message was not lost on Amy. On Monday morning, when their Grandpa strode out of the kitchen and onto the back porch, Amy had asked, "Is that food basket you're carrying for old Mrs. Isay?"

"Yes, for Mrs. Isay," he nodded.

"We'll take it to her, Grandpa," Amy said, reaching out.

Gert had yelled, "You're not intending to let them go near that crazy woman's cabin, are you Pastor?"

The Pastor had replied, handing over the basket, "Oh, there's no harm to her, Misses. You can't listen to rumors. We should encourage the girls to do good."

Amy led Effie outside by the hand. It seemed only right that they deliver Mrs. Isay's food to make up for their sinful disrespect. So, for weeks to come, the penitent sisters took over the chore, walking down the hill and through the woods, across the brook, and up the hill again with Mrs. Isay's food baskets, setting them down on the cabin porch, but never once laying eyes on her again.

On the way over to the old woman's cabin, many weeks later, Effie had asked hopefully, "Do you think God forgives us by now, Amy?"

"Doesn't matter. We'll still take the old woman her food," Amy had replied.

"Why doesn't it matter?" Effie had asked.

"Cause God's still looking down to make sure we stay good. He has his eyes on you every minute, you know." Amy didn't say so, but she also wondered if, somehow, her father magically knew about their good deed, as well. Maybe he'd come back if he did.

"I guess we'll keep taking the baskets to her, then," Effie had sighed as they trudged up the hill toward Mrs. Isay's cabin, a ritual they continue to this day.

Effie's eyes fill with tears just thinking back on those years. She sits all alone on her bed, and she pines, *I feel so much safer with Amy around. Now things are changing, and I'll have to fend for myself.* Effie can picture her father's warm smile, she can still hear him laugh, and she remembers how handsome he was. Amy says he looked like their Grandpa with wavy hair and blue eyes—and she can tell that it's true from that picture in the spare room—the only photograph picture they have of their father. Yes, her daddy was a loving man, but why did he leave her?

Effie's thoughts jumble together and things start to turn dark, *I'm all alone with what I'm trying to forget—the bad things about how Mama died. I shouldn't have done it.* She shivers uncontrollably. *If Amy could be with me more, my bad thoughts would vanish.* The dark memories that haunt Effie at night time are creeping into daylight now, but no one will know, because she'll never tell. She reaches for the tattered rag doll that her mother made years ago with a red gingham apron cut from her own apron scraps. The doll's apron is wrinkled and frayed now, and her yarn hair is gone. Effie cradles the helpless doll fragment as tears roll down her cheek. She can't stop them.

Amy is outside the kitchen when she remembers the locket that she left upstairs. Her mother gave it to her just before she passed away, and she misses her mama more than ever today. *Things would have been different if Mama was down there at the river. She would have had a sweet hug for me by the water's edge and put her arms around me. Nothing bad ever happened with mama around.* Amy tries not to think about such warm things.

Effie hears her sister mounting the steep stairs. She sits straight up in bed and scrambles over to the window to stand looking out as Amy walks in.

Amy sees and rushes right over, "Effie, what has you so upset?"

"Nothing," Effie sniffles.

"It must be something. I can tell that you're crying," Amy coaxes.

"It's just—well sometimes I get so lonely, and I miss Mama and Daddy. I'm afraid I'll forget them."

"I know. Me too," Amy says, and then, trying to cheer her sister, she adds "We still have each other. Right?"

Effie is silent.

Amy coaxes again, "I know it's not the same without them, but I'm always here for you. Right?" Amy repeats.

Effie stands mute with her head hanging low. Finally she rasps, twisting her skirt around in her fingers, "We used to play more—you and me."

Amy hugs her little sister and whispers, "I know it." She walks over to the bureau, reaches into the top drawer, and gently lifts out the glistening metal chain with its little heart dangling down from the center. It's not real gold, but it's all that she has of her mother's, and it is precious beyond telling. She holds the locket out to her sister.

"What is this for?" Effie asks.

"It's for you," Amy smiles.

"Mama gave *you* the locket. It's yours as the oldest," Effie protests.

"Yes, Mama wanted me to have it, but I'm certain that she'd want you to have it now, Eff. I'm called away for chores more and more, and, it's true— I leave you alone frightfully long. No wonder you're sad. Whenever that happens, Effie, I want you to grab hold of the locket and think of Mama and me. That way, we'll both be with you, and you won't feel so alone."

Effie trembles reaching out for the little heart that sparkles in sunlight sifting in through the window. She pulls the thin chain carefully over her head, and she desperately prays, *Please God, let Mama's locket take my bad thoughts away.*

Amy hugs her sister again. Effie feels so helpless and small in her arms.

CHAPTER 2
SWEET AMY

The six o'clock train from Hoxie howls along in the distance—folks set timepieces by it all over town. April's only half over, but the porch thermometer boils up to nearly eighty degrees. Grandma Gert hovers over her old wood stove in the kitchen, throwing thick slabs of bacon into a big iron skillet—the very same pan that cooked "vittles for our brave Civil War soldiers," but then the Boswell women tell that story about *every* pot and pan passed along. "It means nothing to me," the Pastor's wife always says, "It's just an ugly ole' black skillet, for all that I care."

Gert is a short, stout woman, freshly starched and ironed, and, as far as anyone can tell, she never perspires. Her hair is pulled back in a bun, a style that accentuates her facial features, most memorably her nose. Actually, its average size, but her nostrils flare out like a bull set to rage—that's what draws the attention. Her petite mouth softens the look when drawn up in a smile; however, that's not very often. Gert and her older sister, Minnie Mae, from Mountain Home could be taken for twins, but they can't tolerate each other and hardly ever visit back and forth. Nonetheless, when Gert can't have her way (seldom as that is), she threatens to leave for Minnie Mae's—a threat that no one takes seriously.

Gert begins the daily ritual by pouring a thin stream of hot bacon drippings into batter, the way the Pastor likes it. Cornbread is one of her specialties. Sometimes she bakes it in her corn stick mold, but today she fills her eight by eight-inch pan with the batter for the Pastor to cut into freshly-baked squares and slather with butter and honey. That reminds her. Gert rushes out to the ice chest on the back porch. She's in luck. Her bowl of churned butter is still nice and firm sitting atop the last bit of ice. "We'll need Mr. Hamm to deliver us a new block tomorrow," Gert sighs. Seems like they go through at least a block a week, winter and summer just the same.

The wooden staircase creaks and Gert calls out, "Is that you, Pastor?"

"Most surely, it is," he calls back.

"The girls ready?" Gert calls out again.

Popping his head in though the door, the Pastor says, "They're still stirring around upstairs, Misses." He is already dressed in his suit pants that're hitched up with wide black suspenders, and his white shirt billows out on the sides. He sniffs toward the massive stove consuming the kitchen's sunlit corner and says, "That sure smells good."

Gert has no interest in his flattery. "Those two girls need to get down here and start shelling these nuts. Not much time 'til your service, and I want my pies baked before church."

The Pastor turns quickly, lest Gert find work for him too, calling out as he exits, "I'll be in the parlor Pastor thinking on my sermon, Misses."

"You spend your *life* in that parlor," Gert snaps.

The sisters bound down the stairs a few minutes later. Amy has been awake since dawn completing her chores. First, she lit corncob and sassafras kindling to fire up the stove, and then she joined Grandpa out in the barn to feed their hungry cows and horses. Finally, she pumped water into tin buckets and hauled them up to the porch—they'll use the water for wash basins and cooking, and they'll need more pumped by noon. Now Amy is washed and ready for church in her new rosebud print dress. It's the same one as yesterday but freshly washed and ironed. Effie marches in behind her sister wearing her blue cotton church dress and her hair tied back with a blue ribbon to match.

"Morning, Gramma Gert," the sisters harmonize.

"Sit down and pick out those nuts for my pies right away, girls. Don't fool, now. It won't take long with two of you at it."

Amy and Effie flash frowns behind their grandmother's back, grab nut bowls and kitchen cloths, and head out to the porch, alighting in side-by-side rockers. They're cracking the tough brown shells when Effie starts teasing, "Good golly! It's too warm for the picnic today, Amy. You'll get wilted over there looking for a beau."

"Don't be a silly goose, Effie. No one's going to be over there except the

Jasper twins, and ole' Ned." Amy considers the Jasper twins far too silly, and Ned is their gawky neighbor, the Fitzgerald's youngest son. "Besides, I have to help out like usual—I'm not wasting my time chasing beaus today, nor any other day, neither," she adds, looking down at her hands callused from garden chores, nails bitten down to the quick, and fingers now turning nut brown. *There'll be no fellas' over there that I don't know already, and it'd be a miracle if the one I fancy shows up again.*

The nuts are almost all shelled when Grandma Gert shouts out from the kitchen, "Breakfast is ready! Pastor! Girls!"

The group dutifully files inside right away, and the Pastor begins his prayer: "Thank you for this day, Oh Lord, and for our daily bread...." He serves himself first and starts the plates around, but waits for them to complete the circle before taking one bite himself.

Breakfast is solemn. The girls fasten their eyes on their plates, and the Pastor and his wife share only a few words about the girls' manners and such. At last, breakfast is put away, and Gert bakes her pies. As usual, they're luscious and fragrant and bubbled right up to the top with pecans roasted dark in the golden corn syrup.

"There'll be no finer pies over there today; that's fer sure, girls," Gert crows, setting the pies out on the kitchen table to cool.

The Pastor disappears up stairs to finish his dressing for church. Effie starched and ironed his shirtfront on Saturday, and he closes it down center with round metal studs handed down from his father and grandfather. Gert made his suit from brown homespun cloth, and it fits him well—not too tight. He returns to the parlor looking handsome in his preaching garb, and he calls to Amy, "Come help me ready the service," adding over his shoulder, "Misses, you come over directly with Effie. Don't you dally."

Gert shoots back, "When was the last time I dallied, Pastor Blackwell?" (She adds the "Blackwell" when she's truly annoyed.)

Amy is almost out the door when Grandma Gert bellows out from the kitchen, "Come back here and get these pies for the picnic, Miss Forgetful."

First Sunday every month the Pleasant Hill faithful picnic out on the lawn after church, those closest bringing plenty to eat for those without. They travel along the old Military Road and park their wagons in neat rows alongside the church. Some fall asleep during the sermon, some even get saved, but they *all* look forward to feasting, laughing and singing after the service. It's a good cooling off before dusty rides home. Church regulars don't dare miss the get-togethers except for illness or death. But Amy doesn't enjoy the picnics these days. "More questions, more explaining about my future. It's no one's business except mine," she sulks and then feels bad for being so selfish.

Amy juggles the pies as she trots alongside the Pastor crossing the dusty road to the church. The silence is awkward, so she thinks up to say, "Grandpa, what will you preach about today?"

The Pastor pays her no mind as he barrels along, eyes fixed on his beloved Pleasant Hill church just ahead. He enters first and breathes in the familiar musty aroma. Church founders carved the twin-peaked entry doors almost fifty years ago, and the Pastor props them wide open to let in fresh air. Amy follows behind and stashes the pies on a back pew.

An old wooden pulpit commands the center in front, and, slightly behind to the right, sit the rock-hard choir benches. Twenty pews for worshipers face the pulpit, ten on each side, and Amy scurries around, checking that each one has a hymnal, though most know the music by heart. White cardboard fans shaped like tulip poplar leaves are stapled to stubby wooden handles, and they lay here and there on the pews. Amy turns the picture of Jesus' holding a lamb to the top, relegating the side printed "Harney's Funeral Parlor" in bold letters to the bottom. She sighs, *These'll get waved about plenty in the roasting heat today.*

Sunday sounds soon fill the air as worshipers slide onto pews and choir members shuffle in through the side door and sit down on their benches. There's a cough here and there and a rustling about, but everyone settles down quickly.

Little three-year-old Richie, neighbor Fitzgerald's only grandchild, toddles in with his mama and daddy, Thomas and Janet. Grandma Gert gripes that the child is downright spoiled, but he's plenty cute today with his curly brown hair and big brown eyes. Effie is standing by the entry when Richie passes by and begs, "Sit wif me, Effie. Sit wite here wif me," pulling on her arm hard toward the last pew.

Janet Fitzgerald eagerly motions Effie to sit, plopping Richie at once on her lap, pleading, "You mind, Eff? He'll keep out of trouble back here." Then she whispers, "There'll be an extra nickel in it for you, next time you mind Richie over at our place."

Old Mrs. Thompson begins jerking her flabby arms up and down directing the choir in a squeaky rendition of "Amazing Grace." Grandma Gert accompanies on the tinny upright piano. Soon, the sweltering worshipers are spellbound by the Pastor's inspiring sermon, and, around noon, the heartfelt invitation begins, "All ye who are lost, won't you come forward and be saved?"

Effie has nodded off in the heat on the back pew, and little Richie hops off of her lap. He toddles out onto the church lawn and back into the church through the side door. The poor child is lost and trying to find Effie when he spies the backs of the choir benches and wanders over for a good look around. Little Richie stands tippy-toe on his pudgy little legs, but the only thing he can see is the back of Grandma Hamm's head. Reaching up with his plump little fingers, he grabs hold of her hairnet bound bun and shakes it hard to get her attention.

Grandma Hamm cries out, "Oh, my God, Oh, my God in heaven!" as she flings her hands up over her head.

The Pastor is elated to hear the old woman answer his call, and he shouts, "Hallelujah, Praise the Lord!" The whole flock rejoices over Mrs. Hamm's salvation until she climbs up on her bench to swipe her hymnal at poor little Richie crouching behind.

Effie snaps awake from all the commotion, and she spots Richie running around up in front of the church, Mrs. Hamm now in chase. Red-faced, Effie races up the aisle to grab her wayward charge.

There is nothing to do but laugh as the Pastor proclaims, "Richie is the youngest soul ever lost and then found here at Peasant Hill. Praise the Lord!"

Amy whips checkered cloths over the old picnic tables still chuckling over Richie's finale. "Amens" completed, the churchwomen scramble past her to their wagons and reappear moments later with baskets stuffed with fried chicken, breaded okra, and corn bread. Others flaunt fragrant apple tarts, peach cobblers, and sweet pastry baked in hot kitchens all over the countryside. They chatter away proudly spreading their yummies out on the tables under black walnut trees. The church ladies take these picnics as a personal challenge—a call to show off old family recipes and to boast that theirs is a blue ribbon winner, or it *was* one year or another. "The best I ever tasted," their husbands feel compelled to proclaim out on the lawn.

Her granddaughter isn't moving fast enough to suit Grandma Gert, so she hurries over to bark out her orders, "Fetch those folding chairs, Miss Amy. Go get more cloths. Bring over those boxes right away."

Embarrassed in front of the others, Amy furrows her brow, eliciting an even louder chastisement from Gert, "Don't you look at me that way, young lady." Amy wants to slink away, but she knows better.

Gert is carefully placing her prized pecan pies out on the table when a young man walks over and asks, "May I offer to help you some, Ma'am?" Gert has never met the lad before.

Amy turns to see who belongs to the familiar voice, and her heart jolts when she recognizes the handsome young man that she's been dreaming about.

"Well, son," Grandma Gert croons, "There's a great big ole' crate of preserves over yonder, and I sure could use some help toting it over. That would be mighty nice of you." It's clear that Gert's partial to polite young men. She adds, "My name is Mrs. Gertrude Blackwell, the Pastor's wife, and this here's Miss Amy Blackwell, my granddaughter."

The young man nods at Gert, "How do, Ma'am. I'm Ernest Lee Herald from over Success." He smiles and nods in Amy's direction, too.

Amy knows full well that they've met before, but he's not letting on, so she doesn't either.

Gert gushes, "I know of Heralds that have the big ole' grain mill over those parts."

"Yes'm. Those're my people. That's our mill and our farm—my dad runs things along with my Gramps."

Gert cocks her head, all too obvious, "You belong to a church, Mr. Herald?"

"Yes'm. Belong to First Baptist Church over in Success, Ma'am. My whole family does," he assures, turning back for a longer look at Amy this time. "I'm over this way helping Uncle Marlin fix his silo roof after a wind tore it off. I don't get over this way too often."

"Well, then, we're mighty glad you came here today, and thank you for offering to go get my crate." Gert grins as the newcomer heads toward her best strawberry preserves.

Amy's eyes follow the young man as he lopes across the lawn; she judges that he's around eighteen years old. She had wanted to speak up but held back. *It wouldn't do to be forward, being the preacher's granddaughter and all.*

"He's a nice young man. Don't you think so, Amy?" Grandma Gert asks.

"Yes'm," Amy nods.

"Wouldn't hurt you any to be polite to him, young lady," her grandmother growls.

Now, this shocks Amy, because Grandma Gert never pushes her out front like this. "Yes, Grandma," Amy replies.

Ernest Lee is back in no time with the crate. He sets it down next to the table and asks, "Is this a good spot here, Ma'am?"

"Yes, son. That's just fine," Gert replies and then clears her throat and raises her tone several octaves higher, "Since you're new to the area, you need to come over to our house, Mr. Herald. We'll show you around our land and down by the brook. You'll learn more about Pitman that way. You like fried catfish?"

"I like catfish any *way* and any *day*, Ma'am. Even like fried catfish tails." Ernest Lee crows.

Amy smiles at his rhyme. *He isn't one bit put off by Grandma Gert like most folks are around Pitman, and he even got a smile out of her.* This time Amy takes a longer look at the lean young man standing there by the table. He has thick wavy blonde hair and is a lot taller than she is, probably six foot, near the same height as her Grandpa. He's good-looking for sure, with blue eyes that laugh when he talks—just like she recalls from church weeks ago. She looks down at his hands. They're strong but curiously uncallused for the son of a miller. Amy quickly hides her own nut stained, callused hands under her apron.

Answering Grandma Gert's kind invitation, Ernest Lee explains, "Thank you, Ma'am, but I'm heading home to Success tomorrow, Ma'am."

Without a moment's hesitation, Gert insists, "Then, you must stop over and share our table on the way out of town, Mr. Herald. You'll ride right down the road past our house, and we'd be mighty proud to have you stop over and visit. We eat around noon—plenty of time for you to have a meal and still reach Success before nightfall."

"Yes'm. That's right; I could at that. I'll arrange to be at your place by noon Monday, Ma'am." Ernest Lee grins back at the Pastor's wife, and then over at Amy.

Amy can scarcely believe her ears. Grandma Gert can be persuaded to do most anything the Pastor asks, but she's not one to be social herself, much less one to invite a virtual stranger to share their table. This is incredible.

For the rest of the picnic, Amy casually gazes across the churchyard in Ernest Lee's direction. She thinks she catches a look or two back, but she can't be sure. *Best not to be too obvious. Wouldn't do to be forward.* Amy serves big squares of coconut cake and pecan pie, nodding politely at neighbors, "Yes, that sure was a mighty good sermon, Mrs. Hamm," or, "Yes, little Richie is quite a hand full, isn't he Mrs. Fitzgerald?" she says, but Amy hears nothing of their replies. Her body tingles, her mind races, and she feels happy in a way she never has before. *Smile nice; maybe he's looking right now.*

Effie bounds over from playing Blind Man's Bluff with children from her Sunday school class. "What's the matter, Amy. Cat got your tongue?" she mocks.

"I'm just busy, that's all, you silly. I don't have time for games right now, Effie."

First thing Monday morning, the sky clouds up and spring rains pour down. The Pastor works in his study, Grandma Gert works away at scouring her kitchen, and Effie, as usual, makes herself scarce. Amy looks out the window every few minutes, though she's not quite sure for what. The church still stands across the street, the hen house is still out back, their spring garden is still growing, and farmland still stretches out as far as she can see. Everything is accounted for, same as yesterday, yet it all looks so different somehow. Even in the rain, the barn is redder, the flowers are brighter, and the little church looks whiter today. Farmers are glad for the rain on their spring crops, so what could be better? Amy feels so happy that she can hardly sit still from excitement.

However, the longer it rains, Amy begins to fret, *Why did it have to pour down today? It'll spoil everything and Ernest Lee won't come by. I just knew it was too good to be true.* Her morning chores are complete, but she decides to keep busy or she'll get sick from the worry. *I'll darn Grandpa's socks and mend my spare apron—good rainy day work.* Amy sits down in the front room with her sewing basket, but before she can get her needle threaded, the clouds finally part and the sun shines brightly up in the sky.

Grandpa emerges from the parlor and looks out in awe, "Look at this, Misses. It's just like in the picture books. Brilliant rays for the Almighty to walk down upon." A hint of a rainbow forms, making the sight out their window truly magnificent.

Salvation is the farthest thing from Grandma Gert's mind. She snorts, "Stop that gawking, Pastor! We need a big mess of catfish. They always bite real good after a rain muddies up the river."

These are the sweetest words Amy has ever heard coming out of Grandma Gert's mouth. There *will* be a catfish fry today for the caller.

The Pastor muses on the way out the door, *There's a perfectly good rainbow up in the sky, and Gert doesn't care a fig about it. And what's all her ruckus about company coming? That's not like her.* He met Ernest Lee the day before and, while the boy was nice enough, he puzzles, *I wonder what she's up to—inviting him over so quick like that?* Anyway, he slaps on his old fishing hat and mutters under his breath, "I guess this is as good as any excuse —I hardly ever have time to go fishin' any more." So, Pastor Blackwell rolls off in his wagon, heading for Current River with his best cane pole and a can of wiggly red worms scooped fresh from a rain puddle.

Amy is so happy that she doesn't mind Grandma Gert's stream of orders. "Amy, get out to the hens and bring in some eggs—and grab some of that early parsley on your way in." As usual, Effie gets no assignment, but Amy doesn't mind that either today. This noon event will be most extraordinary, and she can't wait to lay eyes on their very special guest once again. Amy feels her cheeks flush, and she hopes a cold isn't coming on.

Gert flutters around the kitchen like a plump busy bee. She can't help but marvel at how beautifully things are unfolding, *Just when I was wondering what to do about Amy, Ernest Lee appears out of the blue.* She really isn't all that surprised, for, she's known all her life that she can "will" things to happen. Gert doesn't do it too often—only to test her powers now and then, just to make sure that they're in good working order. She smiles and hums as she works, *Ernest Lee Herald is just another one of my successful willins'.*

It came to Gert in a flash when Ernest Lee introduced himself at church yesterday. *Pairing up those two up will straighten out my Amy problems, for sure. The child's getting older, and her independent attitude is annoying of late. I'm growing real weary of it. She's a real aggravation, and it's not good for my blood pressure.* That part is true. Even a strong brew of sarsaparilla tea can't stop Gert's blood from boiling every time Amy doesn't follow directions exactly. *I must do something about this situation. Amy's getting much too uppity, and it's time that she strikes out on her own. Anyway, what can she do for the Pastor's work that I can't do myself?*

Gert's own mother would never have allowed behavior like Amy's. Mrs. Boswell used to scold Gert growing up, "You've got a sharp tongue in your head, Miss Gertrude," or, "I'm going to take you down a peg or two, young lady." Gert is adamant that sparing the rod will spoil a child, but she can't find a Bible verse to prove it. In any case, her husband forbids her laying a hand on the girls—even when they need a good paddling. Gert feels her blood pressure rising just thinking about it. *Anyway, I'm not even Amy's real Grandma,* she huffs; though, most folks in town don't know it.

The truth is that Gert has only herself to blame for Amy landing in her lap, for it resulted directly from one of her very own "willin's". Right after the pastor's son, Gideon, was born, the Pastor's wife, Mary, came down with scarlet fever and died practically overnight. It was then and there that Gert "willed" the Pastor to take *her* for his wife. His first wife was nice enough, Gert thought, but she was far too soft for a devout Christian woman.

Gert's mother used to sneer, "The Pastor's wife has no organization about the house, and the whole church knows it. What's more, that woman spends every waking moment tending to other's problems, do-gooding at birthings and sitting up nights with sick people. No wonder she took sick herself. Don't you think so, Gertrude?"

Gert would reply, "That is definitely so, Mama." Gert would never say one bad word about the preacher's wife outside of the house, but she agreed wholeheartedly with her mother—the Preacher deserved better. Yes, Preacher Holloway Blackwell deserved Miss Gertrude Boswell!

Day after day, following Mary's untimely death, Gertrude made it her business to bring food and fresh milk over to the Pastor and his baby. "Here's a nice fresh beef broth, Pastor, with plenty of blood-rich juice for the baby," she'd say, or, "I fried up a little extra chicken for you, Pastor, with a little mush for baby Gideon." Pretty soon Gert was sitting down and feeding the child herself, and, in short order, she was indispensable to the good Pastor's household.

That was when Gert made the "willin'." Even though she was five years his senior, she set her cap for the preacher. After all, he was a man in good standing in Pitman, and he already had a child. Gert had never been married, and she abhorred that messy business of begetting a baby—she knew all about it. Once walking through the woods as a girl, she saw a man pulling at his red thing through his pants front. He wagged it up and down at her, licking his lips, motioning her over with a grinning leer, and she had run hollering all the way home. No, she wasn't going to go near anything nasty like that, especially after her mother told her what it was for. She figured that Pastor Holloway Blackwell and his ready-made family would be just perfect, and she "willed," right then, that he would take her for his wife.

Sure enough, within the year the Pastor proposed. "Miss Boswell, I know we haven't courted like a man and a woman should, and I know that my short comings are many, but will you take my hand in marriage, considering how close you've become to me and the boy?"

Now, there were those in the congregation that knew this union was a big mistake, and many who suspected what Gert and her mother were up to. And there were more than just a few in town who would give anything for Gert to get her come-uppence for meddling about in their dear Pastor's life. A few went so far as to whisper that Gert was a crazy woman, calling her "nuts." However, no one dared to say anything to the Pastor directly, and few cared to tangle with Mrs. Boswell and her snotty daughter Miss Gertrude, so everyone let it alone.

What's more, the Pastor took Gert's appearance in the center of his life as a sign directly from God. One day he proclaimed, "Miss Boswell, the Lord must have brought you to me and my boy in our hour of need. He meant for us to be together following Mary's untimely passing."

Gert accepted the Pastor's proposal of marriage on the spot, agreeing whole-heartedly that, "Yes, our union is most certainly by God's own design." However, she secretly had another view, really, *The Pastor's marriage proposal was due to my 'willin.' It had nothing to do with the Lord, whatsoever.* Gert enthusiastically went about the business of planning their wedding, congratulating herself, *It's just as well that Holloway Blackwell believes our union was God's doing; I'll do nothing to dissuade him of that notion.*

Now the tables have turned. Gert's beautiful plan was spoiled when the Pastor's son Gideon grew up, married, and dumped his two daughters at their house in Pitman after his wife died. Actually, in Gert's view, Effie is no bother at all—only Amy. Gert's more convinced than ever, *Why should I have to put up with Amy's aggravation? We took her in after her mother died, and we let her stay on when her no-count father took off, but this is long enough. She's old enough to make it alone in the world and to leave me in peace with the Pastor and Effie.* So that's why Gert isn't Amy's true-blood grandmother at all, and why she feels no hesitation in putting Amy out of their life.

Gert's blood pressure pulses just thinking about Amy, so she fans herself with a pie pan sitting handy on the table. *There is no doubt about it. Young men don't come around every day to pawn off a sassy one like Miss Amy, much less a church man from a family of means, and especially now that the country's at war. I'd better grab this prized bird in the hand!* Gert starts feeling better with her latest "willin'" decided.

The Pastor returns with his catch of silvery catfish strung on a line. He cleans them under pump water out in back of the house, staring down at their bulging bug-eyes and the ugly black protrusions mounted on top of their heads. "Catfish are just about the homeliest creatures on God's earth," he mutters. The heads come off first, and then he cuts them open clear down the stomach and peels their thick, scaleless skin back like a banana. "You ugly bottom feeders," he snorts, pulling out their innards stuffed with river debris. Then, he conjures up the fried fish aroma that'll waft out from the kitchen at noon, and he concedes, *These critters may eat river garbage, but they'll sure taste good when the misses fries them up nice n' crispy.* Washing them vigorously under the pump water, he churns them around in the bucket one last time and hauls his bounty into the kitchen.

Gert inspects the Pastor's brimming bucketful. "Beautiful," she exclaims dragging the slippery wet catch over to the wooden side table. Wielding the cleaver like a veteran fish monger, she chops the cat fish into fat chunky pieces. Today she decides to take the extra steps. She cracks open two eggs fresh from the hen house, beats them furiously around in a bowl, and dips the fish chunks into the frothy yellow slime. *Now the cornmeal will stick on there good and thick,* she smiles to herself. Gert drops the meal coated chunks into the hot skillet one by one, jumping back as the grease bubbles up, spitting and spattering, burning her arm. Unfazed, she wipes the blisters on the apron that encircles her middle-age girth. "This fish'll be brown and crispy in no time at all—bound to put young Ernest Lee Herald in a friendly, good mood," she chirps, humming a snappy rendition of "Soldiers of the Cross."

Gert is mixing up the leftover cornmeal and with grease for the hushpuppies, and Amy is putting plates around on the table when there's a knock at the screen door. Ernest Lee stands out on the front porch with his hair nicely combed, smiling and twirling his hat around in his hands. The Pastor ambles over and swings the screen door open wide.

"Good day, Pastor Blackwell," Ernest Lee says, extending his hand out cheerfully to the Pastor.

"Come in, young man," the Pastor replies blandly, shaking the hand.

"Yes, sir. Thank you, sir," Ernest Lee replies, his voice cracking a little.

Gert hurries out from the kitchen, all aglow. "So good to see you Mr. Herald," she gushes. "Glad y'all could come visit a spell."

"Thank you kindly ma'am," Ernest Lee replies.

Amy is frozen with her hands clasped in front and her eyes glued to the newcomer's face. Words fly out of her head, leaving her dumb by the table. *He's exactly like I remembered, even better. Look at him. He's warm and charming with Grandpa, just like he was with Grandma Gert over at church yesterday. Nothing scares him at all.* Amy's body turns warm all over and she worries again that she's coming down with a cold—or, worse yet, influenza.

Gathering courage, she forces a small smile and nods over in Ernest Lee's direction.

Gert's feast is as fine as ever graced an Arkansan's table. All during dinner, Earnest Lee keeps up a nice flow of table conversation. Passing platters heaped up with fish, cornbread and fresh garden vegetables, he compliments the Pastor's wife, "Fish sure is good and crispy, Ma'am. I even like those nice and crispy tails." His eyes sparkle, pleased that she remembered about it. For the Pastor, he brings news from his church in Success. "Yes, sir, Brother Rahm is a real good man, sir. We get him first Sunday of every month. He's a blessing for sure." He remembers Effie too, "I saw you playing Blind Man's Bluff over at church. I like that game myself. Do you ever play Red Rover?" Ernest Lee smiles but never speaks directly to Amy, except to say, "Can I pass you more of these peas sitting over here by me, Miss Amy?" or "Hush puppies, Miss Amy?" Amy sits tongue-tied, transfixed by the guest.

Grandma Gert has to size up her prospect, "You work at your father's mill now, do you, Mr. Herald?" Gert sings the words, raising her voice up at the end.

"Yes'm, mostly in the summers the past two years," he replies, eyeing Amy as well.

"Oh, do you have other work the rest of the year?" Gert sings again.

"Well, Ma'am, I've been up at the Business College in Springfield the past two years. I just earned my business degree. I have some nice prospects for the fall, or I might stay home and help run Dad's business."

"Oh, imagine that," Gert coos, "a nice young man and so well-educated too."

Amy blushes at Grandma Gert's over-friendly tone, almost flirting with Ernest Lee, it seems.

"And your Mother?" Gert asks.

"My mom is ailing, but she does what she can about the house, and her sister Glory comes down from Missouri to help now and then."

The delightful meal flies by in no time at all. Pastor Blackwell pulls his napkin out from under his chin and stands up to signal the end.

Ernest Lee stands up right away, too, and says, "Well, Mrs. Blackwell, Pastor Blackwell, it sure was good of you to invite me to share your table today. That was wonderful catfish."

"Do you have to rush off, son?" Grandma Gert coyly lowers her gaze.

"Well, ma'am, I must be leaving soon to get home by dark, but I do have time for a look around, like you said yesterday. Do you suppose you could spare Miss Amy?" He asks, smiling in Amy's direction the same warm, friendly smile as yesterday.

"Of course, of course," Gert gushes again. "Amy, you go on and show Mr. Herald around, and don't forget down by the brook."

"Yes ma'am," Amy whispers, feeling nearly faint.

"I'll come too," Effie springs up.

"No, I'll need you to help in the kitchen, Little Miss Effie," the Pastor's wife snaps at the child in a rare moment assigning her chores.

"Aw, shucks," Effie moans as Ernest Lee opens the porch door and exits with Amy.

First, Amy leads Ernest Lee down by the barn to show off their horses munching hay and three cows contentedly mooing. Then, they walk on through the barn and out the back door, on through the apple orchard, and head down the hill toward the brook. Amy's confidence is reviving, and she starts gesturing this way and that. "This is our family's land where Civil War battles were fought over yonder. Effie and I found genuine musket bullets up on the rise, lots of them. I can lead you over to take a look, if you like."

Ernest Lee isn't answering or smiling right now. Amy is sure that he's bored.

Finally, they come to the brook that some might call a small stream—a lively wide path of water, quite deep in places, bubbling past mossy rocks and under hundred-year old oak trees.

"Here's where Effie and I used to play house, right under this ole' tree; we hardly ever come down here any more," Amy says, feeling silly for even talking about little girl's play to a fine young man like Ernest Lee Herald. There is only one rock on the bank large enough to sit on and rest, so she sits down.

Ernest Lee hovers next to her and stares down at the water. He is still mute.

Amy stops talking, too. Now she is positive that Ernest Lee has lost interest.

Neither one is speaking when Ernest Lee slowly brushes his hand across Amy's back and then up higher, resting it up by the nape of her neck. His soft touch tickles the skin above her new dress, and an electric chill goes through her body, feeling so new.

"Well, I guess I need to be going on along," he says, still watching the brook babble past.

Amy sighs and slowly stands up as well.

Ernest Lee's hand stays put on her neck, and he gently turns her to face him. He rasps, "Miss Amy, do you think I'm too old of a fellow for you?"

Now Amy tingles all over. "Well, how old-how old are you?" she replies.

"I'm eighteen, going on nineteen," he says earnestly, studying the tops of his boots.

Finally, after what seems like an eternity to Ernest Lee, Amy whispers, "I'm going on sixteen next month. That doesn't sound like much of a difference to me, Mr. Herald."

Ernest Lee closes his eyes and softly exhales. He slides his broad hand up even higher and onto her long, lovely neck, feeling her warm flesh in his palm. He slowly draws Amy toward him and breathes in the sweet scent of her pink clover soap. Holding her close, he kisses the side of her forehead, "You're the sweetest thing I ever did see, Miss Amy. I've thought of little else from the first moment I saw you over at church."

The couple's hands touch and their warm gazes melt sweetly together. The moment is over in a flash, but Amy reels with excitement, wondering how things can whirl around when she stands still by the brook.

Ernest Lee kisses her hand and gently leads Amy back up the hill toward the house.

Amy can barely think straight. *Is Ernest Lee my true love like I pined for? I could fly right up in the sky.*

Grandma Gert is out on the porch waiting and gushes as the couple approaches, "Oh, Mr. Herald, what did you think of our land? Isn't it just as pretty as you've ever seen?"

Amy lets her hand drop right away, but Grandma Gert has already seen. Amy doesn't know how to act, so she stares down at the ground.

Earnest Lee doesn't feel one bit shameful, and his outgoing nature is back. He smiles his wonderful smile and replies, "Yes'm, you have mighty pretty land here, indeed. I sure am obliged that you let Miss Amy show me around."

Grandma Gert beams and walks closer to offer, "Here, I put up a little food sack for your ride home. I've got some ginger cookies and a jar of lemonade in there for you—it should stay cool for awhile 'cause I've had it sitting in the ice chest since before-noon," she beams, handing over the bag which he stashes in his saddle bag. "I put some of my fresh apple butter in there for your mother and father with my regards. We've never met, but folks hereabouts speak highly of them," she croons. "Now you'll come back and visit us real soon won't you, Mr. Herald?"

Ernest Lee turns toward Amy's grandfather, "Pastor Blackwell, I was planning on coming this way next weekend to help out Uncle Marlin again. I'd sure be pleased if I could visit with Amy a bit on Monday before I head home," adding quickly for the frowning Pastor's benefit, "I'd come by *after* your noon meal this time, and we could sit up there on the swing."

Butterflies flutter around inside Amy's stomach, and she waits for something bad to happen from Ernest Lee's boldness.

The clueless Pastor turns to Gert, and she replies without hesitation, "Why, of course. That would be just fine, Mr. Herald. You'd like that, wouldn't you, Amy?"

Amy gives a little nod, "Yes ma'am." *Stay calm, don't let on how tickled you are.*

The Pastor stands there befuddled, but Effie catches on right away and she lets loose of a giggle.

Ernest Lee mounts his horse, tips his hat to them all and takes a parting gaze at the girl he will marry. "Miss Amy," he nods as he trots off on his horse into the late afternoon haze.

Ernest Lee wakes up Tuesday morning with a smile on his face. He never fell for a girl before. Growing up he always made fun of the notion. Any guy seen holding hands with a girl over at the schoolhouse got razzed; maybe even humiliated in front of the teacher—Ernest Lee usually razzing the loudest, but this is so different. He knew Amy was for him the very first time he saw her—his heart pumped so fast and he had a burning down low.

He reluctantly rouses to start another day at the mill. By the time he gets dressed and walks into the kitchen, his father holds out a letter addressed to him from the post box. Ernest Lee rips open the letter and reads rapidly.

"What is it?" Mr. Herald asks.

"It's a head book keeping position," Ernest Lee says in a flat tone.

"Where?" Mrs. Herald asks excitedly.

"In Tuckerman—at Marshall Brothers Mercantile," Ernest Lee stares down at the letter.

"What does it pay? Mr. Herald inquires.

"It pays more than I ever imagined I'd ever make right out of school," he says, folding the letter back in its envelope and stuffing it inside his shirt pocket.

"Oh, Ernest Lee," his mother squeals. "This is your big chance. Think of it." She claps her hands together. "Aren't you excited, son?"

Ernest Lee walks off somber-faced as he replies, "Yes, I am, Ma."

"What about breakfast, son?" his father calls after him.

"I'm not hungry now, Dad," he answers over his shoulder. He reaches the door agonizing, *This is dreadful. I can't believe that I've finally found the girl of my dreams, and now I'll have to move so far away? Maybe I won't consider this offer. Rats!* He sputters and grumbles to himself all way down to the mill, knowing that his mind will spin around this dilemma all day.

CHAPTER 3
COME AGAIN

The following Monday is like most other days, except Amy hums cheerfully going about her morning chores. She glances into the parlor where her Grandpa bends over his papers, writing furiously, as usual. There's a knock at the front door, but she knows it's way too early for Ernest Lee to arrive.

The Pastor directs, "Amy, let in Brother Charles."

Brother Charles is from the nearby town of Maynard which is slightly south and a bit to the west. His congregation joins with Pleasant Hill's in campaigns against gambling, drinking and other good Christian causes. The two men of God get along very well in these endeavors. Also, they mutually support the Current River Baptist Association, a collection of small area churches that have banded together—Ernest Lee's father was one of its founders. Unfortunately, the Association has had problems lately, and the friction finds Brother Charles right in the center stirring up the dissent. Pastor Blackwell has been dreading his visit.

"Amy, bring us some lemonade from the ice chest, please," the Pastor instructs, motioning his guest into the chair by his desk. "What is on your mind today, Brother Charles?"

The visitor gets right down to business, "Well, Pastor, I've been an Association member since arriving in Maynard five years ago from St. Louis."

"Yes, indeed, both of our churches go a long way back with the group. That's a fact," Pastor Blackwell nods in agreement.

"Well, as you know, Pastor, I don't hold with a lot of politickin', but a certain Association matter won't lie still," Brother Charles continues.

Pastor Blackwell knows at once where the conversation is going, *It's the almighty dollar again.*

Brother Charles drawls, "Remember that cantankerous meeting not too long ago when the Association refused to fund our State Baptist Convention?"

Pastor Blackwell is the Association's President, so this subject is not news to him. Brother Charles' faction was most unhappy with that no-funding vote, and they've been itching to reverse it ever since. "Yes, I thought you might bring that up," the Pastor replies. "I have the minutes right here," and he reads, "'The churches of the Association vote to discontinue financial cooperation with the State Baptist Convention.' Says plainly that...."

Brother Charles cuts in, "Sir, I intend to turn that vote around. There's no reason in God's creation why we shouldn't support our State Convention."

Pastor Blackwell tries a diplomatic approach, "As worthy as the Convention's goals may be, Brother Charles, surely they have resources far beyond our little group. It might be different up in St. Louis, but members down here favor spending our funds right here at home. The unsaved around *these* parts come first." He pauses, lightly brushing his palms together, "Anyway, I'm afraid the matter is out of my hands. It rests with our Association members, and some churches have severed relations with the State Convention already."

Brother Charles studies the old elm out in the yard through the window. "Well, we're *all* serving our Lord, Pastor Blackwell. I wish no strife in our ranks, but I fear there'll be a split if things don't change around soon. My concerns about that vote must be addressed!" Brother Charles says, his face flushing to an exasperated red.

Pastor Blackwell tries another approach, "Surely our little group of a mere seventeen churches isn't essential to the State's survival, considering all the churches left to give funds, especially those wealthy big city churches."

Brother Charles looks the Pastor full in the face to launch his harangue, "You know good and well Pastor Blackwell that your objection goes *far* beyond funding. What you folks *really* object to is the State's supporting foreign missions abroad. Isn't that so?"

"I do have to question the practice," the Pastor concedes.

Brother Charles becomes even more vehement, "We're not pioneer preachers any more, sir. We can't only find converts by blazing trails through the back woods or holding revivals in tents. That's noble, but not nearly enough. We must turn to foreign lands for our converts—especially with our great nation just entering the war. God needs us to spread his message abroad now, more than ever. Just think of those heathens running around over there without knowledge of God. No, your old-fashioned ways'll never get through to them."

Pastor Blackwell feels his visitor's challenge in the pit of his stomach. He counters, "Sir, I preach God's word in the way that I do because the *Bible* directs it. And so should you."

Brother Charles snipes back, "Well, I suppose that all depends on *who* interprets the scriptures, Pastor Blackwell. I believe we serve not only by what we *say*, but more by what we *do*. We can't go preaching there's only *one* way to salvation, and then not tell half the world about it. Can we?"

The Pastor studies his father's well-worn black Bible sitting out on his desk, and his voice is firm, "Well, as far as I am concerned, the rest of the world can wait, Brother Charles, because there's no end to what needs doing here in Randolph County." Pastor Blackwell picks up the Gazette from the desk and waves it about, "You know the issues well right here in this paper."

Brother Charles leans back in his chair prepared for the onslaught.

The Pastor expounds, "For one thing, there're misguided folk obliged to stir up trouble for coloreds living out on the edge of our town, and that's against our good Christian principles. We've got to fix it so those coloreds can live there in peace."

Brother Charles shows no reaction, so the Pastor continues expounding, "And then there's the destitute that can't clothe or feed their family. If money is short, you and me can get paid in corn meal or feed for our preaching, but there's poor folk with no way to find work, let alone to pay bills."

Still no reaction.

"Then there's those guzzling down alcoholic spirits at stills out in the woods, dragging bottles back to their cabins, and, the next thing you know, they're getting in bad with the law. They need to be saved from that demon."

Patience dwindling, Brother Charles cuts the Pastor off sharp once again with a challenge, "What about the unsaved heathens abroad, Pastor? Do we just pretend that they don't exist?"

Sensing no prospect for a sympathetic ear, Brother Charles rises to leave just as Amy walks in with the lemonade. He fumes, "All due respect, Pastor Blackwell, I'm growing tired of your arrogance." Smacking his palm flat on the desk, he insists, "I'll have my say at the next meeting, and I *will* get some action or my group will pull out. Good day, Pastor. Miss Amy." Brother Charles storms out of the room.

The screen door bangs shut and Amy's mouth gapes open. She sets the tray down on her grandfather's desk and blurts out, "Grandpa, I thought preachers were brothers working together for the Lord."

The Pastor shuffles his papers and mumbles, "Sometimes even brothers can't agree…" Then, his back stiffens, "…but it's not your place to question such things of grownups!'

Amy's mind races. *I never thought preachers, much less Grandpa, would argue like that. He never lets Effie and me argue without making a fuss.* She summons up the courage to ask, "Doesn't God want us to set a good example, Grandpa? What about being a 'sunbeam' like you always said?"

The Pastor looks like an important thought just flew right out of his head, but he manages, "Well, all I can say is that things are going badly with our Current River Baptist group. Now I'll have to work *twice* as hard to help our misguided brothers see the light." Then, he points his finger at Amy, "…and *you'll* have to help me out more than ever. Understand?"

Amy's heart sinks. Now she'll be under her Grandpa's thumb longer yet. Her eyes glaze over as she summons up her numbing blank shroud, but it doesn't work this time—she can't stop the turmoil inside, *Grandpa is adding another link to my chain and nothing will deaden the pain. How will I ever get free of this parsonage prison?* Her sadness turns into anger and she fills with remorse for being so hateful, scolding herself, *I shouldn't have such selfish thoughts after all that Grandpa has done for me and for Effie. I own him my help.* She pours her grandfather a cool glass of lemonade and races out onto the front porch to cool off herself.

A few hours later, Amy picks at the food on her lunch plate.

Grandma Gert scolds, "Land sakes, Amy, you'll faint dead away if you don't put some food in your stomach. Ernest Lee will come by right after we eat and you won't be ready."

Effie has been teasing, "Amy's got a beau; Amy's got a beau a callin'," leaving Amy more upset than ever.

Amy manages to eat something, cleans up Grandma Gert's kitchen, and then retreats to her room. She plops down on the bed and tries composing her self, but her body tingles at the thought of Ernest Lee's visit. *He's so perfect. He's everything I need.* Sadly, even if the young man fancies her, Amy knows that she'll never be free for him to court. She is sure to be tied to her Grandpa and his church work forever. Amy lies back to ponder the injustice, when a rumbling noise intrudes from outside. *That sounds like a wagon load of scrap iron spilling out on the road,* she thinks. She runs over to the window just in time to see a black automobile rolling down Military Road and right past the church.

Effie yells up the stairs. "Amy, hurry down to see! A whirlwind's coming down the road!"

Amy races down the stairs two at a time and finds Effie, Grandma Gert, and Grandpa already out on the porch. The automobile churns up a brown trail of dust on Military road, heads up their farm road, and stops at the edge of their lawn. The huge machine lets out one final gasp before resting. There sits Ernest Lee Herald looking as handsome as ever behind the wheel of the huge metal monster. Smiling his sparkling smile, he ducks low to exit the tiny door and tips his hat to them all.

"Goodness gracious," Grandma Gert cries. "Pastor, it's one of those fancy automobiles from the city."

Amy gasps, "Oh, my heavens." She has never seen one close up before, but she is quite certain that only its mother could love this awkward assembly.

"Folks, this is a genuine Model T automobile right off Mr. Ford's assembly line," Ernest Lee boasts.

Sure enough, Ernest Lee propelled the "new-fangled contraption" all the way over from Success, over to his uncle Marlin's Pittman farm, and now over to their house. The metal conglomeration sports a flat-nosed hood, a knock-knee angled frame, and an odd assortment of cranks, springs, flywheels, and gears. Ernest Lee lifts the hood to show them off.

"Where did you get that 'T' thing, Mr. Herald?" Effie begs, running toward the auto, but not going right up to it.

"Come on over and take a look. Don't be afraid," he encourages. The others slowly move down off the porch.

"Well, I'll be," says Grandma Gert. "Is this automobile yours, Mr. Herald?"

"Practically so. My Dad has an admiration for gadgets, but this is the biggest one he ever did purchase. We had the first telephone in Randolph County, the first indoor plumbing, and now we have the first automobile, too. Folks in Success don't know what to make of us Heralds lately," he chuckles. "Want a ride?"

The invitation barely leaves Ernest Lee's lips when Grandma Gert clamors up on the running board and hops in the front seat on the passenger side, plopping herself down on the pleated leather cushion. The pastor squeezes in alongside her next to the door. Effie hangs back, but Ernest Lee coaxes her onto the back seat and boosts Amy up next to her.

With much flourish and fanfare, Ernest Lee plops back behind the wheel, turns on the ignition, tugs at a mysterious lever, tweaks a gauge or two, and announces, "Now for the moment you've been waiting for." He bounds around front, closes the hood, gives the big crank a mighty turn or two, and every inch of the automobile begins vibrating vigorously. Racing back to his position behind the wheel, Ernest Lee shouts over the roar, "Everyone ready? Hang onto your hats." He bangs the door shut and they're off.

Grandpa, Amy and Effie frantically clutch at the sides, but Grandma Gert, with uncharacteristic lack of decorum, throws her arms up, and squeals, "Wheeeeeeeeeeee!"

Down the farm road they roll and then right onto Military Road, the route of the first overland mail, the route that guided Civil War soldiers into battle, and now the route of Ernest Lee Herald's remarkable journey.

They roll along past the Pleasant Hill church and head up toward Hamm's General Store. Ernest Lee calls over his shoulder, "She'll travel up to 35 miles in an hour's time—on a good stretch of road." Fields of spring cotton and corn sprouts slide past like in some sort of dream. A mare whinnies at the "thing" barreling down the road, and Brother Fitzgerald leans on his plow out in his field and scratches his head as familiar faces roll past. The Model T's spinning wheels sway around every corner and bounce up and down, but Henry Ford's magnificent machine is the darling of the road, and Ernest Lee Herald relishes her limelight and all that goes with it.

A half-hour later, the merry group pours out of the car and dusts themselves off at the edge of the Blackwell's yard. "That was more fun than a basket full of piglets at the county fair," Grandma Gert cries out, a bit shaky but exhilarated.

Then, according to her plan, Gert leads everyone up onto the porch, grabs Effie by the hand, and directs Amy and Ernest Lee, "You two sit down. Effie and me have some rinds to pickle out in the kitchen." Then, single-handedly pulling her husband up by an arm from his rocker, she continues, "…and the Pastor has a sermon to write." Gert reappears moments later toting a tray with lemonade and ice chunks swirling around in her very best pitcher. She pours two tumblers full for the couple, cooing again before exiting, "You two have a nice visit, now."

Ernest Lee saunters over to the swing and sits alongside Amy. They sip lemonade forever, it seems. Finally, Ernest Lee speaks, "Miss Amy, I have something to tell you."

Amy's heart begins racing, just like it did last week down by the brook.

Ernest Lee continues, "This is a lot sooner than I expected, but I've given it considerable thought all week long. Anyway, I'm given to making quick decisions—always have been." He picks up her hand and cradles it between his.

Amy feels flushed but resists the urge to check for a fever. His eyes are so kind.

"Well, I got a letter this week from a company down in Tuckerman. They asked if I'd be their head bookkeeper. Can you believe that? They want *me*— just out of school! They asked my business school up in Springfield to recommend someone who has a talent with numbers. The school sent them my name, and they wrote right away."

Amy doesn't speak, so he continues, "Look at my hands, Miss Amy. These aren't the hands of a farmer or even a miller like my Dad or my Gramps. Even the military doesn't want me—I'm not fit enough to suit them, much less to fight in this war. These hands mostly pushed pencils for the last two years, and, anyway, pencil-pushing is what I do best."

So this is what he wants—it's a career and not me in his thoughts. Amy stutters, "You...you're good at numbers, Mr. Herald?"

"I can figure numbers out in my head that'd take others hours. I figure, if God gave me that gift, then I should use it, just the same as those with the gift for farming or milling."

The prospect of loosing Ernest Lee, just when she has taken to him so strong, devastates Amy. Tuckerman is over 35 miles south as the crow flies— too far for courting. Anyway, he didn't say one word about courting just now. *How could this be? There will never be another like him; I know that.* Her eyes are filling with tears when he takes her chin in his hand.

"I want to take you for my wife, Miss Amy. I want to take you down to Tuckerman with me. I know this is sudden, but I know that it's right. I won't go without you." He hesitates, for this is the most serious thing that he can ever remember doing, and he wants to say it just right. "I'll ask your grandfather for permission—surely he won't refuse a fellow with a new Model–T—at least that's what my dad said," he flashes his smile, then grows serious again, "Just give me the nod that you care for me too."

Amy leans forward. *Maybe I didn't hear right. Did Mr. Herald just ask me to marry? Even such a forthright young man wouldn't be so bold. There must be a courtship first with lots of visiting back and forth, and then, after a lot of church going together, then and only then, maybe Grandpa might consent to it.* She barely knows Mr. Herald, and she's shocked that he's thinking this way at all. It's much too soon. But refusing is only a fleeting thought. Her Grandpa may never agree, but at least her true love is asking for her hand. Her bright smile flashes her answer.

Ernest Lee stands up, and lets out a big, "Whoop, yippee!" Before he realizes what is happening, Effie, Pastor Blackwell and his wife rush out onto the porch.

"Everything all right out here, Amy? Mr. Herald?" the Pastor asks.

Ernest Lee looks down at Amy and gets the nod that he wants to see. He beams, "Well, sir, I know this is quite unexpected, but, with all respect, may I ask you a most urgent question?"

"Yes, Mr. Herald?" The Pastor can't imagine what, short of being saved by the Almighty, could cause the boy such a gleeful exuberance. But he knows Ernest Lee was saved long ago over in Success, so what else could it be?

"Well, you see, sir, very soon I'll be leaving for Tuckerman to take up a fine position as head bookkeeper. I am asking your kind permission to marry Miss Amy. I wish to take her with me as my wife, sir."

The Pastor hadn't added it up this way at all. In fact, this wasn't even in the *back* of his mind. However, he learned a long time ago not to speak until he's sure of things in his head. He clears his throat to respond, "I'd like to think this over a bit, Mr. Herald." The Pastor isn't smiling. In fact he is frowning.

This isn't what the young man wanted to hear. The marriage makes perfect sense to Ernest Lee, and he spent all week planning it out to be four or five (at the most) weeks from now. Sure, it's soon, but it is so right. He figured that it would be such an easy decision for a man of God like the Pastor. Ernest Lee's father had even agreed that, as much as he needed his son's help in Success, this position was the chance of a lifetime for a business school graduate. In the end, he wished Ernest Lee well. However, about the proposal that his son had confided, Homer Herald had cautioned, "Remember, Son, if the Pastor says, 'no,' don't burn your bridges behind you."

So, Ernest Lee musters all the calm that he can and replies, "Yes sir, I understand." However, the forlorn look on his face belies his conciliatory words.

Gert can hold her tongue no longer. She's not about to let a perfectly good "willin'" be thwarted by her thick-headed husband. She furiously motions for the Pastor to follow her inside and drags him into her kitchen. Propping her fists atop both ample hips, she looks her husband straight in eye and spits out, "Pastor Blackwell, I thought you were a man of God."

The Pastor is startled. He's about to speak, "I…" but Gert cuts him off.

"Don't you believe that God brought Mr. Herald to us here in Pitman for a reason? Don't you know that God wants this union to be?" Waving her hand toward the porch, she shames her husband, "Look at poor Mr. Herald standing out there on the porch. Have you ever seen a sadder look on a lad? You've taken all hope away from the young man—and him with an ailing mother back home." Gert shakes her head slowly side to side, lamenting the dreadful injustice.

The Pastor has never known his wife to be this passionate about anything—or to make such an open display. He's about to speak once again when Gert scolds, "You stand up there in front of the church, week after week, calling on folks to be saved that very minute. Tell me, then. Why can't a fella' decide to take a Baptist wife quick like that too? I say that there's nothing wrong with it, and I'll not have you turn this fine boy away from our home!"

"Our Amy's only fifteen," the Pastor sputters.

Gert fumes, "You know perfectly well, Pastor, that you've married young-uns before. Don't be so silly."

"What about Amy's work for the church?" he counters.

"Hang the church work! We'll get it done. It's nothing the three people left here in this house can't manage."

Gert takes his breath away. The Pastor never thought about any one but Amy helping out with his church work, much less about Amy getting married and leaving so soon. He decides that he won't yield and inch. "What's got into you, Misses? You never rush into things like this, and we hardly know this fellow at all. Get hold of yourself—we'll have to give it more time."

The pastor marches back out onto the porch with Gert fuming behind. He clears his throat and begins, "Nothing personal 'gainst you Mr. Herald; you're a fine young man as best I can tell. It's just that our Miss Amy has more growing up to do. And then there's the church work. In due time she'll take a husband and raise up a family, but not yet. It's too soon."

Gert is determined, *This willin' is going to be tougher than I thought.* Her only hope lies in beating her husband at his own game. Mustering her very best strategy, Gert preaches passionately for everyone to hear, "Pastor Blackwell, since the Almighty is leading this fine young man to down to Tuckerman, mighten it be that God needs our Amy down there too?" Turning quickly to Ernest Lee she croons, "Do they have a nice church down there in Tuckerman, Mr. Herald?"

Ernest Lee chirps up right on cue, "Yes ma'am, a good church, a big church, with lots of folks needing saving down that way. We'd be in that Tuckerman church every single Sunday, Ma'am—and at prayer meetings, too. I personally guarantee it."

Amy holds her breath and Effie is shocked, *What ever will Grandpa do?* The tension is as thick as molasses out on the porch

The Pastor gazes up at the fluffy clouds floating by. *I vowed to bring Amy closer to God—I wonder if this is what the Lord's has in mind.* He looks over at Amy. She's the picture of his dear Mary right now. Long forgotten feelings well up inside as he recalls the burning passion that he had for his late wife. He has pushed it out of his mind all these years, but it floods back right now. He can see that Amy's blank look is gone and that her eyes have come sparkling alive. Pastor Blackwell heaves a deep sigh and reflects, *After all, Amy'll soon turn sixteen, the same age she Mary was when we were married.*

Pastor Blackwell finally turns to his granddaughter and says, "Well, I suppose I should ask. Is this what you want?"

Amy's eyes are brimming with tears, "Yes, Grandpa Blackwell—more than anything I know."

The Pastor drawls at last, "Well, I guess it's God's will that you two should marry and go down to Tuckerman...."

"Yippie, yahoo," Ernest Lee shouts once again, grabbing hold of Amy and planting a kiss full on her cheek.

"Welcome to the family, Mr. Herald," Gert slaps him hard on the back.

Ernest Lee is overjoyed, "Marrying Amy—it's more than I could ever hope for, Mrs. Blackwell. I thank God." Smiling, he proudly adds, "And now, please call me Ernest Lee Ma'am—all of you."

"Ooooooh!" Grandma Gert gushes, knowing one thing for certain, *This here union was my willin.' God had nothing to do with it at all. Nothing whatsoever!*

Everyone disappears back inside the house, and the couple is alone on the porch once again. Ernest Lee takes hold of his future wife's hand and asks, "Shall we go down by the brook?"

The two happy souls romp across the field, but Amy stops short to solemnly ask, "About the church, Mr....I mean Ernest Lee. How strict are you about Bible teachings?"

Ernest Lee grins, "Well, I'm faithful to the Good Book, but I don't make a huge commotion about it."

"Don't you wonder all the time what God is thinking, or if he's happy with what you are doing, or not?"

"If I did that all day long, Amy, I'd never have time to get anything done. Anyway, I figure that's what God gave me a brain for—so I can think things through for myself. Why worry about *him* every minute, as long as I follow the Good Book the best that I can?"

"But don't you worry about going to hell if you don't get things right?"

"As long as my heart's in the right place, why on earth would God send a good person to hell?"

Amy feels a huge boulder roll off of her shoulders and away down the hill. As soon as they pass by the barn, Amy grabs Ernest Lee's hand and drags him around to the back. She beams, "Things are going to be wonderful with our new life together; that's what I think." She gives him a big hug, marveling at the thought, *I won't have to run away from home now. I'll leave peacefully with my love Ernest Lee.* The sad thought of leaving Sister Effie behind quickly dances through her mind, but it dances out just as quickly—this happy moment must not be diminished. Standing on tiptoes, Amy grabs Ernest Lee tight around his neck, and the couple shares their first real kiss together, body to body, pushing together hard against the back of the barn with mooing cows the only witness to the passion.

The days fly by, and chores seem so mundane to Amy as she counts the days until her wedding. Nonetheless, Brother Fitzgerald dropped off a load of plump strawberries yesterday—the very first of the season. There are far more than the four of them could eat in a week, so Grandma Gert directed the sisters to make strawberry jam. They fat red berries are so plump and juicy. Some folks have a strong preference for jelly, but the Blackwells prefer jam—fresh fruit cooked down until it's nice and soft with no extra sugar at all. "Pure fruit, just like God intended," Gert always says.

The sisters promised Grandma Gert to have the preserves put up by noon, so they laboriously stir the strawberries around in the kettle, taking turns as they chat. Amy says, "Remember when Mama used to make jam, and she'd let us lick spoons?"

Effie grins and nods that she does.

Amy continues, "She even let us stir the hot mixture a little, too."

Effie rolls here eyes and says, "I used to love that."

Amy laughs, "You were always more agile at it than me, Effie—even as a little tyke you were. Mama even said so."

"Really?" Effie loves to hear the old stories.

"Most certainly you were, Effie! Remember how clumsy I was at pouring fruit in the jars?" Amy envisions their tiny kitchen back then. All the rooms in their cabin were small and the furnishings were sparse. But their little hands were always "helping" Mama, and that was what mattered. "Remember that time I sloshed cherry jam on the floor, and Daddy walked in without looking?" Amy chuckles, "Our kitchen floor was sticky for weeks!"

Effie takes her turn stirring and smiles thinking about the sticky red floor. She was only four when their mama died, but she can remember things too—too many things. It is true that Effie was always good with her hands. She was especially good with scissors and her mama was so proud that she'd brag, "Effie can cut shapes of just about anything." They'd save old paper, and Mama would play, "Hmmm. Now let me see. I think I need me a cute little birdie. Can you cut me out a bird, Effie?"

The little hands would get busy and, next thing they knew, a little sparrow shape appeared at the end of Effie's scissors. Then, it was a mouse, or a bunny—or anything her mama asked for.

"Oh, lands sake. Look at this, Buck," she'd call out to her husband.

Now Amy is the one who stands out—cooking, sewing, gardening, and most everything else she touches. And Effie is happy with this. After their Mama died, Amy took charge and Effie willingly followed. Effie's special talent was forgotten, and she grew to hate artwork and never cut out her little shapes again—not even at school art time. Instead, she'd stare out of the window into the schoolyard.

"What captures your fancy out there?" the teacher would ask.

"Nothing," Effie always replied.

The heat from the fruit boiling up is turning the kitchen into a sauna. Still, Amy adds another stick of wood to keep the kettle bubbling and says "Keep on stirring, Eff. I need to catch a breath." Amy steps out onto the back porch and draws in the sweet morning air. Then she glances around the back yard and calls out excitedly, "Come look at this, Effie!"

The smokehouse door is ajar and, curled up just inside, a fat red cat tends to her litter. She appears to have three kittens that they can see. One is solid red like the mother and the two smaller are red spotted all over with white.

"Where on earth did they come from?" Effie is amazed.

The kitten's eyes are wide open, and they work away sucking on their mama's nipples, but pretty soon the largest red kitty wants to play and rolls over in dirt. Mama cat lunges, clamping firm jaws firmly around her wayward kitten's neck. The startled ball of fluff rolls back to Mama Cat's belly. Soon the red kitty becomes bored again and starts to stray off, but Mama Cat's swift leg swipes him right back to her side.

"Isn't that cute? Can we bring them inside, Amy?" Effie begs hopefully.

Amy shakes her head, "No. Grandma Gert would never allow it. Anyway, she'll be back at noon expecting this jam to be cooling off in the cellar."

"Oh, shucks," Effie says as the two girls walk back into the sweltering kitchen to keep stirring the fruit.

"I'm sure that Mama and her kittens will find their way home," Amy soothes.

The girls diligently stir the kettle as the berries turn to mush, but Effie can't stop thinking about the kittens nursing out in the smokehouse. She yearns to take them all up to her room. Watching a mama lovingly care for her babies would be such a joy—even if the mama is only a cat.

It's well after midnight and Effie sneaks down to the porch like she does on nights she can't sleep. She curls up on the swing, clutches her rag doll to her chest and stares up at the moon. She tries to keep her mind on the sweet kittens sleeping out in the smokehouse, but soon the bad thoughts creep in. Night time is always the worst for remembering. *Some say I can't remember back that far back 'cause I was only four, but they're so very wrong,* she thinks. She squeezes her bedraggled rag doll tighter trying to block out the bad thoughts, but she can't, and now she has a new worry, *With Amy going off to get married, who will watch out for me? And who will take me to find Daddy one day?* The worries spin around in her mind with new ones piling on top, *Why doesn't Daddy come back? Maybe he knows about my bad deed— that's probably why. If only I hadn't done it, Mama might still be alive and I'd still have my Daddy.*

A sick wave runs through Effie's body. Not even the rocking porch swing can comfort tonight.

CHAPTER 4
TRIP TO TUCKERMAN

The Heralds' white farmhouse nestles south on its grass covered knoll. Fluffy green willows shade their lawn all around and fragrant spring honeysuckle twines up the porch rails. At the foot of the knoll rests their weathered red barn with pastures surrounding, a haven for tail-tossing horses and cows munching hay. There isn't a cloud in the sky and a warm breeze is blowing—the perfect day for a wedding in May.

Excited and jovial, the two families ring the Herald's modest front room. Martha Herald sits in her spindle-back chair, grateful to rest at home and still witness the service. Martha's sister Glory, a squat, cheerful little woman with fuzzy gray hair, stands on her right, and Martha's husband Homer, a lanky and awkward fellow wearing a jacket too tight under the arms, stands close on her left. Gramps Herald, a quick-witted fellow given to corny one-liners, leans back on the wall between Homer and Uncle Marlin.

The Pastor commands the center of the room, proudly clutching his Bible. He chats with Ernest Lee who is all decked out in his best Sunday suit, grinning from ear to ear and nervously shifting from foot to foot.

Grandma Gert signals Effie to bring in her sister, and the coy bride floats in from the kitchen. Crisp white ribbons now encircle the waist of her new rosebud dress, and her hair is tied back with a huge satin bow at the nape of her neck. She cradles a fluffy bunch of Baby's Breath in her arms and smiles demurely.

Pastor Blackwell escorts Amy over to Ernest Lee's side. The groom beams.

"Oh, doesn't she look pretty?" Martha Herald whispers so loudly that the modest bride blushes.

Pastor Blackwell faces the couple and begins, "Dearly beloved, we gather here to unite this couple in holy matrimony." Then, being a creature of habit, he launches into God's plan of salvation—in detail. Gert finally catches his eye and glares, motioning toward poor Mrs. Herald ailing in her chair, so the Pastor quickly skips to the wedding part.

Amy is surprised at her Grandpa's good spirits today, considering that his religious indigestion has been brewing all week. She tried calming him with promises like, "Don't worry, Grandpa. I'll never forsake your mission," and then she tried, "Effie will be so helpful with your church work, Grandpa, better than I ever was." But the Pastor's mood remained sour all week—sorry that he ever gave in to Gert about Amy's marriage. Then, Amy hit upon a better approach, reminding him, "I'll be a soldier for Christ down in Tuckerman, Grandpa—just like it directs in the Bible." How could any Pastor argue with that? He reconciled, once again, to the marriage, conceding that his wife *was* the better judge of these things, *Gert's so perceptive.*

The newlyweds complete their "I dos" and kiss smack on the lips. Everyone smiles into their hankies at first and then chuckle out loud when the kiss lasts too long.

Incredibly, Grandma Gert parts with a compliment, "This was the nicest wedding I ever did see."

The happy clan feasts on Aunt Glory's fragrant casseroles, fried chicken and fresh garden greens until the platters are bare. Finally, they devour her two-layer wedding cake decorated with sugar icing and little strawberry hearts on the top.

The Pastor, mellow from feasting and glad that it's all over, thumps his belly and declares, "What a wonderful feast; the best ever."

Gramps Herald chimes in, "That meal was *so* good, I won't be surprised if the Governor bills tax on it!"

Ernest Lee laughs the loudest, grateful for Gramps' mild witticism in front of his new father in law.

The happy family mills about, and Ernest Lee follows Pastor Blackwell out onto the porch intending to thank him for such a fine service, but the Pastor speaks first. "I'd be pleased if you and Amy would settle in Pitman, son. And I wouldn't object if you were heard as a preacher. You have a good way with people, and...."

Ernest Lee waits until the Pastor concludes, but respectfully replies, "Well, I'll be working with numbers for some time to come. However, I'm a man of my word, and we'll stay close to God down in Tuckerman. You can count on that, sir."

The Pastor heaves a deep sigh, "My son left home, you know."

"Yes, sir. Amy told me."

"I always thought he'd come into the ministry," the Pastor trails off. "Anyway, it would be good to have you and Amy around if you ever rethink it," he says as he heads toward the door.

Ernest Lee calls after him, "Sir, may I ask—why did your son leave home?"

"Because of me. That's the truth of the matter," the Pastor sighs once again.

Ernest Lee thinks fast, "I don't see how that could be, Sir."

The Pastor looks down, "You don't need a sad tale on your happy wedding day. It's just that you remind me...."

"I *would* like to hear," Ernest Lee encourages.

The Pastor wanders back over and continues in low tones, "His name was Gideon, but everyone called him Buck. Anyway, I never saved him, you see. I'd look deep into his eyes asking, 'Son, do you hear Christ's call?' His reply was always the same, 'Perhaps one day I will, Daddy. Give me more time.' He never did see the light. But he did bring his bride to our home, and Amy was born in the room at the top of the stairs. I thought we were all living together in peace, but after awhile, you see, I couldn't resist."

"Resist, sir?"

"You know, I'm an ole' preacher, and I kept on trying to save him. Finally, resentment most likely drove him away—at least that's what I gathered, though, no words were exchanged at the time."

"What did he do?"

"He just pinned a note to his pillow—said they left early that morning to lead a life on their own. By the time I arose, they were gone." The pastor shakes his head like it all happened yesterday. "Buck wrote home once or twice after that, assuring me they were all right. He said that he was working down state as a carpenter, and then he wrote me again after Effie was born."

Ernest Lee hopes he's not too bold in asking, "When did Buck bring the girls back home to live with you Pitman? Amy never exactly said."

The Pastor leans against the porch rail, "It was right after his wife Mary died of pneumonia. Amy was only six, and Effie was four. I was proud when he came home for his girl's sake. However, we argued just like before, so he took off again—but this time he left home alone. That was nine years ago, and we haven't heard from him since."

"May I ask—why didn't he take the girls with him that day?"

"I'll never know for sure. He said he'd be back for them, but he never returned."

Ernest Lee starts feeling comfortable with the closeness, so he asks; "Do you imagine that Buck will ever come back home?"

The Pastor stares straight ahead and straightens up slowly. He pats Ernest Lee's shoulder and, without saying a word, he strides back inside to join the jabbering wedding party. The door bangs behind him and Ernest Lee is alone on the porch with his question.

It's late in the afternoon. Ernest Lee smiles over at Amy who is chatting nearby with his mother. "Well, *Mrs.* Amy Herald, it's time we get along to Tuckerman."

The new bride nods eagerly at the suggestion.

With good byes and hugs all around, the newlyweds lead the group out to the front of the house. Homer stops short on the lawn, clears his throat, and proudly announces, "If you're determined to take off for Tuckerman, son, I want you to drive off in style. I make you a gift." He beams as he motions toward his beloved Model T Ford parked alongside their wagon.

Amy gasps and Effie squeals with the surprise. All hands transfer the couple's baggage over to the shiny black automobile, and, with a few hefty turns of the crank, they are off.

Effie rushes back inside the house as the couple drives away. She clutches her mother's golden locket for comfort, but she still feels alone, so she dives at once into a flurry of activity, clearing off the last of the food sitting out on the table. Effie is stacking up the platters and plates when Grandma Gert marches back into the room with the others.

"What are you doing, young lady?" Gert gasps.

"Just clearing things off, Grandma Gert."

"Stacking dirty plates up so high up, one on top of the other? You've been taught better than that!" Gert makes a grab for the plates.

The stack shifts to one side, and Effie tries to right them, but it's too late. The group stands aghast as the Herald's precious china crashes down onto the hard wooden floor in a deafening clatter, food-caked shards flying clear across the room.

"Now look what you've done, you clumsy girl," Gert shouts.

Effie pleads, "I was only trying to help, but when you grabbed...."

Gert turns to the Pastor and wales, "See that Pastor! Look at how she talks-back to me. She'd never dare do this back home in Pitman. What the Heralds must think!"

The Pastor steps in, "See here, Effie. You should be more respectful than that to your grandmother."

"I didn't mean...." Effie pleads once again.

Gert rages on in front of the Heralds, waving her arms all about, finally concluding, "You're such an ungrateful child. I praise God every day that you're not my *own* flesh and blood! I'd hate being a true kin to the sorry likes of you!"

The wedding group is stone silent as Effie runs out the kitchen door and heads down toward the barn.

Amy sings loudly as the couple rolls along. She leads Ernest Lee through all four verses she can remember of, *"Blest Be the Ties That Bind."* Her thoughts float along, *Who would have thought it—just over one month ago I was so lonely and sad, and now I'm a new bride with a new handsome husband, riding in our new automobile on the way to our new home."*

Folks wave and call out as the couple passes through town after town, many seeing an automobile for the very first time.

"Tell me about the house that you found us in Tuckerman," Amy begs.

"Oh, it's no bigger than a hen house, but you'll like it that small. It'll be less to sweep up," Ernest Lee grins.

Amy has been asking about their new house for weeks, and, every time, Ernest Lee thinks up something worse to describe it.

"Oh, it's just an ole' shack, but we'll make do," he says now.

Amy decides to give up.

The afternoon fades and they're rolling through Walnut Ridge when Ernest Lee spots a clearing ahead. He winks, "Well, Mrs. Herald, what about resting up there?" They pull off of the road and stop in the center of the round grassy spot. Ernest Lee can't resist—he playfully grabs Amy's shoulder and pulls her close for a peck on the cheek.

Amy smiles coyly, "Ernest Lee! Anyone passing out on the road will see us!"

"No luck this time, but I'll get you yet," he laughs, content to sit in the front seat with his bride as they munch on apple butter sandwiches and smack down Aunt Glory's bread and butter pickles. Wagon after wagon rolls by, but the couple relaxes, happy to be off the road and alone.

"We'll be in Tuckerman before nightfall. It won't take us too long once we get going," Ernest Lee ventures. They're enjoying themselves so, that they sit dreamily watching the sun sink toward the horizon. Pretty soon the tired couple nods off. Amy's head rests on Ernest Lee's shoulder when the odd noises start.

"What's that?" Amy sits upright. The tinny noise sounds like "ting, ting, ting" graduating to "pling, pling, splash," before raining down.

"Just a little shower, sweet," Ernest Lee reassures.

Before long, the little splashes turn into big heavy drops pelting down and zinging in all directions off of the shiny black metal. "Quick, let's put the side curtains up," Ernest Lee shouts, digging under the seat for the panels and snapping them on top all around. The wind picks up, blowing torrents of rain, and the Model T vibrates in the wild assault. The lovely blue sky of just an hour ago is now black as night, and strong gusts howl like wolves through the trees. Water trickles in through curtain gaps, so Ernest Lee presses the panels down tighter yet.

"Slide closer Amy and we'll stay dry in the center," he says, gathering Amy toward him with a sweep of his arm.

"I'm scared, Ernest Lee," Amy cries.

"Oh, I've been out in storms worse than this before," Ernest Lee brags. "This'll blow over fast as it started."

The angry storm doesn't let up. Lightening brightens the sky like a mid-summer morn and loud thunderclaps deafen their ears. "I never figured we'd spend our wedding night like this," Ernest Lee grumbles, pulling Amy even closer and reaching in back for a blanket that's stashed on the floor.

Soon others pull off the road too—frightened travelers in covered wagons, and some towing mules braying loudly at their plight. Wild sparks fly through the sky, and the newlyweds cower together.

"We're 'hold-up' just like in pioneer days," Amy whispers.

"Yes, except for our odd metal wagon," Ernest Lee scoffs.

Around midnight, the rain lets up and the wind is still at last. "We'll I'll be," Amy exclaims, "Do you think the storm's finally over?"

The night is pitch black except for a sliver of moon and for stars popping out as the storm clouds move off. Tree frogs start chirping, and it's more peaceful than ever before. The two nestle together, relaxing for the first time since the ruckus began.

"You see, Amy? We're warm and safe," Ernest Lee whispers, squeezing her hand gently.

"It's nice and cozy in here," Amy whispers back, feeling snuggly close on the narrow front seat.

"And it's our wedding night," Ernest Lee rasps, kissing Amy's nose, then her ear, clinging her tighter and tighter under the blanket in the blackness of night. They can't stop kissing now on the lips and then down on the shoulders, covering each other with their warm loving touches, then stroking and finding new places, lying down on the seat.

"I wanted…." Ernest Lee whispers.

"It doesn't matter," Amy whispers back, "I love you."

The sun is high when the couple finally reaches Tuckerman the next day. They haven't gone far when Ernest Lee turns right onto the first gravel road they cross and rolls to a stop. "Here we are, Amy," he says.

Amy is overwhelmed at the sight. "You didn't let on."

The charming two-story, white clapboard house has wide windows with pretty yellow shutters upstairs and down. A handsome brick path leads up to the porch. It's not a grand house by any means, but it stands out like a gem with its modest proportions and tasteful design.

Amy looks at the house's pristine condition and gasps, "Ernest Lee, this house doesn't even look lived in!"

"That's because it *wasn't* ever lived in before," Ernest Lee laughs. Amy begs an explanation, so he continues, "My dad called everyone in Tuckerman that he knew, and the Mayor told him about this house sitting empty."

"Land sakes! How come?" Amy can't wait to know.

" 'Cause the poor fellow that built it went broke. So, Dad bought it and did what little fixing up was left. I wanted to surprise you. You like it?" he asks.

"Do I like it? Ernest Lee, I love it!"

"Well, let's go on inside." The couple trots gingerly up the front path, but Ernest Lee pauses at the door to whisk Amy off of her feet, just like he promised his mother he would. Swinging his squealing bride over the threshold, he declares, "There. Now we're officially married in our new home." He tries for another wet kiss, but Amy is moving too fast for him now.

"My gracious, and we have furniture too, Ernest Lee?" Amy excitedly rushes around, running her hands over the upholstered sofa and chairs.

"Yes, Dad bought us that too," Ernest Lee boasts.

The couple walks around and discovers that the front sitting room opens onto a small dining room with the kitchen adjoining off to the side. A little sunroom runs along the back of the kitchen, and Amy notices a closed door on one wall.

"Where does that door lead?" Amy asks.

"Wait till you see." Ernest Lee proudly pulls the door open and announces, "We've got our very own indoor plumbing room."

Amy shrieks, racing over to take a good look. There in the middle of the tiny little room sits a white porcelain pedestal with a wooden ring for a seat. An odd wooden box is affixed to the wall just above with a chain that hangs down.

"Go ahead and pull it," Ernest Lee coaxes.

Amy walks over, and gives a little tug to the chain. Nothing happens. She gives the chain a heftier tug, and the bowl emits a loud "whoosh" as water furiously churns around inside the bowl. "Land sakes, that sounds like a tornado!" Effie cries.

Ernest Lee chuckles, "That, my sweet, is gen-u-ine siphon jet action. Just remember, that giant 'whoosh' caused that poor fellow to run out of money."

"Was the bowl-contraption all that expensive?" Amy asks.

"No, it was digging the deep hole that ran up his bill!" Ernest Lee chuckles.

The pair continues exploring, this time heading up the narrow staircase where two rooms face each other at top, one looking out on the front road and the other looking out on the back yard.

Ernest Lee notices, "This sunny front room has a nice big feather bed—perfect for our new bedroom."

"What about the other?" Amy asks about the facing room sitting empty.

Ernest Lee grins sheepishly, "For our 'wee ones' some day?"

Amy teases, "Not *right* away," knowing full well that she intends to teach school a full year before having a family.

Nightfall comes all too soon. The weary couple unpacks what they can, snuffs out the lantern, and snuggles down on the soft mattress that's washed in the moon light. A warm breeze blows in through the windows, and the thin cotton sheets feel so cool. Amy rolls over into her husband's arms, content with their love. But the soft whistle of a far off train brings new thoughts to mind, *How can I forget about poor little Effie back in Pitman? She's all alone tonight with no one to talk to.*

"What's wrong?" Ernest Lee looks over and frowns.

"I was just thinking of little Effie all by herself tonight. We've never been apart even one night before."

"She's a big girl now," Ernest Lee assures.

"Still, I feel bad about leaving her all alone."

"Well then, you'll just have to go home to Pitman for a visit real soon," Ernest Lee grins.

Amy sits straight up in bed, "You'll take me back to Pitman, Ernest Lee?"

"Of course I will," he whispers, kissing her cheek.

Amy feels so much better now. "How did I deserve a wonderful husband like you?" she says. "I haven't felt this happy since my…" She pauses.

Ernest Lee guesses, "Since your Daddy was home?"

"How did you know?" Amy asks.

"I figured it out from what your Grandpa said."

"He spoke about my father?" Amy is surprised.

"He sure did—we talked out on the porch right after the wedding."

Amy whispers, "Did he ever say why Daddy left?"

"He didn't say exactly, but he said it was between him and his son. He said that for sure. They'll patch it up one day, and your father will come home again. It happens like that even in good Christian families. You'll see."

Amy feels warm and wonderful with Ernest Lee's reassurance. She snuggles back down beside him, but has only strength left to kiss him goodnight before drifting off to sleep in his arms.

Ernest Lee tosses and turns, and he can't fall asleep. He hears another train whistle blow, but it provides him no comfort, and the warm breezes blowing in bring no relief. Even Amy's soft breathing doesn't calm him. Tomorrow he'll meet his new boss and start working at his very first job. *What if I'm not as good as I thought? What if I fail and Mr. Marshall decides to fire me? Then what will we do?* The excitement over his new job turns into agonizing worry. *What made me think I could do grown up work after only two years at school? I should have stuck with farming and milling like the rest of the Heralds.* Ernest Lee fixes his eyes on the ceiling. Worries rumble around in his head like last night's fierce thunder.

Amy is alone in the kitchen the next morning, tea cup in hand, looking out at her lovely back yard. Ernest Lee left for work after downing only tea and a single slice of bread with jam. He looked terribly tired. She assured him, "Don't you worry one bit, Ernest Lee. Concentrate on your new job. I'll get things done around here."

"Don't overdo, sweet Amy," he replied. "There's nothing that can't wait until I get home tonight." He patted money into her palm and bravely reassured her on the way out the door, "I'll do just fine."

Amy wanders about the kitchen figuring what to do next when she hears, "tap, tap, and tap." Peeking out through the side window, she can see a woman standing out on the front porch and clutching a package. Amy races into the front room and opens the door.

"I'm Mary Randolph, the Pastor's wife," the visitor smiles. "We got word you folks were coming, and I brought you a little welcome gift," she says holding out the box neatly tied up with string.

"So glad to meet you. I'm Amy Blackwell—I mean Amy Herald. Please come on in," she invites, blushing at her mistake.

Mary laughs, "Oh, we heard you're newly married. Congratulations! It took me months to get used to my new name too."

Her guest is older, no doubt, but Amy doesn't feel any difference as they talk on and on over tea. She learns that Mary and her husband Rob moved down from Tennessee just three years ago, they live just up the road, they have two little boys not yet in school, and her widowed mother lives with them. Mary is short and plump (but not overly), with a kind, caring face and dark brown hair that she draws back in loose wavy curls. It amuses Amy how outspoken Mary is, considering that they just met. Amy finds herself thinking, "I hope we'll be truly good friends."

The two enjoy Mary's freshly baked "welcome" cake, and Mary asks, "Will you be shopping today?"

"I was planning to. In fact, I was figuring out where to go first when you knocked at the door," Amy laughs.

"Goodness!" Mary exclaims. "You won't get lost here in Tuckerman. You folks have the best lot in town so close to Main Street. My mother is minding my boys. Let's quick go get you stocked up."

Amy likes Mary's go-getting spirit, her laugh, and the way she listens attentively when you talk. It's been a long time since Amy felt so lighthearted—or had a friend. The two spend the rest of the morning filling Amy's shopping list. They buy a bucket and a fry pan from Jake's Hardware, staples from the Smith's grocery and soaps and salts from Miller's Pharmacy. They're walking further down Main Street when Amy spots bolts of bright yellow gingham in Hassack's Fabric Shop window.

"Oh, I wish I brought my sewing machine with me from Pitman," Amy sighs. "I'd make up some pretty curtains with a table cloth to match."

Mary is quick with an answer, "That's no problem at all. I'll put my Singer machine in its case and bring it over this very afternoon."

Amy grins, "My Grandpa always says that the Lord can work wonders, and the Lord sure has today, Mary Randolph." The two hug with delight like they've known each other for ages and march inside the store to buy yards of the bright gingham cloth.

They're laughing and joking, heading home down Main Street when Amy gasps, "Look, Mary! That's were Ernest Lee works."

Sure enough, across the street stands a two story brick building with "Marshall's Mercantile" printed across the front window. Amy quickly crosses the street with Mary trailing behind. They peek in Marshall's window from the side, careful not to be seen. Ernest Lee is standing inside chatting amiably with a kindly looking gray-haired gentleman.

"My husband looks like he's worked there ten years already," Amy whispers, feeling a burden lift right away.

Effie sits on the front porch swing by herself anxiously looking up and down Military Road for no good reason. The porch is a lonely place since Amy left to get married. Amy sends her long letters to read, but it isn't the same. Last week Effie turned fourteen years old—Amy used to make a big fuss over her birthday, but this year it was only mentioned in passing. No one even sang "Happy Birthday."

"Come in here, Effie," Grandpa calls out from his parlor.

Effie scuffs inside, and the Pastor commences to instruct the minute she enters the room.

"Effie, here are my church diary notes. Now, I want you to fill those things in on this printed list for me and to add up the numbers to date. I'll be needing it for my meeting today."

"Fill in *all* of these lines. Grandpa?" Effie's brows raise.

The Pastor frowns, "Yes. Your sister Amy helped me at your age, so you can help me too."

Effie begins reading his printed list entitled, "Weekly Statistical Table:"

# Miles Traveled___	# Public Praying___
# Churches Founded___	$ Collected___
# Sermons Preached___	# Membership___
# Rec'd. By Baptism___	# Excluded___
# Rec'd. By Letter____	# Died___

Then she tries to make out the hen-scratch in her grandfather's church diary:

Sunday, June 15, 1917. Brought apples and corn over to Union driving 15 miles; Preached 9 AM to 10 AM; Sunday school 10AM- 11AM; Main Sermon-"We Are All Disciples" from 11 AM-Noon; Prayer Meeting 6PM-7PM. Saved 3 souls.

"Grandpa, why did you take apples and corn to that church up in Union?"

The Pastor answers, "Because they might have to make do for my supper. I never know if I'll be invited in for a meal after church, Effie." He turns back to his work.

Effie continues reading his weekly diary:

Monday, June 16, 1917. 10 AM Public Prayer in Pitman. 1PM, drove to Oak Grove to see about setting up a church; 6PM Public Prayer at Masonic meeting, Pitman.

"Grandpa, what's a Masonic?"

"That's one of our leading Orders—like a club. Our best citizens belong and they do good works around town for the poor and the ailing."

"Doesn't our Church do good works?" Effie persists.

"Yes, but Masonic folks come from all *different* churches. We all work together." He adds in a burst of impatience, "See here, Effie. I must get on with my reading—you get on with that countin'. No more questions for now."

Effie finishes inserting the numbers. She adds them up with last week's and places the neatly filled-in list on her grandfather's desk. He doesn't look up, so she quietly exits and heads up the stairs.

The privacy of her bedroom is most welcome these days, for Grandma Gert has been more demanding than ever, owing, no doubt, to the wedding day plate-clearing incident. Then, in the evening her Grandpa says, "Effie, follow me over to church to set up for prayer meeting." It never ends.

Effie looks over at Amy's empty bed and ponders her lonely life now. *Now Grandpa wants me to add up his records? With me so poor at math? How will I manage?* Worse yet, school started last week, and she still has no friends. Effie sits all alone at recess watching the others have fun, girls whispering back and forth, and boys playing ball or performing silly pranks. Without Amy to share her problems with after school, Effie doesn't know where to turn.

Last week Effie woke up with a black cloud hanging over her head, and it has been up there for days. Everything looks colorless and bland. Yesterday, she was out in the garden and couldn't help thinking, *It's not worth it,* though she didn't know why she ever thought such a thing.

This morning Grandma Gert shook her finger, "If you don't eat something, Missy, I'll send the goblins over to get you." Effie stared down at her plate, so Grandma scolded again, "Where's your sense of humor, young lady?" Effie didn't laugh then and she isn't laughing now. In fact, Effie can't remember laughing since before Amy's wedding.

Nights are the worst, lying awake. Sometimes she thinks of her mother and feels warm all over. Her mother was just a little thing with a pretty heart-shaped face and the same blonde hair as hers. Then, just as quickly, Effie's thoughts switch from fond remembering to the bad thoughts about the day her mother died, and she lies there in terror.

Effie grabs her rag doll now and presses it close to keep from crying, but it doesn't work. The doll gets wet and more face paint flakes off. *My poor doll is pitifully faceless. Just like my life.* She can hear her Grandpa hitching up the wagon and heading into town for his meeting. Grandma Gert is way out in the garden trimming lilies and cutting back weeds. She'll be out there until supper no doubt.

Effie sits on the edge of the bed in a patch of afternoon sun. How did things get so confusing? She stares down at the little rag doll remembering how her mother cut it out of muslin, stuffed, dressed, and stitched it up, painting the little face on, and then giving it to her on a cold winter morning that was her birthday. She starts longing so hard for her mama that she can feel her warmth in the room. *That's impossible, those days are gone.* Now the bad feelings start coming on again—the ones that she's trying to forget, and Amy isn't around to distract her. The intruding thoughts ring loudly again in her ear, *It's not worth it. No, it's not worth it at all.* This time they're much more insistent.

Grabbing her doll by its tattered little arm, Effie slumps down the stairs. The screen door slams closed and she crosses the lawn, wanders down the green grassy hill, and on through the leafy orchard, but there are no colors today and no familiar scents. Finally, she reaches the shade, and the babbling brook beckons. Soon cool water will stop her sad memories and end all her pain. The peaceful thought strikes her, *By the time I reach Current River, I'll be with my Mama.*

Effie sobs as she lowers her beloved little playmate into the water, letting go of her arm and watching her float down the stream. The doll's bright red gingham apron bubbles up in the flow.

Now Effie begins what she must. She unlaces her shoes and places them neatly on a rock on the bank and tucks Mama's precious locket safely inside. Her sobbing subsides. *Yes, this is right. It won't be long now.*

Effie wades in past the rock tops, the deepest part where they were never allowed to play growing up. The coldness climbs up her thighs, and she slowly crouches down into the swift moving flow. She finds a solid rock on the bottom, curls her toes tightly around it, and, with one determined push, she snaps her legs straight out behind. Her body shoots forward—but she's floating, not going under like she planned. The thought comes to her, *Just let go and be free. God will take you under further down stream.* Effie squinches her eyes up tight for the journey in the numbing cold water.

A white light dawns ahead and God's angels beckon. Effie floats closer to see. It's peaceful and so utterly serene in the water. Her minds floats, *This is how it'll be up in heaven. Please take me home to my mother to rest.* The angels beckon again, and she floats further down stream, eager to join them.

But, something pulls her up from her soaking wet bed now. *Don't! Please let me sleep. Leave me alone. Can't you see this is right?* The jerky pulls won't stop, pulling at her again and again, jarring Effie awake. Her knees rake over rocks and then drag over wet mossy ground. Her chest feels on fire as it heaves up and down, and she gulps for air between plegmy coughs. Her squinting eyes find light that's dotted with green. Somehow she turns over now, and a spongy coolness slides along her back until the pulling finally stops. Effie squints up again, this time into a grayish vision with two eyes peering down. Someone strokes the side of her face. Effie lies quietly as the patting continues and a soft tune floats through the air:

Hush little baby don't say a word, Mama's gonna' buy you a mockin' bird. And if that mockin' bird don't sing, Mama's gonna' buy you a wedding ring....

The words are familiar to Effie. It has been a long time since her Mama once sang them. The sun beats down, warming her cold flesh, but she's helpless to rise.

After a long while, the kind voice asks, "Are you ready to sit up now?"

Effie squints up into a face that she recalls from long ago, but she doesn't answer. She remembers little by little—it is old Mrs. Isay. This time, Effie isn't afraid. She lies there awhile longer on the grassy spot in the sun and then asks, "Why—why didn't you leave me be?"

"You don't want to die, now. Nothin's that bad, child," the old woman rasps.

"How did you know I was here?" Effie cries.

"I was comin' down to fill up my bucket, when I saw you let loose of your doll and you waded in after. I rushed down the hill as fast as I could, but it took me a bit to catch you down stream."

"I *wanted* to die," Effie cries, her tears streaming down, "Why didn't you leave me alone?"

Mrs. Isay pats her cheek again, and whispers, "Week after week, I look out my window when you leave food on my porch, and I say to myself, "Something is bad wrong with that poor child.""

Effie wants to throw herself back in the brook, but her body is limp and the lilting cadence of Mrs. Isay's words lulls her to rest. The old woman strokes her face softly and the sun beats down on her cold, wet body. *I'll just lie here for now until I figure out what to do.*

"Let me walk you up to your house, child." Mrs. Isay intones.

"No! I'm never going home," Effie chokes.

Mrs. Isay is quiet for awhile and then tries again, "Well then, let me take you up to my cabin for a bit. Surely that will do."

"No—I don't know."

The old woman slowly drawls, "Well, if we stay here, and if your Grandfather passes by, you'll be goin' home with him right away; that's for sure."

Effie tries to prop herself up on an elbow, but fierce coughing dislodges more phlegm.

Mrs. Isay pounds on her back again and gently props her up against a tree. Spotting Effie's shoes across the brook, the old woman wades over the rock tops to retrieve them and returns right away. She finds the locket inside her shoe and carefully loops the chain around Effie's neck and then slips the shoes onto Effie's cold feet. With no further words spoken, the two stagger up the hill until they reach Mrs. Isay's one-room cabin off in the trees.

Effie slumps down on the thin log bed that stretches under a tiny curtainless window.

"Here's a quilt I made all myself. Put this 'round you while I spread your dress out to dry on the porch," Mrs. Isay says, holding the old patched quilt up between them and looking away as Effie disrobes.

Effie wraps herself up tight in the quilt and leans up against the pine headboard. She's exhausted and chilled to the bone, and she slowly sips the hot brew of birch tea and honey that Mrs. Isay boils up. The cabin feels strangely familiar to Effie.

The old recluse sits in her rocker by the bedside and begins telling Effie about things that she's never heard of before—how to pound roots into medicine and flowers into dye, how to survive in the woods during winter and how to live all alone. Mrs. Isay never once asks Effie what troubles her that day or why she waded into the brook. Likewise, Effie never asks the old woman why she hides in the woods, talking to no one. They unlikely pair speak in unhurried, soft tones until the afternoon sun sets pink in the sky.

"If I get your dress, will you put it on now?" Mrs. Isay gently asks. "You can be home by suppertime if you leave soon."

"I don't know what to do," Effie whispers.

The old woman smiles, "Can we talk now and then when you leave food on my porch?"

Effie wishes that Amy were here, and she tries clearing her head, but she's all alone and her thoughts jumble together. *What do I have in common with this old recluse? She spoiled my plan, so why should I speak with her ever again?* Yet a force draws Effie to the old woman like a moth to a flame. *Well, the poor old thing has been so nice to me. It wouldn't do to hurt her feelings, I suppose.*

Before she can think further, Effie finds herself saying, "Alright, we'll talk more when I bring up your basket next time."

"Well then, I'll fetch your dress, and you'll come back to talk whenever you like," old Mrs. Isay smiles, and she disappears out the front door to grab Effie's dress from the last sliver of sunlight on the porch.

Effie dresses quickly and shuffles off through the woods pondering what has just happened. True, the old woman is strange, but she isn't the sinister person that Grandma Gert has warned about all these years. *Grandma Gert never said outright what was unholy about the old recluse. One thing's for sure, though: Grandma wouldn't like my visiting Mrs. Isay one bit if she knew.* Effie shrugs. *Why does it matter what Grandma Gert thinks? She probably never even met the old woman!*

It has only been one month since their wedding, and things are more wonderful than Amy ever imagined. Their little brick house is bright and cheerful inside, and her crisp gingham curtains now trim every window. She talked to the teacher about helping out at the schoolhouse fall term, and she's active in church doings, just as she promised her Grandpa she'd be.

Ernest Lee loves Mr. Marshall's mercantile business. In fact, from the tales he regales over supper, the man is more like a father than a boss, bestowing accolades daily such as, "Wonderful work, Ernest Lee," or "We've never had our accounts in as good order as this before, son."

As Amy hoped, she and Mary Randolph have become very good friends, shopping, talking, and sharing prized recipes almost every day. Amy invited Mary and her husband over for dinner one night. Amy was so nervous about having the new Pastor in the house, Mary's husband or not.

The minute he walked through the door, Brother Randolph charmed them by being as courteous as he was kind, laughing right away, "You can drop the 'Brother,' just call me Rob and feed me anything you have in your kitchen." The couples are drawing closer and closer. Amy notices something else, too. Rob Randolph looks so somber in his pulpit, but he's so outgoing and friendly in person—and he's quite funny too, not to mention handsome, much like Ernest Lee in these traits. After Rob Randolph's first visit, Amy remarked to her husband, "He's the first pastor I've known that's a *real person.*" She was thinking of her Grandpa, and Ernest Lee knew what she meant.

As far as Amy's concerned, there's only one thing wrong in her life right now. Despite her happy life in Tuckerman, she can't stop worrying about her sister Effie in Pitman. Her nagging guilt grows stronger each day. *How can I have such fun here in Tuckerman and leave Effie all alone back in Pitman? It isn't right. I hope no harm will come to her.*

Effie's last letter was odd when she wrote, "Don't worry about me. I have a new friend to visit with, and I'll be just fine." How strange that Effie didn't mention her friend's name. Amy knows everyone back home, and she can't think of anyone Effie is close with, or of anyone new who moved into town. And why did Effie make such a point about her not worrying? That makes Amy all the *more* concerned. She shares her fears with Ernest Lee, but he says, "There's nothing we can do from here. It's no good to borrow trouble like that."

Amy admits, *Ernest Lee is probably right—there's nothing to get so upset about. I'm sure Effie is just fine.* Still, Amy vows to visit her sister very soon like Ernest Lee offered—just to make sure for herself.

CHAPTER 5
STITCHES IN TIME

The neighborhood rooster greets daybreak, and Amy snuggles up against Ernest Lee until he rouses, too. It has been over two months since the wedding, and the couple has developed a set morning routine. First, they scurry around getting washed up and dressed, Amy fixes a nice breakfast, and Ernest Lee leaves right after slurping it down. Then, Amy puts her kitchen back in order, and she starts some kind of project she's dreamed up. Today she'll sew on her new Singer machine for the first time.

Last week she announced to Ernest Lee, "My rosebud dress was nice for the summer, but I'm ready for a new dress this fall." The fact is, with all of her cooking and baking, the rosebud dress is a bit tight these days, too. Ernest Lee grinned and gave her extra money for fabric, and she raced over to Hassack's to buy the brown cotton print just in from New York. Amy smiles at the thought, but there's no time to daydream. She's got to get busy.

Amy smoothes her fabric out on the table and pins the pattern pieces down in place. Then, she carefully cuts out around them and stacks up the pieces in neat piles on the side. Amy loves the precision of sewing. She plops her spool of thread over the stubby little peg, pulls the chocolate brown thread across the top, loops it in and around the levers and down to the sewing foot, scoring a needle-threading bull's eye on the very first try. Finally, she brings the bobbin thread up without any snarls. She exhales.

Good so far, but now for the tricky part. Positioning fabric beneath the needle, Amy steadies her feet on the flat iron treadle, and, with a hefty turn of the wheel, works her feet furiously forward and back. Her Singer click-clacks as the fabric flows beneath her fingers, so lovely and cool. The needle flies up and down, *click, clack, click,* quickly stitching the dress pieces together. Amy plops the sleeves into place, then she sits back to admire her work, *My seams are as straight as railroad tracks.*

Amy has worked hard on her dress all day. She'd love to finish up now, but it's time to fix supper. This time she's concocting Ernest Lee's favorite chicken and dumplings, and she has it simmering on the stove by the time he walks through the door.

"Amy, that smells like chicken and dumplins'. Biscuits, too? Wonderful, my love," Ernest Lee licks his lips.

Amy knew he'd love this meal. With any luck, it'll satisfy sufficiently to get him chatting tonight, because she'd like to hear more of his stories from work. Amy sets the steaming tureen down in front of her husband.

Ernest Lee is barely through with his prayer when he begins ladling the chunks of sweet chicken breast over lumpy white dumplings and helping himself to fresh peas along with a huge buttered biscuit. Gobbling up forkful after forkful, he smacks his lips and winks over at Amy, "Mighty good, Sweet."

Amy casually asks, to get him talking tonight, "How were things at the mercantile today, Ernest Lee?"

"Very good, very good," he says, same as always.

"Good as last week?"

"Couldn't be better. Mr. Marshall said so today." Ernest Lee proceeds with his story.

Amy beams, "I knew you'd do well, as smart as you are."

She marvels at their good life in Tuckerman, but she takes nothing for granted. Every night she prays, *Dear God, please don't take this wonderful life away to pay for my sins. And can you please let me know soon if my baptism took?* Thus far, she hasn't heard back. So, in the meantime, she thinks up ways to find reassurance from Ernest Lee. She always scolds herself later, *See there! Everything's just fine and dandy. Stop pestering poor Ernest Lee and enjoy the new life that God granted.* Then, the very next day she worries all over again that she'll lose everything due to her failings.

Ernest Lee leaves for work Monday morning after a wonderful weekend at home. On Saturday they planted a patch of marigolds in a sunny spot out in the front yard. It's not much of a garden, but it reminds him of his mother's flowers back home. He hustles over to the mercantile and enters through the side door.

Mr. Marshall stands there eager to share weekend stories. The man started his business in 1875, advertising in the *Herald* that he sells, "a *selected* stock of quality general merchandise," and now he sells most things including furniture, clothing and even farm equipment. He never lets on, but Mr. Marshall is also a most generous man—the first to volunteer for charitable work, a trait which Tuckerman's citizens hold in the highest esteem.

Mr. Marshall starts talking first, clearly enjoying his Monday morning disdain, "What a slave driver my good wife Mrs. Marshall is. She had me planting box hedges all weekend!"

Now it's Ernest Lee's turn, and he screws up his face to complain, "My good wife, Mrs. Herald, had me planting flowers all over the place. It'll look like a meadow in our yard." The jovial pair swap their stories until work begins.

Ernest Lee is eager to start working on a project assigned just last week. Mr. Marshall had walked into his office and announced, "Let me tell you all about my *other* business, son—my real estate holdings. I'd like you to keep those books for me, too." Then he chuckled, "Of course, there'll be an increase in your salary. You won't mind that, now, will you?"

The young bookkeeper had responded without even knowing what was entailed, "I'm truly honored, sir." The timing couldn't be better, as Ernest Lee has the mercantile accounts whipped into shape, and he's ready for more challenging work. Before their morning chat ends, he assures Mr. Marshall, "I'll get going on your personal accounts right away, sir. I'll have them assessed by the end of the day. "

Mr. Marshall is pleased.

Ernest Lee busies himself nonstop all day with scarcely time out for lunch at his desk. However, he has lots of questions, so he's glad to see Mr. Marshall wander in to his office just before five o'clock.

"How did it go, Ernest Lee?" his boss asks, plopping down into the oak chair by the desk.

"Well, Sir," Ernest Lee says, "Your personal accounts are reconciled and in mostly good order. However, something is puzzling me."

"Yes?" Mr. Marshall leans closer.

"Well, sir, some of those prices you paid for real estate in town...."

"Yes, yes. I know which lots that you're talking about. Well, I don't always consider market value *alone*, son. It wouldn't show up in the paperwork, but some folks I bought lots from needed the money, some had illness and others lost crops. I pay a bit too much from time to time for my land, but I figure the value'll catch up eventually. Don't you think so?"

"Perhaps so, Sir, but I also noticed some personal loans you made that are quite overdue. Shouldn't those notices go out right away?" Ernest Lee asks hopefully.

"No, I'll send them out when those folks can pay down the balance." Mr. Marshall adds with a twinkle in his eye, "Wouldn't do any good to ask them right now, since they don't have the money. Would it? You just add things up they way things stand, son." Then, seeing the concerned look on his young bookkeeper's face, Mr. Marshall reassures him, "Don't worry any, Ernest Lee. I can carry the load."

"Well, yes sir, but...." Ernest Lee starts in, hoping he isn't overstepping his bounds, "...but it wouldn't do to let things go uncollected too long. We should keep a close eye on these accounts."

"Yes, indeed we should, and we shall," Mr. Marshall says jumping up almost euphoric. "We will keep a *strong* eye on things—now that we have such a sharp mind as yours around here." He slaps Ernest Lee's back, "Good work, son," he commends and struts out of the office.

Ernest Lee wonders how a smart businessman like Mr. Marshall can overlook past due accounts. Then he figures, *the man is happy and well off, so why should I worry?* Ernest Lee puffs up his chest and talks to the mirror on the way out the door, "Yes indeed, you keep a good eye on things around here with that 'sharp mind' of yours, just like the boss said!" *Maybe I can't figure out Mr. Marshall's accounting logic, but at least I'll have an accolade to share with Amy over supper. She'll rest easy tonight.*

The day zips along for Amy, but she isn't feeling very zippy at all. It is mid afternoon, and her stomach turned sour again right before breakfast—she hasn't eaten one bite since then. She tried to make tea cakes for her company, but her stomach got queasy when the eggs slimed around in the bowl. She's glad Mary is coming over to soon embroider—she'll ask her for sick stomach remedies. Amy sits at the table feeling nauseous when Mary taps on the kitchen door and lets herself in.

"You look dreadful!" Mary gasps.

"I can't make the tea cakes today," Amy apologizes.

"Are you ill?" Mary asks.

"My stomach is off, and the look of raw eggs made me feel even sicker."

"You're probably catching the grip from last night's cold air," Mary says, "And there's plenty of influenza going around too."

"Whatever it is, I've had it all week, but it was much worse this morning."

"Especially bad this morning?"

"Most especially this morning—yesterday morn was bad too," Amy frowns.

Mary whispers, "If you don't mind me asking...when was the last time...you had your 'friend,' if you know what I mean?"

Amy knows what Mary means right away. When she was thirteen she woke up one morning with blood on her nightgown "down there." Grandma Gert was most annoyed at the mess and explained, "You'll get this curse once a month, now—it's a woman's cross to bear, and you'll clean it up."

She answers Mary, "It hasn't come for awhile, now. Why do you ask?"

"Why?" Mary repeats, smiling.

"Would the 'curse' cause my stomach to sour?" Amy asks.

Mary replies, much amused, "Did Grandma Gert ever say where a 'curse' goes when you're 'with child'?"

Amy's eyes widen as the connection sets in. "I feel so silly—me growing up on a farm and not figuring this out about nature!"

Mary chuckles, "Never mind about that now. Let's go over to Dr. Wallace's office and see about this."

Embroidery is the last thing on Amy's mind as she hustles along to Dr. Wallace's office with Mary. It's just down the road, and they enter the small brick-front building through a side entry where Doc Wallace makes his office. The sparsely furnished wait room boasts a blue muslin sofa next to the door and two ladder back chairs at the end of the room. There are some text books in a cabinet next to the chairs with the Doctor's framed diploma hanging above. The two women sit down on the sofa—they are alone in the room.

After what seems an eternity, Doctor Wallace walks in and asks jovially, "Who is my patient today?"

Amy shakes in her shoes. Finally, she turns Mary's hand loose and follows the doctor into the examining room.

Amy is bustling around the kitchen fixing supper when her husband bounds in from work.

"Hello there, sweet Amy!" Ernest Lee gives her a big hug and a kiss.

Amy chirps, "We're having biscuits and ham hocks tonight, Ernest Lee."

The pair eats heartily, and supper is nearly over before Ernest Lee realizes—Amy hasn't made her nightly inquisition. So, he clears his throat and begins, "Well, Amy, I have some good news from work that you might like to hear." He proudly relates the latest accolade from his boss but, curiously, he gets no response. He sits pondering the situation.

Amy pipes up, "Now, I have some news too."

"Yes?" he looks over at her.

"Well, you know the spare room upstairs?"

Ernest Lee can figure it out already. "Yes, I know the extra room upstairs, and I'll bet company is coming."

"That's right," Amy nods.

"I'll bet its Effie!"

"No, it's not Effie."

"Is it Grandma Gert?" he asks, dreading the answer.

"No, not Grandma Gert either," Amy teases.

Now he's stumped. "Well, who is it?"

"I'm not sure yet. I'll let you know in seven months time!"

Grandma Gert insists on retrieving all mail from their metal box out on the road. Today she's taking too long, so Effie sneaks down the path, and grabs the letter she's been waiting for. She races back up to the house and bounds up the stairs to her bedroom. It's a hot Saturday morning in July between chores, and she'll have plenty of time to read every word—twice if she wants. She stretches out on the bed, tears open the envelope and reads a few lines.

"Goodness, gracious," Effie shouts running back down the stairs, waving the letter about. "Grandpa! Amy's having a baby! In February!

Grandma Gert rushes out from the kitchen with a look of disdain," It didn't take those two very long to go at it. Couldn't they wait a decent length of time?"

"Hush now, Mrs. Blackwell; just listen to you," the Pastor says rushing out from the parlor. "What else does she say in the letter, Effie?"

"She writes that she'll visit us for Thanksgiving and at Christmas time too." Effie hops up and down clutching her letter, "Imagine that—At last Amy having a baby."

"Well, I hope she doesn't expect me to go down there to Tuckerman and help out with a screaming infant," Gert snorts.

Effie clasps her hands together, more excited than ever, "Oh, I *want* to help out. I hope she asks me to come help. Can I go down to Tuckerman when the baby comes Grandpa?"

The Pastor can't get over Effie's change for the better, of late. Not too long ago, he commented to his wife, "Effie seems most sullen—keeps a lot to herself. Have you noticed it, Gert?"

Gert had replied, "No, I can't say that I have, not at all. She's just goldbricking, like usual."

A few weeks later, Effie began chatting again, just like her old self, and the Pastor asked his wife, "Effie's had a turning around. Don't you think so? Maybe the Lord spoke to her."

Gert had replied, "I haven't noticed anything different at all."

The pastor shrugged it off at the time, but now he's sure there's been a positive change in the girl, whether his wife notices or not. "Yes, you can go help Amy out when the time comes," he agrees.

Gert breaks in, "Well, we'll just have to *see* about that Tuckerman visit. Only *if* it fits in with school and *if* your work gets done around here— that comes first." She taps her foot and adds, "Another thing, Effie. *I'm* supposed to bring up the mail from the box. Don't you do that again. You're much too careless," Gert fumes.

Effie is far too happy mind Grandma Gert's snit. She can hardly stand the excitement, and she wants to share the news right away. "Grandpa, I'm going to take that basket of food over to Mrs. Isay now. Alright?" Effie half-asks.

Effie romps down the hill and up the other side to the cabin, sets the basket down on a porch table, and waits until Mrs. Isay appears out on the porch. The old woman motions Effie to sit down in a rocker beside her, and she begins telling of yesterday's woodsy exploration and about a new herb she discovered. The trees fan a warm breeze as they rock back and forth on the porch. Mrs. Isay soon finishes her story, and Effie takes her turn.

"Mrs. Isay…" Effie begins.

"Yes, child," Mrs. Isay says. The old woman knows, full well, her young visitor's name, but she prefers calling her "child," which Effie has come to enjoy.

"Well, my sister Amy is going to have a baby next February."

"Isn't that nice," the old woman looks over and smiles and nods.

"And she's coming for another visit at holiday time," Effie starts rocking faster.

"Wonderful, wonderful," Mrs. Isay is still nodding.

Now that Effie's gleeful news is out, she turns quiet and stares down at the floor. After a while she asks, "Did you know my mother, Mrs. Isay? Did you ever meet her?"

"No, I didn't know her, child."

"I wish my mama knew about Amy's baby," Effie says.

"Maybe she does," the old woman nods.

"My Mama is up in heaven, Mrs. Isay."

"Yes, I know, child. She passed on when you were but four," the old woman says.

"How can she know about the baby, then?" Effie asks. She also wonders how Mrs. Isay knows precisely when her mother had died. They've never spoken of it before. The old woman doesn't reply to her question, so Effie asks louder, "I say, how could my mama possibly know about Amy's baby, Mrs. Isay?"

Mrs. Isay answers with a question of her own, "Do you ever feel her presence?"

"My mama's presence?" Amy asks, surprised by such a question.

"Yes, child, do you ever feel like she's in the same room?"

Effie sits up straight in her chair and blurts out, "Yes, it's exactly like that!"

Then, she slumps down, "...but I know that's impossible."

The old woman whispers, not meaning to be heard, "*Is* it impossible? I only wish I could tell you."

"Tell me what?" Effie begs. "You can tell me, really."

Mrs. Isay vowed that she would never tell what she knows, so she says nothing.

"What can you tell me?" Effie pleads again.

The old woman hesitates, but then whispers, "Sometimes I *see* things." Mrs. Isay speaks so low that Effie can barely make out her words.

"I need to know," Effie moves closer, touching the back of Mrs. Isay's old weathered hand.

Mrs. Isay speaks hesitantly, "People that passed on...they speak to me, sometimes. It happens like that." The old woman turns to Effie, "I use to call it 'my gift,' but it has made me an outcast, so it's really a curse. I try not to use it."

Effie looks into the old woman's eyes that have grown suddenly fearful. Effie encourages her gently, "You can tell me because I *will* believe you. I *need* to know."

"Your mother....," Mrs. Isay begins.

"Yes?" Effie leans closer.

Mrs. Isay stares into Effie's eyes, "That day you waded into the brook…the truth is…a figure appeared in my cabin and led me down there to save you." She slowly continues, "I didn't know who the figure was at the time, but I knew that my 'gift' was intruding again. I just couldn't stop it." She sees the confused look on Effie's face, so she explains further, "I didn't know for sure who the figure was until *you* entered my cabin for the very first time, child." Mrs. Isay pauses before telling all. "It was your mother…her spirit…that led me down to the brook, and she appears when you visit my cabin. She appears here today."

Effie looks all around the cabin to assure herself that they are very much alone. Then she looks back at the sad old woman, wondering what in the world she is talking about.

Mrs. Isay goes on, "Your mother says things to me, things that she wants me to tell you."

Effie gasps at the thought, *This pathetic old creature is addled—probably from living alone in the woods for so long.* Still, Effie is puzzled, because Mrs. Isay has never been confused like this before. Why now? One time, Grandma Gert had called Mrs. Isay 'a crazy old witch,' but Effie had thought nothing of it. What if it is true? Effie looks outside. A wind is whipping up the hill and the leaves are blowing upside down on their limbs. She decides, *I'll tell Mrs. Isay that I must rush home to beat out the storm, but I'll take care not to hurt the old woman's feelings.*

Effie walks over and finds Mrs. Isay staring blankly at the wall now. Her face is frozen as she speaks.

"Your mother is saying something important, child. Listen. She says I should tell you, 'It's alright. It wasn't your fault.'"

Effie's blood pulse hard through her veins. She tries to speak calmly, "What was that you just said about my Mother?"

"Your mother says for me to tell you, 'It's alright.'" Mrs. Isay turns to look right at Effie.

Effie shouts out, "No! I won't hear any more. You never even knew my mother, Mrs. Isay. Don't you say one more word about her!" Tears stream down Effie's cheeks and her throat hurts from shouting so loud.

For years, Effie has blocked out the bad memories about the day that her mother died. How could Mrs. Isay know? The urge to flee this insanity is more than Effie can bear. She races over to the door but trips over a large basket that sits nearby on the floor. The basket's wooden top flops open revealing red gingham fabric inside—just like her old rag doll's apron! *That can't be!*

"Child, let me explain...." Mrs. Isay rushes over to pick Effie up off the ground.

"Get away! Not one more word, Mrs. Isay! Don't you ever speak of my Mother again!" Effie bounces up off the floor and flings the cabin door wide open. She runs out onto the porch and shouts back into the cabin, "How could you?"

Effie bolts down the wooden steps and starts running down the hill, but her foot catches on a tree root and she tumbles to the ground, rolling over and over and onto her side. The summer storm brews and tree limbs thrash together. The wind tangles her hair and blows leaves into her eyes.

Mrs. Isay catches up, finally. She grabs hold of Effie's shoulders, but the girl cries out, nearly hysterical, "Don't you touch me! Leave me alone! You *can't* know anything about it!"

"Of course I can't, child," the old woman soothes, struggling to stand Effie upright against the fierce wind.

Effie desperately tries to figure things out, *I've never said one word. Grandpa and Grandma Gert don't know. Not even Amy.* Effie's head spins and the air is turning white. She tries calling out, but a pulsing starts in her ears. She falls backwards whispering, "I'm not feeling...."

"What happened?" Effie blinks awake in a haze.

"You fainted dead away, child, out on the hill." Mrs. Isay is sitting on the edge of the thin wooden bed, pressing a wet cloth to Effie's forehead.

Effie tries to sit up, but the pulsing starts again in her head. She's wobbly and weak, so she lies back on the pillows.

"Here, drink this cane sugar water for strength," says Mrs. Isay, tipping a little tumbler of the liquid onto the girl's lips.

Effie takes tiny sips and lies back again in awkward silence. Finally, she whispers, "Explain what you said."

"I am sorry child. I'm sure it was a shock," Mrs. Isay replies. She's eager to right her wrong, so she tries to explain once again, "You see, your mother's spirit gave me those very words to tell you. Were they important to you?"

Effie understands now—reality has finally set in—poor Mrs. Isay has gone crazy! Effie answers at last, "No, Mrs. Isay. The words weren't important at all. I'm so sorry that I carried on so. I'm feeling lots better, now, so I'll just rest a bit more and be going along home before the storm gets any worse."

Mrs. Isay nods understanding more than Effie realizes, "Yes, you rest a bit, child, till the wind dies down some. I'm sure it was just the excitement. Those words I spoke were just an old lady's ramblin's. Just put them right out of your head. Don't pay any attention."

"All right, Mrs. Isay," Effie sighs, feeling safe in knowing that there'll be no more visits with old Mrs. Isay. She won't listen to any more ramblings about her dear Mother.

Effie is deep in thought as she walks home through the woods. She's only fourteen, and not as good as Amy is at figuring things out, but she tries to make sense of it all, *Mrs. Isay must be crazy if she thinks she sees spirits, but it's curious that she never seemed so before.* Still, Effie resolves once again, *I'll keep my distance from now on.* She reaches the house just as the summer rain pelts down.

The Pastor is bending over his Bible as Effie walks past in the hall. For once, he looks up with a little smile for Effie, but he quickly turns back to his work. He looks up again and Effie is lingering, so he says, "You beat out the rain, I see."

Effie's question is out before she can think, "Do good Christian people ever visit from heaven, Grandpa?"

The Pastor is startled at first, but he's growing used to Effie's impulsive questions and chatter, so he answers, "Well, the Bible says that God's angels carry out work here on earth."

Effie presses on, "I mean *real* people we know, like the people in someone's own family. Do they ever come back to earth after they're dead?"

The Pastor is amused, *A question straight from the schoolyard, no doubt— they've been debating the Bible again.* Considering that his answer will settle a score, he answers Effie most seriously, "We all know that God's Angels appear on earth from time to time, Effie. And Hebrews teaches that they can take on human form. There have been reports hereabouts."

Effie sits listening, so he goes on.

"Like Deacon Fitzgerald—he tells of the time his wagon got turned over in a ditch way out in his field, knocking him unconscious and pinning him to the ground. He woke up with buzzards circling above him. He knew he was a goner for sure, so he started praying hard as he could for God come to save him. In no time at all, a young man approached from behind. He righted the wagon and freed up the Deacon, saving him from certain death out there in the hot sun all alone. The Deacon says that when rose to his knees, he was all alone in the field, and the young man that saved him was nowhere to be found."

Effie is amazed, "Truly, Grandpa?"

"I tell you, that young man was an Angel sent by God to save Deacon Fitzgerald and nothing less." The Pastor stares hard at Effie, "Now, mind you, Effie, such Angels are of *God's* own making. God *never* makes Angels out of mortals he saved here on earth. Earthly man can *never* come back as an angel."

Effie rasps, "You mean, real people don't *ever* come back after they're dead?"

"No, they do not, except by the work of the devil himself," the Pastor intones with a most severe look in his eyes, "...the *devil* himself, Effie," he shouts, snatching the Bible from his desk at the thought, thumping the Good Book as proof.

"Yes, Grandpa," Effie's voice shakes. She excuses herself and disappears up the stairs to recover in the quiet of her room. Her mind starts whirling again, *Something isn't right. Mrs. Isay may a bit strange, but she would never consort with the devil. I just know that in my heart.* Effie starts listing in her head the old woman's good works, *Didn't Mrs. Isay stop me from drowning in the brook that day? And didn't she minister to me when I fell and fainted up there on her hill just now? That wasn't the work of a body in league with the devil.* Effie figures that Grandpa must have the devil thing figured out wrong. She wishes she could ask Amy.

Amy is turning the spare room into a nursery done up in yellow. Mary gave her a hand-me-down white bassinet, baby clothes, and blankets for the arrival. Amy has them all laid out on the bureau. The project is growing bigger — just like her tummy — day by day.

Ernest Lee looks into the room one evening, "There's so much stuff in there, Amy. You sure we aren't having triplets?"

"Hush up, Father hen," Amy chides.

The truth is, Doctor Wallace had examined Amy in June, weighing and measuring again and again.

Amy had finally asked, "What is it, Doctor Wallace?"

"I won't know until next month, but let me ask you something. Do you or Ernest Lee have any twins in your family?"

Amy went numb. She couldn't think of any twins on either side. She told Ernest Lee when she got home, and then she was sorry she had. He didn't seem happy.

Now it's the middle of August, her third month of pregnancy, and Amy visited Doctor Wallace this morning. This time he announces, "Well, you're too small to be having twins. There's just one big healthy baby in there." Amy is relieved. One baby will be plenty to handle.

"I told you this morning—that was a false alarm, Ernest Lee," she says as he looks into the baby's room.

"Just as well," he replies flatly.

She knows what her husband is thinking. It's less for him to worry about right now, considering the bad news that he's had about his mother. Dad Herald wrote just last week that Martha is getting weaker and weaker these days—tuberculosis most likely. Ernest Lee has been worried sick, but he tries not to let on.

"Were you and your mother close growing up, Ernest Lee?" Amy asks outside the nursery.

Her husband looks downcast, "I was always a worry to my mother at home. I wasn't strong or agile like most Herald men, but she never made a fuss. Instead she got me busy with my pencils and books."

Amy can't stand the sadness in his voice, "Ernest Lee, would you like to go see your Mama now in Success?" She adds, "We don't have to wait for Thanksgiving."

"No. Dad says she's weak but still getting around. There's no need to go home right now."

Amy feels uneasy about the matter—even selfish. However, she needs Ernest Lee now too, so she doesn't dissuade him. She continues fixing up her pretty yellow room for the baby as her husband disappears down the stairs.

91

CHAPTER 6
CHRISTMAS SPIRIT

The shop windows on Main Street are trimmed holly red and green. A wooden Santa waves at the townsfolk hustling along with Christmas lists in hand, chatting and enjoying pine scents wafting through the air. Tuckerman's First Baptist Church members will worship with white candles in windows, fresh evergreen sprays by the pulpit, and little Christmas angels that Sunday schoolers cut out. Amy leans over her big belly to attach the angels onto the ends of pews.

"Did you cut those Angels out all by yourself, Amy?" Brother Randolph walks up and smiles.

"The Sunday schoolers are more talented than I am," Amy laughs. She admires the man for being so genuine with no put-on airs—the perfect match for her good friend Mary. Next to her Ernest Lee, Rob Randolph is the nicest man that she knows. He returns to his church office and Amy touches her cheek, embarrassed to feel that it's flushed. She gets right back to her work of holiday decorating.

Grandma Gert never allowed Christmas decorations back home in Pitman. "Christmas is a holy day, not a decoratin' contest," she'd say. Now Amy can decorate all that she wants. Ernest Lee fastened a Christmas wreath to their front door and Amy tied a red bow on top, and they picked out a little pine tree to sit by the window in the front room. Amy couldn't resist the shiny glass ornaments at Mr. Miller's store, and now they jiggle back and forth in the breeze when the door opens and closes.

Thanksgiving seems like ages ago, and Amy can't wait see Effie at Christmas. Amy has been making her Christmas gifts for weeks. She stitched a crisp white apron for Effie's Sunday dress and a yellow gingham apron for Grandma Gert out of left over curtain scraps. Grandpa will get an embroidered cover for his Bible, and Ernest Lee's mother will get a quilted lap blanket. Aunt Glory will open a cheerful cotton duster, and the Herald men will get scarves. Amy has one last gift to make—a pair of slippers for Ernest Lee from the wool scraps she saved. Her handiwork is wrapped up cheery Christmas paper with bright colored bows, and the packages nestle in a basket next to the tree.

Amy hurries home from the church, but her Christmas chores are not finished—she has more baking. She mixes up two loaves of fruit bread right away and puts them in the oven—gifts to give Mary who'll arrive any minute.

"Good morning, Amy," Mary enters quickly to keep out the cold.

The two are chatting and sipping their tea when Amy feels a little "catch" in her side. She has felt the pains all morning, and they go as quickly as they come. Now a sharper pain stabs, and this time she grabs her side with both hands.

"Youch," Amy cries out.

"What is it?" Mary asks, alarmed by her friend's expression.

"Just a little stab, maybe a kick—I'm in my seventh month now. It's nothing,"Amy assures.

"You should stay quiet today," Mary leans over, "Don't overdo before your big trip on Friday."

"You're right about that," Amy agrees as they continue their chat.

Mary leaves mid-morning with a cheery hug. "Have a blessed Christmas, and thank you for my wonderful Christmas bread," she says, sniffing the fragrant loafs on her way out the door.

Amy knows that she should stay home and rest, but there are too many errands, so she hurries over to Main Street. She's walking past Marshall's Mercantile when the pain stabs once again.

"Ouch," Amy grabs her sid, but hurries along in case Ernest Lee is looking out the window.

"Wait up! What's your hurry, Mrs. Herald?" Amy hears her husband's voice calling out from behind. Ernest Lee hustles up to where she is standing.

"Oh, Ernest Lee," Amy straightens up taller. "I'm going to Smith's to fetch more citrus for our Christmas bread," she says, affectionately reaching over and touching his hand.

"Don't hurry *too* fast—it'll all get done before we leave town on Friday," he laughs and gives her a peck on the cheek. "Slow down—you're not the St. Louis express," he cautions as she walks off slowly toward Smith's.

The morning isn't passing quickly enough for Amy making her rounds. She's feeling more tired by the minute, so she finally heads for home. Her stomach is queasy, so she heats up a clear cup of broth for lunch in the kitchen. There was a letter from Effie waiting in the post box, so she starts reading it while the hot broth cools down.

My Dear Sister Amy,

I am looking forward to your visit at Christmas. Grandma Gert keeps me busy making presents to give and baking Christmas cookies for her bake sale. I think we're feeding all of Pitman this year. Grandpa takes me over to church every night to help with our Christmas program rehearsal. The songs sound so sweet.

I miss you very much and long to see you soon.
Love,
Effie

Amy sighs, *That's the shortest letter that Effie ever wrote to me.* Then she realizes, *Effie didn't write one word about her new friend. I still can't get her to say who she is.* Amy's feeling so weary now that she can only think about taking a nap on the soft bed upstairs. She slowly climbs the stairs, but midway she feels lightheaded and grabs hold of the rail. She lectures herself, *If I still feel poorly after supper, I'll visit Dr. Wallace's office. I just need a good nap, that's all.* She stretches out on the bed and falls into a deep sleep right away.

Ernest Lee sits at his desk determined to complete the mercantile's accounts by Friday. Everything is in order, but the numbers still trouble him. The basic problem is simple—business is slow. First, there was the war's escalation and then the President asked folk to cut back on choice items—all this when Mr. Marshall's collections are in a big mess. They'll come up short this month if business gets any worse. Ernest Lee figures, *We're just hanging on. One bad crop year, or a drought, or a flood—no telling what could happen then.* Ernest starts getting riled up, *Mr. Marshal must listen before it's too late. I'll have one more word with him.*

Moments later, Mr. Marshall walks by Ernest Lee's door. Ernest Lee only nods, wondering how to bring up his questions.

"Something on your mind, son?" Mr. Marshall asks, walking in to his office.

Ernest Lee looks up, "Well, I've been working on the year-end numbers, sir. I'd like to talk more about your personal holdings, if that's all right. I'll need more information to figure out a plan." Then, worried he might be too bold he adds, "That is, if you don't mind, sir."

"Of course not. I'll visit your office in just a bit. We'll have a good long talk about it," Mr. Marshall rises and walks off down the hall.

Ernest Lee anticipates Mr. Marshall's promised visit all morning, but it's late afternoon and he wonders if his boss will come by at all.

Mr. Marshall hustles into Ernest Lee's office just before closing, apologizing, "I'm here for that talk, Ernest Lee. Sorry to be so late in the day." He sits down in the chair and leans an elbow on Ernest Lee's desk. Looking serious, he asks, "Now, what is it, son?"

Ernest Lee clears his throat, outlines his concerns, and sums up, "The mercantile accounts can carry you for now, sir, but that won't last forever."

Mr. Marshall scratches his head and says at the end, "Things will turn around, surely."

Ernest Lee explains, "Yes, but things won't turn around over night, sir. The war limits our supplies and our customers cut back more every day. Who knows how long this will last, and it wouldn't take much for us to go under before things turn around."

Mr. Marshall scratches his head again, "Well now, I didn't think there was *that* much of a problem with my balancing act. No, sir; I didn't think that at all. If you will just lay it out plainly on paper for me, we'll talk again first thing in the morning." Then, he adds on the way out the door, "Good work looking out for me, son. You'll get a big bonus this month, you can be sure."

"Thank you, sir," Ernest Lee replies as he bids his boss a good evening. He's happy to hear about the prospect of a bonus, but he really thinks, *This is what causes Mr. Marshall his financial problems—the poor fellow gives all of his money away.* He shakes his head, figuring, *I won't take any bonus for now. Anyway, I'll get one twice as big after I get things straightened out around here.*

Ernest Lee begins working away on Mr. Marshall's figures so he'll be ready first thing in the morning. The young accountant pushes his pencil feverishly along, engrossed in his work long after quitting time.

Two fluffy white lambs romp around Grandpa Blackwell's barnyard. They baah softly and snuggle up to one another, batting their big black eyes, so cute and so cuddly. Amy hovers over them, patting their pure white wool as it blows in the breeze. She gazes down at the lambs adoringly, humming a lullaby as they prance to and fro. She can feel God's presence, and she throws her arms about the baby lambs' necks to cuddle and snuggle. Then, faster than lightening, a black wolf is upon them, baring sharp teeth and snatching at the little lamb's throats. Amy stands back aghast as blood gushes down their snowy white fur, glistening red as the carnage proceeds. For the lambs, there is no salvation, and Amy feels helpless.

Amy rouses fitfully from her dream. She's frightened and pale, doubled over with pain. She feels a warm, moist spot on the bed and draws her hand up for a closer inspection—dripping wet fingers dangle grotesquely before her. The stab in her side is sharper than before, and she screams out for Ernest Lee, but he's nowhere about. She tries to sit up, but she can't. Amy stretches out on her back. Her belly is cramping and warm liquid oozes slowly from between her legs, flowing out onto the featherbed. It's growing dark outside, and no lamp is lit. She lies there moaning in the dim light left in the room, soon passing out from the fear.

Time has no meaning when Amy rouses up from her faint. Ernest Lee is holding her up by her shoulders, kissing her cheeks and whispering, "Amy, sweet Amy, I'm so sorry I left you!" He rests her back on the pillow and leaves her side for a moment, racing over to the window and flinging it open. He calls out in panic to a neighbor passing below, "Run for Dr. Wallace. It's Amy. Tell him to hurry!" Then, he races back to Amy's side, wiping the tears from his eyes.

Amy cries out, "Please, dear God, save our baby."

At last, Doctor Wallace bounds up the stairs with his black bag in hand. Mrs. Wallace runs up behind him. "This is sure sooner than we expected!" he shouts, wiping his brow and wasting no time. "Let's get this baby born right away," he announces. Like a precision team, the Wallaces take command of the bedside, unpacking the black bag and laying implements out on the bureau. They bend Amy's legs and instruct her to grab hold of Mrs. Wallace's arm and push hard with each labor pain.

Ernest Lee is dispatched downstairs to boil water and bring up clean cloths. He bounds down the stairs two at a time, stokes up the stove, and races around in a dither before finding a pot to fill up with water. He grabs a stack of clean toweling and paces back and forth with it jammed under his arm until the pot water bubbles. At last, he totes the towels and boiling hot pot up the stairs.

Just as Ernest Lee enters the room, Doc Wallace calls out, "Push, Amy! Push hard now!"

Amy's face is red as a beet. She lets out a milk-curdling howl and gives one final push.

Dr. Wallace pulls the shriveled red baby into the world and clears out its tiny mouth with his pinky. The wrinkled-up body looks like a freshly plucked chicken with its eyes swollen shut, and its poor gangly body could fit inside a shoebox. The doctor smacks the tiny bottom, and the baby boy lets out a cry no louder than a cat mew.

Ernest runs over to the bedside, beside himself with joy. He kisses Amy's hand, but she lies back from exhaustion, veins popping out on her temples.

Doc Wallace cuts the umbilical cord and his wife washes off the infant with warm water from the pot and wraps him in a soft blanket .

Ernest Lee is about to offer a hand when Doc Wallace shouts out again, "Good heavens! Push again Amy! Push hard!"

Ernest Lee whispers, "Oh, sweet Lord. It's twins."

Mrs. Wallace passes the blanket-bound boy to Ernest Lee, and Amy grabs hold of her arm once again.

Amy wales, "I can't. I'm ripping inside!"

"You must," Doc Wallace commands. With one more ear-splitting yowl, Amy pushes her baby girl out into the world. Only, this poor little body is bluish and limp, lifeless in Doctor Wallace's hands.

Tears stream down Ernest Lee's face, "Doc Wallace, please save our baby."

Doc Wallace unwinds the slimy umbilical cord from around the scrawny infant's neck, and puffs a breath into the tiny little mouth. One more little puff, and then two more, and at last the slimy wet body wiggles one way, and then back the other, bleating out a muffled cry.

Ernest Lee hears him whisper to his wife, "She's breathing too shallow, I fear."

Amy barely has time to kiss the babies on their little bald heads before the doctor whisks them down stairs to warm in a basket next to the stove. Amy falls back in exhaustion.

Ernest Lee rushes downstairs to find Mrs. Wallace boiling little bottles and her husband squeezing sugar water from an eye dropper into two smacking mouths. "What do you think, Doctor Wallace? Will they be all right?" Ernest Lee's voice quivers.

"They're a good size for coming two months early—as long as they breathe on their own, they'll likely pull through." The panicked father stares back at him, pale as a sheet, so the doctor adds, "I delivered others this early, and they made out fine. I'm sure that we have the Lord's blessing now, too."

Ernest Lee runs back and forth between the kitchen and bedroom all night. Amy thrashes about, moaning in pain before finding sleep with a few drops of Doc Wallace's laudanum. The sun is rising when she opens her eyes once again.

Ernest Lee whispers, "Good morning, sweet Amy. Doc Wallace said for you to sip this yarrow tea when you woke up."

Amy doesn't care about tea. "The babies?" she asks with alarm.

Ernest Lee beams, "They are wonderful, precious little gifts from God. A little boy and a twin girl. I only wish my Ma could travel down to meet them—they're so precious."

Amy isn't convinced. She grabs her husband's hand so tightly that his fingers turn white. "Are they *really* all right?" she begs, "Tell me the truth, Ernest Lee."

Ernest Lee sits on the bedside, "I wouldn't tell you something that wasn't so, Amy. They're small little babies…especially the girl, but they're breathing nicely this morning. They'll be just fine, Amy—don't you worry."

"Oh, thank heavens," Amy sighs. She takes a few gulps of the tea and lays her head back on the pillow as she drifts off to sleep.

The new father looks down at his wife, scolding himself, *How could I get lost in my numbers and put Amy and our babies at risk?"* Then he vows most sincerely, *Things will change around here with my new family. I'll share more with Amy, just like she wants.*

Ernest Lee races back down to the kitchen as Doc Wallace calls out, "The little one is trembling. More warmth is what she needs."

"Is there anything we can do, Dr. Wallace; a hospital or something?" Ernest Lee pleads.

Dr. Wallace shakes his head, "Hospitals are no place for a baby, son. She'd more likely take sick there, than get better."

"What can we do? There must be something!" the frantic father pleads.

Doctor Wallace rubs his brow. "Well, I have an idea, Ernest Lee, if you'll trust me on this…."

"Yes, sir. I will. Anything at all."

"Is your automobile ready for travel, son?"

"Yes, sir. I have it ready for our Christmas trip coming up on Friday," Ernest Lee shouts, crisp like a soldier.

"Then, let's take this baby over to my office!" Doc Wallace commands.

Mrs. Wallace lifts the baby girl out of the basket and tucks a warm water bottle inside her blanket.

Ernest Lee sees his tiny daughter's peanut-shaped body, so helpless and small. Sheer panic propels him out the door with Doctor Wallace running along as fast as he dares cradling the baby.

Mary approaches the house just as the two men race along. Ernest Lee shouts over to her, "Mary, thank goodness you're here! I'll be back as soon as I can!"

Mary rushes into the kitchen and finds Mrs. Wallace sitting in a chair by the stove. Mary starts chatting, "I just knew I'd be needed. I felt it first thing when I awoke...." She stops short when she sees yet another tiny baby tucked inside the white bassinet next to the stove. "Land sakes! Another baby? Twins?" she exclaims.

Mrs. Wallace whispers, "Yes, the boy is doing well, but the baby girl is so feeble....we can only pray that the poor little thing will pull through. You should go upstairs to comfort poor Amy. She doesn't know."

Mary tiptoes slowly up the stairs and finds Amy opening her eyes. The morning light streams into the room, and Amy smiles groggily. "Isn't it wonderful, Mary? Two little babies." However, Amy can see that Mary is not smiling, and she insists at once, "Mary, tell me. What is it?"

Mary pulls a chair to the bedside and whispers, "Well, the baby girl is quite small, so Ernest Lee and Dr. Wallace took her over to Doc's office just now."

"Why? What will they do?"

"They didn't say, but I am sure she'll be fine, Amy," Mary tries to assure.

Amy knows better from the look on Mary's strained face, and she buries her head in the pillow.

No one could have predicted such pandemonium after the babies were born. Ernest Lee telephoned Hamm's General Store with the news, and Mr. Hamm flew down Military Road toward the Blackwell's with the announcement. The Pastor, Gert and Effie packed up their wagon at once, and the Tuckerman household has been busy as a beehive ever since they arrived.

The new grandparents put down a palate to sleep in the babies' room, and Effie beds down on a feather palette in the front room. Grandma Gert, so reluctant to help at the outset, immediately takes charge of the household, insisting, "I know just what to do from raising baby Buck." She tries to control Amy's nursing too, scolding, "If you don't get that child back on your nipple, he'll waste away to nothing," she fumes.

Amy is so worried about her ailing baby girl, that she has no strength to argue. She readily complies, "That's just fine, Grandma Gert."

Gert shakes her head, not knowing what to make of the agreeable change in her granddaughter.

The week passes by quickly. Ernest Lee spends every day at Doc Wallace's, reporting back home on the progress.

Nonetheless, Amy is beside herself with worry, fretting all day long, "I won't rest easy 'til our little girl is right here in this basket."

Ernest Lee repeats, "Don't worry so, Amy. Doc Wallace is making good progress."

"What all is he doing?" Amy can't understand.

"He's tending Sally and keeping her warm," Ernest Lee says, remaining purposely vague.

"*We* can do that here," Amy insists."

"Not like he can—he's a doctor," Ernest Lee reassures.

Amy imagines the worst, "I hope God doesn't take our baby girl up to heaven, Ernest Lee."

"Why would God do that?" Ernest Lee says, taking her hand.

Amy doesn't reply, but she remembers her shame down at Current River on her fateful Baptismal morning. *God owes me no favors. Perhaps this is his retribution at last.*

Christmas morning dawns and Ernest Lee whispers to Amy, "We never expected to celebrate a Yuletide like this one."

Tears well up in Amy's eyes as she declares, "I've never known such heartache, Ernest Lee. It'll be a sad Christmas day without our twin baby girl." She's about to say more, but someone is knocking downstairs.

Ernest Lee throws on a robe and heads down the stairs, praying that this isn't bad news. Doctor and Mrs. Wallace stand at the front door holding a basket between them that's heaped up with a fluffy pink blanket. Ernest Lee whisks them inside and gently lifts off the blanket. His tiny baby girl nestles inside the basket, wide-awake and peacefully sucking a finger.

"What a Christmas morning surprise!" the jubilant father exclaims. He gives his guests a big hug, grabs the basket and slowly climbs up the stairs. Tip-toeing into the bedroom, he whispers, "Merry Christmas, sweet Amy."

A few days later it's time. "They're all waiting for us in the front room," Ernest Lee says. Amy sits in her bedroom rocker, tears rolling down her cheeks. "I can't bear saying good-bye. I'm going to miss them all—even Grandma Gert. How can we do everything here all alone?" she whispers.

Ernest Lee feels the same way. Having such commotion about the house has been comforting to him, in a strange way, and the thought of being alone with the babies is scary. When he dares to pick up one of his twins, his body turns rigid, afraid that he'll drop or squeeze them too hard. However, it won't do to show this weakness today, of all days, so he puts up a brave front.

"We'll be alright," he Ernest Lee reassures his distressed wife.

Amy shuffles down the stairs and into the front room, where the Pastor, Gert, and Effie cut off a debate as they see her approach.

Amy struggles to speak through her tears, but nothing comes out.

Effie runs over and jumps up and down to exclaim, "I'm staying in Tuckerman with you, Amy! They just said so."

Now, its tears of joy that well up in Amy's eyes.

Effie embraces her sister, "It's just until school starts up again, Amy, but at least I can help until then."

This is more sentimentality than Grandma Gert can abide. She chides on her way out the front door, "Well Miss Effie, you might just as *well* stay here in Tuckerman for all the help you'd be to me back in Pitman—you'd just moon about wanting to fuss over them babies like you do." Gert sniffs the air and heads out to the wagon with the Pastor in tow.

Amy waves a heartfelt good by as her grandparent's wagon pulls away bound for Pitman.

It's a wonderfully sunny morn, and the little brick house is still for the first time since Pastor Blackwell and Gert left well over one week ago. Amy nurses her tiny baby girl in the rocker, and her son sleeps soundly in the basket. The days pass by quickly in their new routine: Ernest Lee walks over to his office every morning, Effie stays busy about the house all day, and Amy stays mostly in the bedroom, tending her babies.

They named the baby girl Sally. For one who entered the world so feebly, she now nurses ravenously every minute that she's awake. Her brother's name is Timmy, and he's always starving, too.

Amy is rocking back and forth, enjoying the gentle tugging at her breast when it first occurs to her—she never asked her husband about something vitally important. So, after the babies are fed and asleep at the end of the day, Amy snuggles up to Ernest Lee on the feather bed.

"Ernest Lee, how did Dr. Wallace help our little Sally? You never said."

"It was a true miracle, Amy," Ernest Lee nods.

"To be sure it was, but I'm asking—what did he do for her?"

A smile crosses Ernest Lee's face, and he stalls, "Oh, it's not that important, sweet Amy. It worked, and that's all that counts."

Amy is growing both puzzled and annoyed now, "You *still* didn't answer me, Ernest Lee. You were over at the doctor's office all those days. What did he do exactly to save our baby's life?"

"I don't think I should tell," Ernest Lee tries to smile.

"Yes, you should, and *right now,*" Amy insists.

Ernest Lee sighs, "All right, but you have to promise to listen the whole way through."

"You know that I will," Amy promises.

"Well, Dr. Wallace knew of those inventions called 'incubators.' Seems they're made for babies born way too early. He said he saw them at an exhibit one time." Ernest Lee nervously twirls the sheet around and around in his finger, trying to explain. "Not many places have them yet, especially 'round here."

"Yes?" Amy is growing impatient.

Ernest Lee hesitates, "Well, Doc Wallace got the idea that, since these new baby incubators were really like small ovens, and, since Sally needed a good warming up…."

"What does an *oven* have to do with our little Sally?" Amy interrupts, looking Ernest Lee straight in the eye.

"Well…the Doc warmed up Sally over at his house…in his oven," Ernest Lee mumbles.

Amy sits straight up in bed and asks, "What did you say, Ernest Lee Herald? He did what?"

Ernest Lee recites reluctantly, "Well, Dr. Wallace, he put little Sally…in his oven…in a cloth basket." Seeing the shocked look on his wife's face, he starts talking quickly, "But not in a *hot* oven, Amy. No, no. There was *very* little heat. *Very little.* Just enough to warm her up a bit—better than we could do over here. Just enough to give her tiny body a chance to catch up for awhile. Dr. Wallace said the idea worked fine for a doctor he knows up in Pocahontas, and it sounded like a great idea to me too, so I said for him to go ahead and try."

"You're surely joking," Amy gasps.

Ernest Lee is in trouble, it seems. "I promise you. Someone watched over baby Sally the whole time, Amy. I was there myself for days." No reaction yet. "You see, the Doc couldn't try it here in our kitchen, because he knew that you'd throw a fit." Ernest Lee leans back against his pillow and stares up at the ceiling. "I *knew* I shouldn't tell you," he rasps. "It's no use explaining."

Amy is fuming. *How could they do such a thing? How could they put my tiny new baby in a...oven? It is unthinkable.* Then, the idea of her tiny little baby nestled inside the Doc's oven strikes Amy funny. She looks over at poor Ernest Lee staring up at the ceiling so forlorn and upset. Amy can't help but smile, "Well, Ernest Lee, we'll have to call Sally our 'little Christmas roaster'," she teases.

Ernest Lee is so relieved to see Amy smile. He laughs nervously.

Then, Amy adds, "Just promise me one thing—don't ever tell Grandpa."

"Why not?" Ernest Lee asks.

Amy chuckles, "Because he'd claim that what Doc Wallace did it at the hand of the Devil. I'd much rather have a 'little Christmas roaster' than a 'little devil' toddling about our house!"

Ernest Lee is happy to be back at the mercantile after all the excitement at home. He shuffles his papers all morning, and at noon he puts his ledgers aside and locks the black metal safe that sits next to his desk. *It's a good thing that I'm an honest man. Mr. Marshall would never miss one scent of his money sitting right here in this safe.*

Not that Ernest Lee couldn't use the cash these days. Last night he told Amy, "Money is really tight now that we need two of everything, and I still owe Doc Wallace for his services."

"Can't you ask your Dad to help out? Amy had asked.

"With Mama's ill health, the timing isn't right," Ernest Lee had explained.

He gives the safe dial one final spin to lock Mr. Marshall's money safely inside.

Just as Ernest Lee is leaving to go home for lunch, Mr. Marshall runs into his office and stammers, "Ernest Lee...."

"Is it the babies, Mr. Marshall?" Ernest Lee is alarmed

"No, Ernest Lee, but your dad's on the telephone. He says it's something mighty urgent."

Ernest Lee rushes over to the telephone on the wall next to Mr. Marshall's office. After only a few seconds he hangs up the receiver and turns to his boss, "Sir, I've got to leave for Success right away. Ma is very sick." He's sheet-white.

Ernest Lee makes a hasty departure in the Model T, leaving the sisters to manage alone in the Tuckerman house. They stay busy the rest of the day. Amy arranges for Whitehall's Dairy daily delivery and Effie prepares their evening meal. The babies fuss after supper, but they are finally still, so the sisters mend clothes by the lanterns until they can't keep their eyes open and turn in for the night.

Effie snuggles down on her soft feather palate on the floor in the twin's room. She pulls the warm quilt up around her and peacefully rests for the first time all day. Effie has just fallen asleep when a storm whips up outside, and she snaps awake from the windowpanes rattling. She lights the lantern and looks inside the baby's basket—they remain blessedly asleep, so she shuffles across the hall in the lamp glow.

"I can't sleep from the thunder," Effie whispers, finding Amy lying in bed, wide awake too.

"Neither can I. The wind is so loud," Amy whispers back, "...and I just had a most troubling thought."

Effie asks, "About Ernest Lee? I'm sure he's off the road by now."

"No, I got a bad feeling about his poor ailing mother. It was so real—like she was right here in this room. Does that ever happen to you, Effie?" Amy asks.

Effie is surprised, "I didn't know you believed in that stuff."

"I think I do," Amy nods, "though, it hasn't happened for many years before tonight."

Effie is amazed at her sister's revelation. Could Amy be talking about their own mama's spirit? She decides not to inquire about that touchy subject. Instead, she sits down on Amy's bed and says, "I would welcome knowing what happened before, if you want to share."

Amy sits up, eager to explain, "Well, right after we moved into Grandpa's house in Pitman when we were little, I used to wake up night after night. One day I told Grandpa about it."

"What did you say, Amy?" Effie is enthralled.

"I told him that I saw a figure at the foot of my bed—not speaking but

105

standing there silently. I could see her fine features in the glow, so kind and loving. A petite little woman." Amy hesitates before admitting the most unbelievable part, "I told him that—I thought it was our Mama."

Effie's eyes open wide, "You did? Our mama? What did Grandpa say?"

Unexpected tears well up in Amy's eyes as she continues, "He said to pay it no mind—it was bound to be the devil's handiwork. Just a trick." Amy composes herself, "So, the next time the figure appeared, I told her to leave, and she never came back again." Amy hadn't thought of it in such a long time. She didn't realize it still troubled her so.

"She never came back?" Effie asks gently.

"No, and the next morning Grandma Gert scolded me—Grandpa must have told her what happened. I'll never forget how she mocked me, saying, 'The very idea. Seeing your mama's spirit up in the bedroom. Ha! That's just ole' Satin himself playing tricks!' Then she wagged a finger at me, 'You haven't gone near that cabin up there in the woods, have you? That old bag living up there thinks she sees spirits too.' Grandma Gert started teasing us about ghost right after that." Amy can see that her story isn't comforting Effie one bit, so she adds, sniffling now, "Don't worry, Effie. I'm sure if it was Mama, and if she ever comes to visit again, it's because she loves us so much."

Effie knows better. The cold wind whips up outside and tree branches thrash against the windowpane as she sadly divulges, "No, Amy. If Mama visits us, it's not why you think," she mumbles.

"Why then?" Amy asks.

Effie starts sobbing, "It's 'cause of what I did...I know it was me that caused her to die." Effie feels so ashamed that she wants to die right then and there, too.

Amy is shocked. She regains her own composure, assuring her sister, "You know better than that, Eff. Our mother died of pneumonia when you were only four. Surely you remember?"

"Yes, and the sickness that took her was all my fault," Effie chokes out.

"What are you talking about? Mama went outside on that bitter cold day because of the brush fire. That's how come she came down with pneumonia and died. You had nothing to do with that." Amy embraces her weeping sister.

The locked up words tumble out, and Effie confesses, "I *did* have something to do with it, Amy. You don't know. I stole the match box from Mama's apron that morning. I took it outside to play." Effie shakes recalling,

"I saw how Mama made a fire with matches that morning in the kitchen, and tried to copy. I made a little spark, too, and the wind started blowing. The spark flew off into the grass, and I ran inside crying. So, I started the fire that day. If it wasn't for me, mama would have stayed warm inside on that freezing cold day." Effie cries, inconsolably.

Amy rocks her sobbing sister.

"There's more," Effie sobs. "My friend Mrs. Isay says our mama speaks to her about it," Effie says.

"Mrs. Isay?" Amy is shocked to hear the name that she hasn't heard in months.

"Yes, Mrs. Isay says that Mama speaks to her in the cabin—she claims Mama was there the last time I visited." Effie leans closer to her sister and chokes out, "I think that, either Mrs. Isay has gone crazy, or our Mama came back console me for starting the fire." Effie sits on the bedside waiting for her big sister's reaction.

Amy whispers, "Tell me, Effie. What did our mama tell Mrs. Isay?"

Effie pulls herself together, still sniffling, "Mrs. Isay heard our mama say, 'It's alright'. Mama told her to tell me that." Effie sits straight up, "See that! If that's so, it proves that Mama knew I did such an awful thing," Effie starts crying again.

Amy takes her sister's chin in her hand and looks into her eyes, "Don't you see? Mama was telling you that 'it's alright' because you *didn't* start that fire that sent her out into the cold."

"You don't know that," Effie cries. "How could you know?"

"I know because I recall that day clearly—I'm older than you, Eff, remember?" Amy looks directly into her sister's tear-stained eyes to free her from the childish notion. "It was a cold day and the wind had whipped up, just like it's blowing outside this very minute. Then, it thundered loud. Mama and I looked out the window and we saw lightening start a little brush fire over there by the smokehouse out back. Mama and I *both* saw that happen. That's when she grabbed the bristle broom and ran outside swatting like mad until she put the fire out."

"You saw that?" Effie wipes her tears.

Amy goes on, "Afterwards, we couldn't find you anywhere. We searched all around and finally found you hiding under the bed. You never said anything, but you must have figured it was *your* little spark that started it all. It wasn't Effie—it was the lightening. That's the truth."

"It *was* my fault. It must have been," Effie shakes her head in disbelief.

"Your little spark went out harmlessly, Eff."

"It has to be *someone's* fault. How could it be no one's fault?" Effie starts crying again.

Amy takes Effie by the shoulders and says, "You always believe me, because I never lie. Right?"

"Right," Effie sniffs back her tears.

"Then you've got to believe me *now*. You've got it twisted up in your head because you were so young."

Effie grabs on to her big sister, and her shoulders shake as years and years of childhood guilt is shed, "If only I told you about Mama sooner, Amy." Effie cries hard until her tears are all gone.

Amy dries her sister's wet cheeks, soothing, "Thank heavens you told me, Eff. I think Mrs. Isay's visions have happened just like she says." Amy sighs. "Anyway, what harm could there be in thinking it's so?"

Effie looks up wearily and says, "That's right. What could be the harm in it, Amy? I don't understand Grandpa's fuss over spirits, anyway." Then she yawns, "I don't care a fig what anyone says—Mrs. Isay *isn't* in league with the devil. I bet, when they wrote that part in the Bible, they didn't know anybody like her. I'm going to tell her so the minute I get back to Pitman."

Then, Effie thinks to ask, "Amy, do you ever think that Grandma Gert adds words to the Bible?

"You mean, that she recites things that aren't really written?" Amy smiles.

"Right," Effie nods.

Amy laughs, "That's what I think, too—just to prove that God's on her side."

Effie drops off into sleep the most contented she has been in years. Even the howling wind doesn't wake her.

Amy drifts off to sleep right after, still clinging to her little sister. They sleep until the twins stir in their basket across the hall, starving again hours later.

CHAPTER 7
DOUBLE SORROW

Killer influenza is sweeping through Arkansas, and now it has Ernest Lee's Ma in its grip. He drives along at top speed, determined to reach her by nightfall.

The land is frozen solid, and the roads are slick with a thin crust of January ice the farther north he drives. Ernest Lee distracts himself by counting the old tin roof shacks dotting the roadside, shaking in the wind like forgotten store signs. He tries to imagine the hardships inside. *They're huddled together, trying to stay warm by the stove. God help them hang on 'til the spring planting.*

The Heralds hire workers just like them, some for generations back, coloreds and whites just the same. His family never owned any slaves back in the days when most did—his dad says they'd never abide it. When Ernest Lee was twelve, Homer Herald sent him out to pick cotton alongside the Negroes he hired with a sack slung on his back just like they had. "Just 'cause we got a mill and a farm doesn't make us any better," his dad had said. "Get out there and see what picking's like in that baking down sun." Ernest Lee didn't mind planting, but picking cotton was different somehow. As hard as they worked with bleeding hands and raw knees, the pickers got no respect and hardly any pay—that work wasn't for him. He thanks God that he wasn't born to it.

Ernest Lee passes more fortunate families living in the larger white houses set back off the road, but they'll still find the winter hard to endure.

When their winter stores are all gone, they'll stock up on credit to plant crops in the spring, harvest in fall to pay off their debts, and start their lean existence all over again. *No thank you, I don't care to be a farmer—or a miller either, for that matter. I have a nice job in a warm office, a sturdy house, plenty of food on my table, a pretty wife and two plump babies at home. That'll do just fine for me.*

The air grows colder inside the Model T, and his breath billows out in front of his face. Amy made him wear his warm coat and take a thick blanket that he spreads out across his lap, but he still shivers inside his thin cotton pants. He passes one filling station and checks his gasoline gauge, but the tank is plenty full. Anyway, he's too cold to get out.

Winter seems to hit Arkansas hardest in the northeastern part where Ernest Lee was raised. Yet, looking back, he doesn't remember winters being *too* harsh—fate was kinder to his family somehow. Even when sleet or snow raged outside, a fire always glowed in their stove, they had warm clothes to wear, meat in the smokehouse and corn meal to bake. *Ma was as fit as a fiddle in those days. God bless her soul.* He smiles remembering back then. The mill and farmland were passed down from his great-grandfathers and has provided a decent living for several generations. He never wanted for anything growing up—give him a pony with a cart, and he thought he'd be happy forever.

However, as much as Ernest Lee loves his family, he was never inclined to take up their farm work—a fact surprising no one who knows his dear Mother. Mrs. Herald always *hated* their life on the farm, dreaming instead of great wealth and a better life for her son. While his friends nodded off to Bible stories at bedtime, Mrs. Herald recited Horatio Alger tales to her darling Ernest Lee. Her favorites were the *Ragged Dick* and *Luck and Pluck* books with their "rags to riches" stories that she drummed into his head. She'd look him in the eye summing up, "Remember, now. No matter who you are, even a country miller's son, if you have a dream and truly persevere, you're bound to succeed. Just be honest, work hard, never give up, and the American dream will surely be yours, Ernest Lee." Then she'd sigh, "Just think, son, Mr. Alger had many a failure, but did he give up? No, he didn't! No, sir. He just went right out and found himself a bigger dream, and now he's a best-selling author up there in the north without a care in the world." At the end, she gave each Alger story the very same moral, "There's a fortune to be made in the city, Ernest Lee—there's nothing down here for you but drought, flood, and disease. Leave the mill and the farm when the time comes—you'll do far better up north." Horatio Alger became Ernest Lee's idol too.

So, right after common school, Ernest Lee abandoned his family's rural farm life, vowing to become a "numbers man" up in the city—any city north of Arkansas would do. He promised his mother, "I'll sacrifice anything until I've made my fortune." It puzzled some that he jumped at the Tuckerman job, even though it wasn't a big town up north, but his mother could see the benefits, too. Yes, he'd be content with a modest bookkeeper's salary, figuring it would be an investment in his future one day up north.

However, that decision was made many months ago, and, now, Ernest Lee regrets it. He lies awake most nights thinking, *No matter how much I figured expenses, having the twins threw those plans right out the window.* Reality has set in. As he explains it to Amy, "Everything's on *my* shoulders now. No more living off of my dad. It's all up to me to make good." He realized too late, *I should have grabbed that big bonus when Mr. Marshall offered—hang a bigger one later. I need the cash now!"* Ernest Lee's mother has been right all along—it's hard to get rich in the south.

The sun is setting as Ernest Lee rounds the bend for Success. Current River winds its way along town, and he crosses the old wooden bridge congratulating himself, *Thank goodness. I'll be home soon.* This road is full of ruts, but he navigates as fast as he dares past iron-flat fields where cotton flourished months back. It feels like he's never been away. Boyhood exploits along the familiar stretch start flashing back, *This is where I rode ole' Trixie bareback to school, holding on tight to her mane.* Or, *This is the lane I trotted down in the summer for a cool swim in ole' Current River.* Or, worse, *This is the dang road that flooded so bad each spring.* The flooding wasn't so terrible years ago, but then the state dug that ditch, like they did all through Arkansas—without even asking. They claimed it would drain off malaria water, but the new ditch flooded the Herald's land worse every spring, and they *still* had malaria in town. He hates the state's ugly dredge ditch that divides up his family's land.

Ernest Lee approaches his folk's house and deep dread replaces nostalgia. As much as he wants to see his dear mother, he knows it will be so traumatic. *I'll never bear the loss if she passes on.* He shivers, recollecting how she soothed every hurt and shooed his fears away growing up. No telling how many schoolyard brawls he was in or how many times he misbehaved at church—she never made a fuss. If he gave up on his homework, she'd encourage, "Study hard, and there'll be an extra treat for dessert." His eyes would light up, and he'd dive right back in to his work. *No one else encouraged me like she did. I owe all my ambition to her.*

Turning up the long gravel driveway, Ernest Lee pulls alongside Doctor Turner's wagon in front—just the sight of it makes his heart beat faster from fearing the worst. He leaps out and dashes up the wooden porch steps. He swings the front door wide open and finds Brother Rahm and Aunt Glory slumped on opposite ends of the sofa in the front room. Their faces are glum.

Gramps Herald hovers by the front door. The old man finds no refuge in one-liners today, simply saying, "Ernest Lee, you go on up to the bedroom. Your dad and the Doctor are up there with your Ma."

Ernest Lee climbs up the stairs, holding on to the massive wood railing to steady himself. He slid mischievously down its polished slick slope as a child, his mother chasing behind. Now, his Ma lies upstairs dying, and he'd give anything to turn back the clock. His legs feel so heavy and the steps seem so steep now.

His mother's bedroom has a warm yellow glow from a kerosene lamp on the night stand and a candle flickering on top of her bureau. Doctor Turner listens to her heart through his stethoscope. His dad sits in chair by her bedside, holding a cloth to her feverish brow. It's freezing outside, but the room is warm as toast, heat rising through the black metal floor grate from the wood stove below. The men turn to Ernest Lee as enters the room, and his mother's glassy gaze meets his own.

Martha Herald lies in bed, thin as a stick, her face void of color, and her salt and pepper hair straggles about her shoulders. She smiles weakly and holds out her trembling hand to whisper, "Son, you've come at last! Praise the Lord!"

The procession winds up the road to Hitt Cemetery, a tree lined spot at the top of a hill. A lifetime of friends and neighbors pay final respects, parking their wagons alongside the thick iron gates and following the pallbearers stooped beneath Martha's thick wooden casket. Pastor Blackwell and Gert arrive last and fall into line. Brother Rahm stands next to the grave chipped out before the bad freeze. Ernest Lee leans on his father, Gramps Herald leans on his grandson, the three men clinging together, waiting to hear it's all a dreadful mistake.

Ernest Lee is grateful for the hours he had alone with his mother until she succumbed at dawn—was that the day before yesterday? He held her frail hand all night, and, as sick as she was, she gazed peacefully up into his eyes.

She was strong-willed right up to the end, straining with every breath, urging, "Ernest Lee, promise me you'll never give up your dreams. I'm so proud of you, son. I know you'll make good in the city...." She had such faith.

Few eyes are dry during the service, and no one pays attention to fluffy white flakes floating down. Martha's sister Glory is crying the loudest, unable to hold back like the three Herald men. Ernest Lee tries to concentrate on Brother Rahm's words, but bitter thoughts rage around in his head. His optimism has vanished, leaving the festering dregs of his hope that once flourished. *Ma dreamed of heading up north one day, but now she's engulfed in the farmland forever. Ashes to ashes, dust to dust—she's right back were she started with the land she despised!* His fist clenches tight beneath his Holy Bible.

Neighbors stack tables high with prized canning and baking back at the house after the funeral. Grandma Gert orders Aunt Glory about and methodically puts the food out on the table. No one is hungry, yet she shuttles back and forth with the platters.

Ernest Lee leans against the wall by the kitchen watching folks mill about but not talking unless someone comes over. His mind wanders, straddling the line between the past and the present. *Just a few months ago Ma sat over there in that chair at our wedding, smiling and looking so happy. If only I knew then that she'd be gone so soon. If only she could have laid eyes on the twins.* Remorse overpowers him. He rushes out onto the porch hoping the afternoon chill will refresh, but the tears cascade down. He can't mop them fast enough.

Ernest Lee's father clears his throat, announcing his arrival on the porch right behind. They shiver together looking out at their land, which is so unimportant at present. Ernest Lee whispers to himself, *Please don't talk about your future now, Dad. That'll be too final.*

His dad speaks up, words drenching in sorrow, "I don't suppose you and Amy would move back to the farm? It'd sure be a comfort to me with your Ma being gone."

Ernest Lee looks at his dad's grief-etched face. He longs to put his arms around the broken man and reassure, "Yes Dad, I'll move back home right away." It's a struggle for him to keep the words from tumbling out, but he can't. His throat tightens. "I wish I could say different, Dad, but I *must* get back to Amy and the babies. They're best off in Tuckerman." He feels dizzy.

Homer Herald lowers his gaze, "Don't stay out here on the porch too long, son. It's mighty cold out here today," he says, turning, and then realizing,

"Funny—that's just what Martha would say." The grieving husband chokes up again.

Ernest Lee stares blankly around his boyhood room the next morning. First light is streaming in through the window. His childish Sunday school drawings are still nailed on the wall next to a framed picture of Jesus. Business school books sit around on his desk, and his dried-out wedding boutonniere pokes out of the vase he once whittled. *Ma saved that boutonniere for me*, he smiles recalling, until reality intrudes. He buries his head in the pillow, but Grandma Gert's voice booms up from the kitchen, so he throws on his clothes and joins the others downstairs.

Poor Aunt Glory bustles around the kitchen under Grandma Gert's close observation. The incompatible pair gets breakfast put out on the table, heads bow, and Pastor Blackwell says the blessing. Platters go around, but few words are spoken. Gert is the only one hungry, it seems.

Eventually, the Pastor pushes back his chair and announces, "Well, the misses and me will head back to Pitman now." Right before leaving, he maneuvers Ernest Lee off to the side. He leans close and asks, "Son, sorry to be askin' about Effie at a sad time like this, but I might not get the chance otherwise—how did things work out with her staying on with you in Tuckerman?"

Ernest Lee wonders where this conversation is leading. "Everything is fine with Effie at our house, Pastor. Why do you ask?"

"Well, I wondered if she'd be more of a burden than a help to you. She starts back to school in two weeks, so, should I could come down to fetch her?"

"You can rest easy, sir. Effie's a big help right now with the twins," Ernest Lee reassures. "Brother Randolph says he can carry her home when he guest preaches in Maynard—it'll be no trouble since he'll be headed up that way."

The Pastor sighs, "Well, when Effie gets back home, I'll have a long talk with her. I know that I don't spend the time like I should. Times like this make us realize." The Pastor rides off with Gert in their wagon.

Gramps Herald heads down to the mill, Aunt Glory reclaims her kitchen, and Homer Herald sits motionless in his chair in the front room. Ernest Lee ambles over to his father, "Ready to walk down to the mill, Dad?"

All at once, his father rambles on like a drunken, half-sobbing sailor, "I don't understand it—not one thing about it, Ernest Lee! Why did God have to take my Martha away?" Then he looks up and spews, "A *lot* of good all that church-goin' stuff did her—all that witnessing and do-gooding for others. Where was *her* reward in the end? All God gave her back was a life far too-short."

Ernest Lee pats his dad's shoulder and whispers, "Brother Rahm says our reward's up in heaven, Dad."

"Yeah? Well let's see how he feels when God takes *his* wife one day!" The dejected widower slumps back in his chair and motions for his son to leave him alone.

Ernest Lee pulls on his coat and walks out back to the chicken coop. They keep twelve laying hens at a time—just enough for breakfast and for Aunt Glory's baking. Gramps spreads a little feed around every day and gathers up eggs, but that's all the attention the poor chickens get now. Ernest Lee used to tend them growing up. He found them so odd, clucking away and eating anything they could find laying around in the yard—stones, and even glass shards. Considering all the garbage they ate, he always marveled at the perfect snowy white eggs they turned out, and he never failed to laugh at their comical laying routine. They'd hunker down on their little straw nest in the box, taking their sweet time disgorging an egg. If he ever dared to invade their nest's privacy, he'd get pecked hard in the nose, or worse, stabbed in the eye with a beak. Eventually they'd sashay backwards out of their box and strut around the yard so cocky and proud—like they owned the whole farm. Ernest Lee mocks their screechy cluck-clucking as he walks past their coop.

He wanders past his father's prized beehives and down to the barn where a new farm hand lazily brushes a horse. Ernest Lee breathes in the musty mixture of straw and manure—it doesn't bother him the way it does some. Aside from Trixie, his own dapple-gray pony, Ernest Lee never had much fondness for livestock. 4H Club friends used to run hands along a horse's back and down on its rump, checking every muscle, then the ears and the teeth, proclaiming at the end, "Now this is as fine an animal as you'll ever see." Ernest Lee always did what he needed to do and got out of the barn quickly–leaving livestock inspecting to those that enjoyed it.

"Howdy," he calls over to the farm hand, but the big hulk of a guy just nods and keeps right on with his brushing. *Funny Dad never mentioned the new guy.* No matter. Ernest Lee doesn't feel much like talking anyway, so he walks on through the barn and down toward the mill.

The closer he gets, the louder the cadence of the giant paddles gliding through water—such a familiar, smooth, and rhythmical sound. His pioneer ancestors bought the land along Current River because it was ideal for a mill site, and that's what they built. At first they milled corn for their own meal and feed, but later they added bolts to grind flour and then farmers started coming from miles around for them to grind their feed and such. Today the Heralds mill any sort of grain—they're busiest right after harvest, but business trickles in all year long.

Gramps Herald spots Ernest Lee walking down the hill, and he comes out covered head to toe with yellow corn dust. "How long are you staying on here at the farm, Ernest Lee?' the old man asks, brushing cornmeal off of his shoulders.

"I'm thinking of heading back today, Gramps," Ernest Lee answers.

"How can you think of leaving us at a time like this? We're so far behind, and I don't think your dad is doin' too well," Gramps scolds.

Ernest Lee looks down and kicks up a patch of dirt. Some things never change.

Gramps goes on, "To tell the truth, I'm not surprised your father's in such a sorry state. He was melancholy for months while he cared for your Ma, and then he took to letting things slide and we lost all those orders. I got so aggravated that I could've...." Gramps bites his tongue, "Finally, I got him to lay-on another farm hand to help out, but he goes out and hires that sorry lug Hank." Gramps Herald spits at the ground, "I don't trust that guy one little bit. He's like one of them sticky boogers you can't flick off your finger."

Ernest Lee tries to keep a straight face, "Why's that, Gramps?"

"Well, because Hank's been a real ruckus-rouser in town. He had trouble with Sheriff Carter awhile back—just small petty stuff, but trouble-makin' just the same. Your dad had some notion of giving him a chance here— he even talked to Brother Rahm about it. Then, he went ahead and hired the fellow despite what I warned."

This doesn't sound like his dad to Ernest Lee. Homer Herald has always expected an honest day's work for a day's pay. "Why do you think he did that, Gramps?"

"I figure that after you left, he needed a kid to take under his wing. That's the honest truth of the matter." Grampa Herald looks up, almost pleading, "You need to stay on to help straighten this out."

Ernest Lee never knew that his dad took his leaving so hard—he should have stayed in closer touch. Nonetheless, he sighs, "Well, I've got to get back down to Tuckerman, Gramps. I made a commitment to Mr. Marshall, and I must finish what I started down there. That's what my schooling was for, Gramps."

Gramps Herald is not pleased, "So, that's how it's gonna be? That Marshall fellow's business is more important than ours? Wish me luck, then. I'll have loads of fun with spring planting—that Hank fella's disposition is uglier than your hairy arm pits!" With this final retort, Gramps walks back toward the mill.

Ernest Lee shrugs, *This is just what I need—Gramps on my back all over again. The longer I stay, the more I'll get drawn back into their farm problems, just like before.*" Grieving for his Ma is all he can handle right now. He planned to walk around inside the mill, just for old time sake, but he conjures up the image of Amy's soft body holding his babies. Soon, the urge to get back on the road overpowers him. Ernest Lee blurts out, "Well, Gramps. I'll guess I'll be heading down to Tuckerman right after lunch. The more I think about it, I need to get back there today."

Gramps Herald walks back over and grabs his grandson's shoulder, "Suit yourself, Ernest Lee. One more thing I should mention, though—your dad doesn't look too healthy today. Let's hope he isn't infected with that nasty influenza that your Ma had. They say it's bad contagious you know—could get even *worse* here in Success before it's all over."

Ernest Lee shakes his head as he walks back up to the house, *How much more bad news can there be on this farm?*

Timmy is working up quite a squall. His little feet are kicking and his fists are waving around in circles.

Amy walks over, puts Sally down, and gently picks up little Timmy. She offers him a nipple, and his rosebud mouth sucks contentedly right away.

Effie surveys the road outside the window and asks, "When do you think Ernest Lee will get home?"

"It's so late now, I don't know," Amy says. "It grieves me that we couldn't be with him at the funeral."

Effie sighs, "Yes, it grieves me that we couldn't pay respects to his Ma." She flops down on a chair.

"Are you tired, Ef?" Amy asks, looking over at her sister slumped in the chair.

"No, not tired—I've just thinking about *all* of our losses, I suppose."

"You mean Mama?" Amy asks.

"I was truly thinking about Daddy. We never talk about him much any more," Effie reminds.

Amy keeps on nursing baby Timmy.

Effie starts to ask, "Do you...."

"Yes, I think about him once in awhile," Amy breaks in softly, "...but I've just about given up hope that he'll ever come back."

"Tell me again, Amy. What happened the day that he left?" Effie asks, knowing the story by heart, but wanting to hear it again.

Amy dusts off the words, "Well, I was only six and you were barely four when our mama died. I thought we'd always stay with our daddy wherever he went, but after he brought us to Pitman...." Amy shrugs her shoulders, stopping mid sentence.

"What happened then, Amy?" Effie persists.

"I just know that one morning, when we came down to breakfast, he had the wagon loaded up ready to travel. I thought we were all going someplace together, but he said it was only him leaving," Amy says.

"Did he say why?"

"I remember him saying we were better off with Grandpa and Grandma Gert for right then—that he wasn't much of a daddy. I tried telling him that wasn't true, but I remember him kissing us good-bye and rolling off down the road in his wagon. He said he'd return when he had a place of his own, but he never came back."

"Never even wrote?" Effie asks, knowing the answer to that question too.

"No. I kept asking Grandpa and Grandma Gert if he sent us a letter. I asked day after day, but Grandma Gert always said the same thing—that they never got any letters from daddy. After awhile I stopped asking."

"What do you think Daddy is doing now? Where did he go?" Effie asks.

"I wish I knew. I'd like to tell him again how wrong he was to leave us behind. I guess he didn't care like we thought," Amy sighs, lifting little Timmy back into the bassinet to nap alongside his sister.

Effie hears a noise out in front. She runs to the window and shouts over to Amy, "It's Ernest Lee! He's back!"

Ernest Lee hasn't the energy to do much of anything lately. It has been weeks since his mother's funeral, yet he can't seem to shake off his grief. Pastor Randolph tells him not to worry, that it will take a long time, but Ernest Lee is impatient. He tells himself every day, *God has given me a wonderful life, and that alone should be lifting my spirits.* He tries talking to himself, *Ma is in a better place with God, so there's nothing to be downhearted about,* but his pep talks to himself don't work. The babies crying at night doesn't help his mood, either. Sometimes he whispers under his breath in the night, "Why doesn't Amy get up when they first start to cry? I'd get more sleep if she did." Most mornings he wakes up exhausted.

It's Friday morning and Ernest Lee is on his way out the door, late for work again.

Amy asks, "Ernest Lee, don't forget to bring home your pay today. We have to go to the grocers first thing in the morning."

"Can't you think up anything that doesn't cost us money?" he snaps.

Amy has a baby hanging on each shoulder and her patience is gone. She snaps back, flushed with frustration after days of her husband's ill-temper, "Well, we have to eat, and we can't eat without food, and we can't buy food without your pay, Ernest Lee!" Then she backs off, "Look, I know you're going through a bad time. Let's not fight."

"You're right," he says, kissing her on the cheek and the babies clutching her shoulders.

Ernest Lee lopes down the front steps. It's cold outside and there's frost on the ground. He walks toward the mercantile, scuffing along, watching his footprints imprinting ice crystals. Bills are piling up. He has never been in debt before, and the question nags at him over and over, *What will I do?* He walks inside the building, but Mr. Marshall is nowhere around—the man has made himself scarce all week long. Ernest Lee mutters, "He better have collected those bills like he promised, or I'll have to have another good talking with him. I bet he didn't—that's most likely why he hides out."

Ernest Lee walks past Mr. Marshall's office, and to his surprise, his boss sits there at his desk. "Mornin', Mr. Marshall. It's...cold outside today," Ernest Lee stammers.

"Mighty cold, that's for sure," his boss says. "Hope you don't mind my barging in first thing this morning, but I'd like to talk again about your accounts," Earnest Lee says stepping into the office.

"Again, awfully sorry about your mom, Ernest Lee...."

Ernest Lee cuts in, "Thank you sir. Mighty grateful, but about your past due accounts...."

"To tell the truth son, I haven't done anything yet, but I'm fixing to, just like I promised. I'll do something this week."

"That'll be good, sir. Orders are slow since Christmas, and you won't be having as much cash come in as you're used to this month." Ernest Lee's plastered-on smile fades the minute he turns around toward his office. *I knew this would happen! I knew Mr. Marshall wouldn't follow through!* Ernest Lee scowls, blood racing through his veins, temple throbbing. By the time he gets to his office, he feels weak and leans against his wall. *I never used to get hopping-mad over things, no matter how bad. What's the matter with me?*

Amy is ready for Mary's visit. The diapers are washed and hung out to dry on the line, the babies are fed, water is boiling for tea, and her embroidery basket is out for the first time in weeks. *For once, I'll relax with my friend and we'll have a good chat, just like old times,* Amy smiles. She arranges her yellow gingham napkins next to the plates, and her best tea cups sparkle ready for service. There's a knock at the kitchen door and Mary walks in, but Amy can tell at once that something is wrong. Mary's color is pale and her mouth is barely a sliver.

"What's wrong?" Amy asks.

"Oh, I've felt strange ever since yesterday, but I'm sure it'll pass," Mary says, slumping onto a kitchen chair.

"No, you don't look well at all, Mary. Here, let me feel your brow." Amy walks over and puts the back of her hand up to her friend's forehead. "Good night, Mary! You're as hot as that teakettle! Come lie down on the sofa in the front room."

Mary knew as she walked over that she didn't feel right. She pressed on ahead, but now she wishes she hadn't. "I better go on home, Amy. No sense getting you all sick if I'm comin' down with congestion." Mary's dry cough hurts, and a thick yellow glob comes up from deep in her chest. She wipes it away in the folds of her hanky, and she forces herself up out of the chair.

"If it weren't for the babies upstairs asleep, I'd walk you back home, Mary." Amy gives her ailing friend a kiss on her feverish cheek and opens the kitchen door.

Mary walks down the back steps holding onto the rail. She takes a few wobbly steps into the yard when the weakness takes over, and she feels herself slipping. "Amy, help!" she cries out.

Amy is clearing the table when she hears what sounds like a cat yowl out in the yard. She parts the kitchen curtains and there's Mary lying in a heap on the ground. Amy races outside and calls out to Mr. Whitehall just pulling his milk wagon up in front of the house. Together they pick Mary up off the ground.

"I felt so weak that my legs buckled out from under me, or I maybe slipped," Mary shakes her head groggily.

"Let's bring her back into the house, Mr. Whitehall," Amy shouts, wiping the frosty dirt off of Mary's flushed face.

"Mercy, no," Mary protests, "Best not spread any sickness around, Amy. Mr. Whitehall, can you please ride me over to Doctor Wallace's office?"

"But Mary...." Amy tries to reason.

"No, she's right Mrs. Herald," the kindly old gentleman assures. Mr. Whitehall wraps his arm firmly around Mary's waist and helps her over to his wagon.

"Hold on tight, Mary," Amy calls to her friend sitting on milk wagon's front seat. She can't believe this is happening—Mary has never been sick one day since she's known her.

Before too long, Mr. Whitehall's milk wagon pulls up outside again, and Amy races out onto the porch.

The old man shouts out, "Doc. Wallace saw her right away, Mrs. Herald. Brother Randolph is coming to fetch her."

"What is it Mr. Whitehall? Did he say?"

"Yes'm. He said it looks like the influenza, and there ain't a thing to do but lie down and rest. So, he sent her home. I come back here to tell ya'—and I forgot to give you these," Mr. Whitehall walks up and holds out two jugs of milk, and climbs back into his wagon. "Doc says it's the third case he's had walk in this morning. I'm sure glad we was here today, Mrs. Herald. The preacher's wife might'a froze to death out there on the ground. That's fer sure."

Amy walks back into the house lamenting poor Mary's illness. Then she realizes, *Oh my golly! I kissed Mary on her cheek—I could get sick, too. And the babies!* Amy stays home all day, and when Ernest Lee comes in from work she shares the bad news.

Ernest Lee has heard too, "It's all over Tuckerman, and Doctor Wallace had five more cases after Mary came in today. You better stay indoors so you don't come down with it, too. I'll do the errands this week."

Over the next few days, influenza strikes households all over town, but the Herald's household is spared. By Friday, school is closed, and, by Monday, all of Tuckerman is under quarantine. Townfolk are crazy from worry. Mrs. Smith ties bags of asafetida around her kid's neck—an old family remedy that she swears works like a charm. Microzone Company over in Hot Springs advertises a patented spray that wards off the flu, and Dr. Jones' Catarrhal Oil advertises slippery stuff to smear on your chest.

Mr. Whitehall insists that *his* doctor knows best of all. "He says to fill your atomizer up with Listerine and give your nose and throat a good spray'n twice a day." So far his family has not been infected.

"No one knows what to do anymore," Ernest Lee complains one night after supper. "I'll drive over to Doc Wallace's. Maybe I can help."

"No, Ernest Lee," Amy warns, "They say to keep inside. Besides, there's sick people over there."

Ernest Lee isn't dissuaded, "Doc Wallace saved our little Sally. The least I can do is offer my help when he needs it." Ernest Lee arrives at the office just as the doctor pulls up front in his wagon.

"I don't need to ask, Doctor. I can tell just by looking that you had a bad day," Ernest Lee sympathizes as they walk inside to the office.

The Doctor takes a chair, and slaps his cap on the table, "I never saw anything like it, Ernest Lee. It's more lethal than the war. I've seen more fever and chest-splitting coughs this week than in all my days as a doctor." Doctor Wallace hangs his head, "The worst of it is, I can't do much more than wipe brows or give out headache tablets, and I can't get from one house to the next fast enough to keep up."

"Does anything help, Dr. Wallace? A garlic clove necklace or the other crazy things folks are talking about?"

"Don't listen to any of it, Ernest Lee. Just stay inside and rest away from the others. That's all you can do."

Ernest Lee wants to offer his help, but he's frustrated, *Amy was right. What made me think I could help out the Doc?"* Then another idea comes to mind, "Did you ever drive an automobile, Doctor Wallace?"

"Never have, son."

"Well, get in mine, doctor. I'll give you a quick lesson."

So, Doc Wallace borrows Ernest Lee's Model T to whip around town and out to the country. Ernest Lee offers to drive, but the good Doctor refuses, "You have the babies to think of. You're better off at home, son." Selfless ladies from the church help out as best they can, but the poor doctor races from patient to patient alone, eating and sleeping on the front seat of Ernest Lee's Model T' in between calls.

"Doctor Wallace will be the next to come down with flu…" Ernest Lee tells Amy, "Just like those poor soldiers lucky enough to get home from war—then die in their own bed from the flu. The nasty germ is spreading so fast." He opens today's paper full with stories about other folks' suffering. Ragan News says:

Flu has passed through our midst, and there's scarcely a home but what the unbidden guest has entered. Among those taken from our community was Grand Pa Simpson. He made coffins for six others, and at the last he needed one for himself.

Ernest Lee shakes his head. "Pocahontas. That's not that far from Success. Who will be next?"

Amy wakes up sobbing. This time it's her turn to attend a funeral. The news came a week after Mary was stricken. At the end, they say she could barely breathe at all—just wheezing and dripping wet with her fever. Amy can't get the horrible image out of her mind. She's determined to pay her respects.

Ernest Lee insists, "You really mustn't go to the funeral, Amy. You could take sick yourself. There's quarantine in Tuckerman for a very good reason."

Amy knows that he's right—some towns have banned funerals outright, but she's resolved, "Mary was my very best friend *ever*. I know it's a risk, but I'll be no good to anyone if I don't get to her service. I'll sit by myself, I promise you, but I really must go."

Ernest Lee agrees at last and stays home with the babies.

Amy walks over to the church by herself, and slides into the back pew sobbing alone. She can still hear Mary's cheery greeting that first morning in Tuckerman, and she can see Mary's smiling face welcoming her to town. She replays their countless chats over tea, the two of them embroidering together, shopping for fabric, and decorating the church up for Christmas. They were as close as two sisters and so cheery just a few weeks ago. *Mary wake up! It's too much to bear.* Her own dear mother was taken by pneumonia, they very nearly lost baby Sally, Ernest Lee's mother succumbed to influenza, and now her best friend Mary is gone, too. All of her grief comes together, wave upon wave, until she's sitting on the pew drowning in sorrow.

Rob Randolph does not perform his wife's service. He sits in the front pew with his sons, head bowed, and silent for once. He's always the calming presence, the man with the answers, but now he has no answers at all, just when he needs them the most.

Amy wants to reach out to the family but doesn't have the strength or the words. She stays on the last pew, weeping quietly as the others depart.

Rob Randolph spots her sitting there on his way out of the church and, even in the midst of his own grief, he comes over whispering, "Are you coming to the grave side with us, Amy?"

Amy looks up through her tears, "No, I know it's just for family. I'll say my good-bye here."

"But Mary would want you to be with us. She thought of you as a sister,"

Rob says gently guiding Amy up out of the pew by the elbow. Amy feels so comforted by his kindness, and grateful for his caring. She walks silently out the church door with dear Mary's family.

CHAPTER 8
DAY OF RECKONING

Effie looks around the bedroom. Since Amy left, she hasn't changed much in the room, really. Her best cross-stitch now hangs on the wall, and she moved the small chest under the window. She sewed a new bed cover to keep out January's chill, and she's working on a bureau runner to match. Effie stays busy, but it's sad to see Amy's empty bed every morning; she's lonely without her sister around. She smoothes her hand over the bright squares and smiles—it was Amy who taught her to quilt. That reminds her. There's still time to work on her bureau scarf before supper, so she romps down the stairs two at a time.

Grandma Gert stands at the bottom of the stairs with her hands planted firm on her hips. "Young ladies shouldn't gallop like horses," she scolds.

"Sorry, Grandma Gert. I came down for my sewing."

"And whhhhhere did you leave it?" Gert sings.

"It's right over there," Effie says pointing to the front room table, but it's not there now. She wonders aloud, "Where did it go?"

Grandma Gert snorts, "That heap of scraps sat around all afternoon, and you've *finally* missed it. Listen here, young lady! Ever since you came back from Tuckerman, you leave things all over the place. Maybe you can do that down at Amy's house, but *I'm* in charge here, and you'll pick up after yourself."

Effie says, "Yes'm. May I please have my sewing?" It does no good to argue—Grandma Gert always wins.

"I put it away, and you'll get it back when I'm good'n ready to give it. Maybe that'll teach you to look after your things. Anyway, you should be finishing chores—not sewing on that silly thing." Grandma Gert sniffs the air, swirls around, and struts back into her kitchen.

"Yes'm, Grandma Gert," Effie calls after. She scuffs back up the stairs and flops down on her bed huffing, *There's not one kind bone in that woman's body.* Then it comes to her, *I bet I can find out where she hid my sewing.*

Effie tiptoes out into the hall. No one is coming up the stairs, so she tiptoes across to her grandparent's bedroom and closes the door. *I heard Grandma Gert up here this morning. Now, where did she hide it? There're only so many places.* It feels like a game. Effie smiles like a six-year-old on a treasure hunt as she begins looking around. There's a wooden chest at the foot of the bed filled with blankets, a bureau under the window, and a tall wardrobe in the corner with a little shelf on top. Effie rummages quickly around in all three, but no sewing turns up. *There must be another place to look. It won't be hard to spot with those bright squares of cloth.*

She gets down on her hands and knees and moves across the old wooden floor like a cat in the weeds. This time she examines the wardrobe down low, thinking, *Maybe Grandma Gert pushed it in back where I can't see it.* She moves Grandpa's Sunday shoes and the spare lantern aside, but there's no sign of her sewing down on the wardrobe's bottom.

Before straightening up, Effie decides, *As long as I'm down here, I'll take a better look in the bottom bureau drawer.* She crawls over, pulls the creaky wooden drawer open and pushes Grandma Gert's old nightgown and shawls to one side, but again, still no sewing. *Shucks, where else can I look*? Effie sputters. She's kneeling on one knee, about to get up, when she spots the corner of a box under her grandparent's bed. She crawls over and flattens out on her stomach to reach it and drags out an old paperboard shoebox. *This can't be it,* she whispers, blowing dust off the lid. Still, she's curious and reasons, *I've gone to this much trouble, so I might as well take a peek.*

Effie lifts off the lid and finds a stack of old letters inside—about a dozen held together with a pink ribbon wrapped around one way and then back the other with a bow tied on top. *Don't tell me that Grandma Gert had a beau way back when!* Effie chuckles, *I can't believe anyone would write her love letters.* This is just too tantalizing, so Effie unties the bow.

Gert is busy in the kitchen when she realizes, *It's entirely too quiet in this house since Effie stomped off upstairs.* She hurriedly chops up the potatoes for supper, but the knife nicks her finger and bright red spirals into the starchy juice on the counter. Unfazed, she licks her wound clean of blood, plops the white chunks into her pot of simmering water, and heads toward the stairs. Just as she plants her foot on the bottom step, the Pastor calls to her from the parlor.

"Misses, come in here and take a look at this list for a minute," the Pastor insists.

"I'm looking for Effie, Pastor; give me a minute," Gert snaps.

"No, I need you to come in here and tell me what you wrote on this list. I can't make it out, and I'm right in the middle."

"Oh, fiddle sticks, Pastor. Hold your horses. You're always in such a big hurry," she chastises her husband and charges into the parlor.

Grandma Gert's voice echoes up the stairs. Effie freezes in place holding the letters in one hand and the untied ribbon in the other. Then, things are quiet again, and she gasps, *Whew! That was close.* Effie's heart beats like a butter churn. She knows that her grandmother will be upstairs any minute, and there's no time to tie the letters up, so she grabs the whole stack and stuffs them deep down into her apron pocket. *I'll put them back in the box after supper.* Effie pushes the empty box far under the bed, tiptoes over to the door, and opens it up just a crack to make sure the coast is clear. She hustles across the hallway into her bedroom and sprawls out on her bed to figure what to do next.

Grandma Gert's voice bellows out as she clops up the stairs, "You need glasses, Pastor. My writing is as plain as the nose on your face."

Effie jumps up off of her bed. She smoothes the spread out with one hand and poses the other over her bulging apron pocket.

In two shakes of a stick, Grandma Gert pokes her head in the door, "What are you doing in here, young lady?"

"Just straightening my room, Grandma Gert. That's all."

"I thought you were sulking. That wouldn't do. Remember, the Bible says, *'In everything, set an example by doing what is good.'* Sulking is not allowed—in fact, it's a sin."

"No ma'am. I won't do that."

"If it's that sewing that you're mooning about, just remember—I own anything that you leave laying about."

"Yes, ma'am."

Grandma Gert smugly concludes, "Finish cleaning your room and then take the basket over to that fool Mrs. Isay, and come right back and help me fix supper. I already cut up the potatoes—I should have made you do it." Gert descends back down the stairs, her ample hips dusting the wall.

Effie collapses into the chair and reaches for the letters that she stuffed in her pocket. She sighs, *These dusty old letters are not worth such a fright. Anyway, I'm too disgusted to care much about them.* But, her curiosity gets the better of her once again, and she justifies sneaking a peek, *Grandma Gert hid my sewing, so she keeps secrets, too.* Effie sets the stack of letters flat on her lap and starts flipping through them, last letter first. She doesn't recognize the handwriting addressing each one to, "Mrs. Gertrude Blackwell." Effie knows she should stop, but this time she rationalizes, *I'll just read one letter—otherwise I'll always wonder what they're about.* She pulls the first letter out of its square yellowed envelope—it is only one page with only a few lines scrawled out in ink.

Dear Mama Gert,

I am sorry for all the trouble I caused before I left Pitman. Dad said he won't write to me since I took off so abruptly, so I'd appreciate hearing from you now and then about my girls' welfare. Please tell Amy and Effie that I'll come for them as soon as I have a place of my own.

Yours truly,

Gideon

It doesn't hit Amy at first. No one ever called her father "Gideon"—he was always called "Buck." Now, reality sets in as she looks at the date—June 24, 1908. That was right after her daddy left town. He *had* written after he left, and he did want them back!

Effie's head spins trying to grasp what has happened, *These letter lay under that bed all these years—only Grandma Gert could be so despicably sneaky.* It staggers Effie's mind to just think about it. *I asked about Daddy, week after week, then month after month, until I finally stopped asking. Grandpa always shook his head that they had no word, but Grandma Gert knew better!* Her Grandpa's unending lessons about being a "sunbeam" for God ring so hollow right now. For years, she tried to spot her daddy in crowds, but she always thought later, *Well, he didn't want us anyway.* Now Effie knows that was a lie!

Effie chastises herself, *I shouldn't judge things so quickly. I'll read through these other letters. Maybe they will me tell what happened.* So, Effie pours over the letters right up until the last one, which reads:

September 15, 1910
Dear Mama Gert,
I was sad to read in your last letter that the girls won't leave Pitman. I prayed that I could bring them to St. Louis as soon as I get a place. I know you warned me not to, but I must visit them soon to hear it for myself.
Yours truly,
Gideon

This final letter has an address printed up at the top, some hotel up in St. Louis. Effie looks at the date and figures, *That was two years after daddy left Pitman—Amy was eight and I was only six. Grandma Gert lied to Daddy until he simply gave up.* Tears of sorrow well up in her eyes as she wonders, *What will I do now?*

Effie stashes the letters back in her pocket. She takes off her shoes, pulls on long woolen stocking high under her skirt, and laces up her warm leather boots. She rushes down the stairs to the kitchen where Grandma Gert stirs a pot of simmering beef bones on the stove. Effie whisks her warm coat off of the peg, grabs the food basket, and calls out racing past, "I'm taking this basket to Mrs. Isay, like you want." She disappears out the kitchen door before Grandma Gert can reply.

The aroma of wood smoke hangs thick around Mrs. Isay's cabin. Effie brushes through the mounds of snow on the porch and peers in through the window. Mrs. Isay sits next to the stove reading a book, slowly turning the pages. Effie bumps against a porch chair, and Mrs. Isay looks up at once. Effie calls out, "It's me, Effie, Mrs. Isay." The door creaks open and Effie squeezes inside. She hasn't been inside the cabin since she fainted out on hill. It seems a bit awkward. Effie sets the food basket down on the table and smiles at old Mrs. Isay who looks so small and frail bundled up in her sweaters.

"Would you like to sit down?" Mrs. Isay asks.

"Yes Ma'am," Effie replies, stepping forward. The old woman's voice warms her like heat from the stove. On impulse, Effie rushes over and wraps her arms around the fragile bones buried beneath layers of knit, and she whispers, "It's so good to see you again, Mrs. Isay."

There's a shy smile on Mrs. Isay's face as she replies, "I'm pleased to see you too, child." She pulls out a chair and motions for Effie to sit down. Then she puts the teakettle on and sits by the stove waiting for the water to boil.

Effie begins at once, "Something at home has me truly upset." She knows that she's talking too fast.

"What is it, child?" Mrs. Isay looks at her visitor quizzically

Effie gulps hard and tells the story, "I found a batch of old letters Grandma Gert had hidden in a box under her bed." She feels her throat thicken, "They were from my Daddy. I know I shouldn't have done it, but I read every one, and now I know why he never came back to get us—Grandma Gert lied. She wrote him years ago that we wouldn't go with him."

Mrs. Isay rasps, "That explains it. I always knew he meant to come back."

Effie's words tumble out, "I don't know what to do, Mrs. Isay. If I question Grandma Gert, she'll skin me alive for getting in to her letters, but I don't know how I can sit quiet either. She's bound to tell something is wrong."

"There'll be a right time to speak, but this isn't it, child," Mrs. Isay says softly.

"You mean I should say *nothing* right now?" Effie is surprised.

"What good would come of it?" the old woman's voice quakes. "Besides, your daddy will make the truth known. Wait'n see."

"Oh, if that could only be true," Effie gushes.

"Well, trust me that it is. I had this feelin' for some time now."

"What feeling, Mrs. Isay?" Effie leans forward.

Mrs. Isay pours the boiling water into her clay teapot, pinches in some dried flakes from a jar and waits for the tea to brew.

"Please tell me now!" Effie begs.

Mrs. Isay strains to find the right words as she strains tea into two mismatched cups. "Well, one day, right after your Grandpa said I could use his cabin...."

"You mean this cabin belongs to my Grandpa?" Effie never knew who built the cabin, or if it sat on their land for sure.

Mrs. Isay nods, "Yes. He knew from the Masons that I had nowhere to live after my husband passed away, so he told me to move in here 'cause it sat empty for years." She blows on her hot tea and continues, "One June morn years ago, I had been out gathering berries. When I returned with my bucket full, I saw a man wandering around outside my cabin. I could see how downhearted he was, so I invited him in. He was so grateful, and he sat in that same chair that you're sitting in now."

"Who was it? What did he want?" Effie asks.

"He said his name was Buck, the Preacher's son, and that he had to leave town that very day." Mrs. Isay looks over at Effie whose eyes bug wide open as saucers. Mrs. Isay continues, "He said he came back here for one last look around."

"My father? Are you sure?" Effie gasps.

"He said this old cabin is where he courted his wife, and …."

"Yes? What?" Effie encourages.

Mrs. Isay looks long into Effie's eyes, "…this is where they conceived their first child—that was Amy."

Effie's mouth drops open.

Mrs. Isay continues, "I never saw a man cry like your Pa cried here in this cabin that day telling his story from the beginning. He told how he married your mother after they conceived and moved into the parsonage. Sadly, he said, the Pastor never forgave him for the sin, and they fought all the time. So your father thought it was best to move on with his wife and new baby."

Mrs. Isay reaches out and strokes Effie's hand, "Then, after you came along and your poor Mama died a few years later, he said he moved back here to Pitman with you girls—but that he fought with his father, just like before. That's why he had to leave again that very day. He said he'd come back for you and Amy when he got settled. Before he left, he wanted one last look at the cabin—to remember his dear departed wife." Mrs. Isay leans closer and whispers, "That's why your father is tied to this place just like your Mama. I feel that strongly."

Effie looks around the sparse cabin room where her Mama and her father found their true love. She turns to Mrs. Isay and asks, "Do you think that's why…."

Mrs. Isay finishes Effie's sentence, "Do I think that's why your Mama returns to this cabin?"

"Do you think so?" Effie asks hopefully.

"I *know* so," Mrs. Isay nods.

"There's one more thing I must ask—that day I ran out of your cabin…," Effie whispers.

Mrs. Isay smiles, "You want to know about the red gingham fabric that popped out of my basket?"

Effie's brows lift hopefully, "Yes, about the fabric. Was it…?"

"Yes, it was," Mrs. Isay smiles back.

"That fabric—it was the same as my doll's…."

"Yes, and it *was* her apron, Effie," Mrs. Isay assures.

"But, how?" Amy is dumbfounded.

Mrs. Isay carefully chooses her words, "That day you nearly drowned in the brook, child—after you left here to go home, I thought about your doll. I remembered how you cried lowering her down into the stream as she floated away."

"Yes, I wish I hadn't done that," Effie moans.

Mrs. Isay continues, "Well, after you left my cabin, I walked along the brook. Not too far down, there she was, as plain as you please—your doll lay there flat on top of a rock. She was soaking wet but the same as you last saw her—only washed clean by the brook water."

"How is that possible?" Effie gasps.

Mrs. Isay whispers, "I learned a long time ago not to question such things, Child. I only know that she was laying there soggy and limp, so I leaned over and snatched her off of the rock. I was afraid that she might mildew, so I picked apart the threads and fished out the stuffing. I lay everything out in the sun to dry the next day, and then I sewed her together and stuffed her back up."

"Where …?"

"She's right over there in that basket, the same one you tripped over last time you were here."

Effie walks over to the basket sitting on the floor in the corner. She slowly lifts the lid and finds her precious little rag doll lying peacefully on the bottom. Effie cradles her sweet doll, tears splashing down onto the doll's plain cloth face. Effie hugs her doll and sways back and forth. She looks over at Mrs. Isay and says," It must have been Mama that set her up there on that rock."

"I don't see it any other way," Mrs. Isay nods solemnly.

The pair ponders the miracle for quite a long time. This time Effie doesn't question it.

Effie looks out at the sun sinking in the sky, and says, "If I stay much longer, Grandma will ask what took me so long. I better go back now, but can we visit again?" She looks over at the frail woman smiling back at her.

"Of course, child," Mrs. Isay says.

The fire in the stove flickers and the cabin is so cozy. Effie hates to leave the old woman sipping tea all alone. She walks over, puts her hand on the dear woman's shoulder, and says, "I'll be back to talk with you very soon, Mrs. Isay."

Mrs. Isay nods, and Effie walks out of the cabin and down the snow-dusted hill with her beloved doll tucked tight inside her jacket. She mulls things over all the way home, *Mrs. Isay is right. What good will it do to ask Grandma Gert about the letters right now?* Yet, something gnaws deep inside, and by the time Effie reaches the ridge she is fuming, *There are too many lies in that house—there always have been! I have a good mind to tell Grandma Gert what I know about her sinister deed! How can things ever be the same, now that I know? How can I ever stay quiet?* Still, she remembers Mrs. Isay's words, and decides to give patience a try.

Pastor Blackwell notices how tight-lipped Amy is during the supper. He's been meaning to sit down to talk with her for weeks, and so, after supper, he waits until she passes his parlor. "Effie," he calls out, "I'd like to see you a moment in here."

Grandpa Blackwell never speaks with Effie after supper unless he has chores to assign, but that's usually in the afternoon when she gets home from school. Or, sometimes, Grandma Gert puts him up to scolding her. Effie imagines that must be what it is, but, then, she thinks of something far worse, *Maybe Grandma Gert found the empty box under her bed. I'll be in a mountain of trouble!* However, she remembers clearly pushing the empty box way back under, so that couldn't be it. She relaxes a little.

"It's been a long time since we've chatted," the Pastor says. He's sitting in his big leather chair behind his desk.

"What about. Grandpa?" Effie fidgets in the chair alongside.

"Oh, nothing in particular." The Pastor can preach for hours, but he's always at a loss for small-talk with Effie.

Effie finally remembers, "How's your Current River Baptist Association, Grandpa?"

The Pastor is relieved to be on familiar ground. "Well," he clears his throat and begins, "Two churches threaten to start a new group—one that favors the State Baptist Convention, no doubt."

"Brother Charles?"

"Yes, he was the first one wantin' leave, but there'll be more I expect. Sometimes I think...." The Pastor pauses to realize, *I am going on too much about my church work.* Just as he's about to switch subjects, Grandma Gert wanders into the parlor.

"What're you two up to?" Her eyes dart back and forth between her husband and Effie.

133

"Just chatting, Gert. Won't you come join us?" the Pastor invites.

"No! I'm far too busy to sit for a chat," she snaps, hustling off.

The Pastor looks over and sees Effie sitting rigid in her chair. "The Misses doesn't mean to be so gruff. She's really a good, Godly person. You know that, don't you?"

Effie falls silent.

The Pastor persists, "Surely you know that Grandma Gert means no harm?"

"How do you know that, Grandpa? I mean. How do you know that she's a...a...a good person?" Effie stammers.

He answers right back, "Well, for one thing, she's been baptized, of course. Isn't that right?"

"I guess so, Grandpa," Effie mumbles.

The Pastor tries to be patient, "You *guess* so? Why do you doubt it?"

As long as he is asking, Effie decides to ask back, "Does being baptized guarantee that you're a good person, Grandpa? Doesn't other stuff count too? Other stuff they like...."

All at once, Grandma Gert bounds back into the room. She is holding out her empty letterbox, and she shakes it at Effie, screaming, "What is the meaning of this, young lady?"

A shock flashes like lightening through Effie's body. Her mind starts to retrace, *I pushed that box back under the bed in the very same place that I found it. And the letters are still right here in my apron pocket. So, how did Grandma Gert know?* Effie sits frozen as the red-faced woman rants on.

"You tried to hide it, but this dried-out old stamp on the rug gave you away! What is the meaning of this?" Gert demands.

The Reverend breaks in, "What's that box that you're shaking about there, Misses Blackwell?"

"I had personal letters here in this box. I had them stored under my bed, and this deceitful girl stole them."

"What? Why would she do that?" The Pastor turns to Effie. "Is that true Effie?"

Effie nods slowly, "I had a reason."

"What reason?" the Pastor asks his granddaughter.

"I was looking for my sewing—my sewin' that Grandma Gert hid. I thought it might be stuck under the bed."

The Pastor turns to his livid wife and asks, "What's missing from your box, Gert?"

"Just some letters that were *mine*," Gert snarls shaking the empty box in Effie's face once again.

Effie's hands tremble and her head rings, but she slowly rises to her feet, "Go ahead and tell him, Grandma Gert. Tell Grandpa what the letters were about and who they were from."

"It doesn't matter *what* they were, or *who* they were from, young lady," her Grandma shoots back. "They belonged to me, and they were none of your business. You have no right to snoop."

Effie scoops the letters out of her apron pocket and smacks them down on her Grandfather's desk, "These letters *do* matter, Grandma Gert, and they *are* my business. They're Grandpa's business, too!" She turns to her grandfather, voice quaking. "Here, read her letters, Grandpa, and you'll find out what she's kept from us all of these years!"

"You wretched girl," Gert yells, lunging for the letters in an irate fit, but then she starts hacking and gagging from shouting so hard. Gert balls her hand up in front of her mouth, trying to catch her breath, but the coughing won't stop. She falls toward the desk like a huge sack of beans in slow motion, phlegmy hacking sounds filling the room as she clings to the desk with one hand and slaps at her chest with the other.

The Pastor yanks Gert up by the armpits and pulls her into a chair.

Effie races out to the kitchen and rushes back into the parlor holding out a full tumbler of water to her choking grandmother.

The irate woman narrows her eyes, purses her lips and flings her arm out like it's on a spring. She swats the glass hard with the back of her hand, and the tumbler cracks hard against the wall. Sharp slivers of glass fly about the room, and the water drips down on Grandpa's precious books inside his pine hutches.

Gert points at Effie and yells, "She got the Devil to gag up my throat. I know what she's up to...she, she's trying to get rid of me, I tell you." Then Gert shakes her fist at Effie, "You'll leave Pitman before *me*; I can promise you that."

Effie looks to her Grandpa for help, but his face is drained white, and he looks near faint, so Effie runs out of the room. Speed is essential. She rushes up the stairs to her room and starts pulling out clothes from her bureau, tossing them onto her bed. Soon exhaustion takes over and Effie rolls on top of her bed, clothes and all. She can hear her Grandpa shouting downstairs and Grandma Gert yelling back, but Effie doesn't care anymore, *I didn't do anything thing wrong except to find out the truth, but it's all over now. I'm going to leave.* She gathers the strength to walk over to her bureau once again.

The Pastor soon taps at the door. He enters the room slowly and slumps down in the only chair in the room. "I read these letters downstairs just now," he says, clasping them tightly in his hands.

"Oh," Effie whispers.

"No wonder you were upset." He shuffles the letters back and forth in his lap.

Effie finds no joy in his words. She gives him a bored shrug.

The Pastor looks at the clothes piled up on the bed, "What are you doing?"

"I'm going back down to Amy's in Tuckerman. Things will be different now that I found out the truth. Grandma Gert won't want me around—and I can't say I want to be here, either."

Holloway Blackwell tries explaining, "I can't imagine what got in to her, Effie. I never thought Gert'd do something like that. It never entered my mind." Even to his own ears, the Pastor's words fall flat. There's no excusing Gert's action. Regardless of how Effie came by her father's letters, Gert had no right to keep them a secret. Buck wanted to come for his girls, and they had a right to know. The Pastor tries to comfort Effie, "You'll stay and we'll pray. Things will be better now that the truth is out. God will show us the way."

Her grandfather's words chill like fingernails screeching across a blackboard. Effie's words tumble out, "Pray? Look at what good *that* did us all of these years, Grandpa…praying for all these years that Daddy would come home, and the answer was stashed right under your bed." Now she speaks slowly, "And, how do you *know* things will get better around here, Grandpa? God didn't move Grandma Gert to tell us the truth, and your sermons never moved her to confess her lie, either."

The Pastor starts in, "God wants us to forgive and go on. The Bible says…."

Effie cuts in, "There's something else, too—Grandma Gert wasn't the *only* one who drove Daddy off. I know all about the morning he left…from Mrs. Isay."

"Mrs. Isay?" the Pastor raises his eyebrows.

"Yes, my Daddy went up to her cabin that morning he left us behind. Mrs. Isay said that he …."

The Pastor rubs hard at his forehead, "Yes, I can *guess* what she said! I've regretted that day ever since, but Buck bolted out the door before I could stop him. I hoped to make it right," he says. Then, he remembers Gert's letters and adds sorrowfully, "but I never got the chance."

"You couldn't forgive Mama and Daddy because of the baby. Wasn't that it Grandpa?" Effie eyes narrow.

The Pastor whispers, "You know about that?" Then he remembers and nods, "Oh, yes...Mrs. Isay." He begins explaining, "You see, I couldn't forgive their sin before marriage, and, then, Buck wouldn't ask for redemption...." The Pastor rubs his forehead again, but the pain won't abate.

Effie challenges, "A sin? They *did* make it right in the end—they got married — not because *you* insisted, but because they were truly in love. Where were your forgiving words for them then, Grandpa? You can find healing words for everyone else—but for my poor Daddy and Mama you found none. That's what drove them away the first time. *That's* why Daddy left us the second time, too."

"I just told him what was in the Bible," the Pastor explains once again. "I never meant to drive him away."

Effie's whole body shakes, but she's not about to stop now, "I don't understand, Grandpa. You say God forgives, so why couldn't *you*? After Mama died, Daddy came back here for comfort, and you *still* couldn't forgive him. Of course he left Pitman!"

Lately, the Pastor catches himself thinking that same thing, too—the dusty old letters make him yearn to right things today.

Effie has never seen such remorse in her grandfather's eyes. She asks softly, "What did your rigid ways gain you, Grandpa? If you gave Daddy some understanding, he'd still be home today, and maybe he would have found God by now."

The Pastor's shoulders slump, "I was too close," he says, "and I had too much pride." He walks over to his granddaughter, puts his hand on her shoulder, and draws her close to him. He hasn't hugged Effie for ages, and now it is time. He whispers, "I want you to stay."

Effie looks into her grandfather's sorry eyes and says, "I don't know if I'll ever understand what happened between you and my Daddy." She pauses to think, "Two wrongs don't make a right. I'll stay here in Pitman if you want me to, Grandpa."

"I'm so glad," the Pastor chokes.

Effie feels her resentment slipping away, and for the first time she says, "I *do* love you, you know, Grandpa."

The pain in Holloway Blackwell's head vanishes and he feels joy in his heart. He sits on the side of the bed with his granddaughter, only this time he is not judging. He asks her, "Tell me, Effie, where did you learn about grownup love and those things?"

"I learned about love in the Bible," she smiles. "It all depends on how you read the Good Book."

"I had no idea…you're so…," the pastor is perplexed.

"Grown up? I grew up a long time ago, Grandpa. We just don't talk very much, so you never noticed," Effie smiles.

The Pastor sits shaking his head at today's revelations and clutching the letters. Absentmindedly, he opens the last one in the stack—it's so good to lay his eyes on Buck's handwriting again. His eyes scan the letter when one word jumps out—nice round letters that he knows so well: "God." Why would Buck be writing to Gert about God? He quickly reads the line—it's on the last page scrawled down at the bottom, close to Buck's signature:

I'm coming to Pitman soon, Mama Gert. We'll let God be the judge if the girls will take me back in their lives.

The Pastor must have missed that note in his hasty reading. If he had seen it, he certainly would have asked Gert downstairs if Buck ever showed up. He'd ask her about that later, but, for now, he just sits and enjoys this time with his granddaughter. They can hear glass shards clinking into a bucket downstairs. Gert is cleaning up her mess.

Gert is madder than a strung-up heifer. She's still stewing about Effie taking her letters, *Something's got to be done about this. That girl's got to be punished,* she seethes inside. Her chest still hurts from all the coughing and the fat vein on the side of her head throbs as she thinks, *The nerve of the Pastor. Couldn't he see it was the best thing for Buck to get out of our lives? He committed sin with that woman before marriage and brought shame on our family. And then he comes runnin' home to Pitman expectin' us to make things easy for him and his kids.*

Gert tosses broken glass into the bucket, imagining good uses for the sharp, jagged pieces of glass. Voices float down from Effie's room, and Gert gets riled again, *Imagine that man not taking up for me in front of Effie! Couldn't he see those letters were mine? It was all Effie's fault—I never would've gagged like that if she didn't make me so mad! Her and the devil; that's what caused it.*

Gert swings the rag around faster and faster mopping water off the floor. The madder she gets, the more resentment she dredges up—it has festered for years, *It's that old Mrs. Isay that's got Effie stirred up. There's no tellin' what the old buzzard said. Everyone in town knows she hides out in the woods because she claims to see spirits.* Gert shakes her rag in the air. *Well, I know what she's really up to—she's working hand in hand with the devil.* A sinister smile breaks out on Gert's face as the idea surfaces from grimy depths of her mind, *It's not too late. I should've willed Mrs. Isay gone a long time ago. That old witch can still disappear—just like Buck did years ago.*

CHAPTER 9
EASY GO

Losing Mary hit Amy hard. It was over three weeks ago, and her eyes are swollen from crying last night.

Ernest Lee rolls over and rasps, "Good morning."

Amy answers, "You too," swinging out of bed and shuffling her feet on the cold wooden floor searching blindly for slippers. Amy used to welcome this quiet time with her husband, the babies asleep, and a nice time to cuddle, but things aren't that way any more. Ernest Lee has been moody for weeks. Amy knows it's from grieving his mother, so she makes allowances and tries to cheer him with small talk like, "Do you want to play checkers, or read a bit tonight?" Nothing gets through, and he sits in his chair, night after night, stewing things over.

However, since Mary's death, Amy's own mood is so low that she doesn't care about Ernest Lee's. They get up every morning, he goes to work, she cares for the twins all day long, and he comes home for supper. Then, it's bedtime and the days start all over again. There's no antagonism between them—in fact, there's not much of anything. Just going on with their life.

On top of everything else, Ernest Lee received another letter from Gramps Herald last week complaining, "Nothing's getting done around here. Your Dad keeps the place like a train wreck, and Aunt Glory threatens to leave for her sister's up in Missouri."

Amy hustles about in the bedroom and grabs the twins from their crib on her way down the stairs. She sets the table for breakfast, lights the wood stove for oatmeal, and sits down to nurse Sally. Little Timmy is propped up in his chair—blonde hair sprouts up like new blades of grass atop his pink head. He stuffs his fist in his mouth waiting his turn to get fed.

Ernest Lee straggles into the kitchen and peeks into the pot Amy put on the stove. He stirs a time or two to keep it from sticking. "It looks done to me," he says finally, dragging the pot over to the table and ladling oatmeal into his bowl. He drizzles honey in from a jar and blows on the hot globs that drip down from his spoon. Dining formalities have all but vanished—there's no time or energy.

Amy reminds him, "Be careful outside on the walk. It snowed again last night."

Ernest Lee nods, "We could hardly keep up with shoveling over Marshall's yesterday. As soon as we cleared, more snow came down."

Baby Sally stops sucking and gives out a raspy little cough. Amy looks down at her worried, "Remember what Doc Wallace said last week, Ernest Lee? If this cough gets any worse, Sally will need that serum. Last night she sounded like a nest of rattlesnakes hissing."

"How much?" Ernest Lee looks up.

"It won't be for free, but Doc says it'll give some relief. Listen to her breathing," Amy says, holding Sally up for him to hear better.

Ernest Lee groans, "Go on over to the pharmacy. We might as well have the serum on hand." He finishes his oatmeal and disappears out the door.

Amy switches babies—it's Timmy's turn to nurse. She walks about the kitchen holding him and looking out at the gray winter sky.

She dreamt again last night about poor Mary lying cold in her coffin. Mary never sat still for a minute in life, and there she was, stiff as a log, staring up at the church ceiling. Amy can't get it out of her mind. It stirs up thoughts of her mama's funeral all over again. She had buried her head in her daddy's lap with her eyes closed the whole time. He patted her curly locks; he was so tender and sweet. Now she wonders if he lies in a coffin somewhere, too. She lectures herself, *For Effie's sake, I have to have hope. For both of our sakes, I must try to find him.* Thinking about finding her father lifts her spirits again.

Ernest Lee scuffs tracks in the snow on his way to the mercantile. When he was a kid, it was such a treat when the flakes drifted down. He'd put out his tongue to catch the cold lacy wafers, and he'd make a little snowman if enough stuck to the ground. He skids sideways on hidden ice and rights himself, barely. "Jeeeeeeeesus," he screeches, looking around to be sure no one has heard. He never used to say things like that.

Mr. Marshall heads out of the mercantile just as Ernest Lee arrives. "Morning Ernest Lee," the boss nods, tipping his wool cap as he rushes off down the path. His breath makes clouds in the cold.

Ernest Lee looks at his watch. It's only 8:30 AM and his boss is leaving the office already. And why not? Customers are few and business is almost at a standstill. Who could have imagined it? First, men left town to fight abroad, then, there was the influenza outbreak last fall—a scourge still taking lives, and now Tuckerman is having the worst winter in years keeping most folks indoors. Yesterday Ernest Lee pointed out to his boss once again, "This time last year, farmers put money down on spring farm equipment. This year they're buying snowshovels—and they want them on credit. It's going to be a bad year." Mr. Marshall's stock is gathering dust in the warehouse, and his unpaid collectibles are still overdue.

Ernest Lee sits at his desk, tapping his pencil and thinking about his *own* growing debt. He starts adding it all up in his head, *There's Doc Wallace's bill, money I owe the mechanic that fixed the Model T, money we owe to Smith's grocery, and now that expensive cough medicine—I've never owed money before.* He's deep in thought when Wanda, Mr. Marshall's floor manager, pokes her head in his office, "Excuse me, Ernest Lee. Mr. Marshall's not here, and someone out front wants to talk about tractors. None of us know much about the heavy equipment."

Ernest Lee heads out to the sales room where a tall fellow stands in the middle of the floor. His boots are all muddy and his thumbs are hooked in his pockets. "I'm Ernest Lee Herald. How can I help you today, sir?"

"Well, it was the darndest thing. Half my barn roof fell in last night from the snow, so I hitched up the plow to my tractor this morning, and the dang thing gave out," the fellow drawls.

"Your tractor?" Ernest Lee asks.

"Yep. Dang thing," the customer repeats.

"I know a good mechanic in town," Ernest Lee offers.

"Naw. It was on its last leg already, and now the motor's burnt up. Only good for parts now. Serves me right."

Ernest Lee makes polite conversation, "I know how that is. When a good tractor goes out, it's like losing a friend."

"What do you have?" the customer asks.

Ernest Lee hesitates with his answer, not quite sure what the fellow has in mind.

The man speaks up again, "Well, what do you have in the way of a new gasoline tractor?" To punctuate his request, the lanky fellow pulls a wad of bank notes out of his pocket and shakes it around like a fan. "Don't worry none about my paying. I never did believe in banks." The stranger cups his hand at the side of his mouth, and whispers. "I don't have no wife nagging to spend it all, neither."

Ernest Lee is amazed. Very few small farmers around Tuckerman can afford their own gasoline tractor. The store keeps them in stock mostly for the big spreads and plantations. This fellow is a rare specimen, indeed. Ernest Lee looks around and the two of them are alone in the middle of the salesroom. "What did you say your name was, Mr....?"

"I'm Norris Gardner from out on Grange road. I stay pretty much to myself out there, me and a few farm hands. I don't get into town much."

"Well, Mr. Gardner. Let's take a walk out back to Marshall's Mercantile warehouse. I have a couple of tractors that will interest you. Either one of 'em will last you a lifetime. I can guarantee that."

In no time, Ernest Lee is back at his desk, flabbergasted at what has just transpired. Out of the blue, this Gardner fellow walks in and plunks down crisp bank notes for the best John Deere tractor they have in stock, "The Waterloo Boy," with a plow and all the attachments selling for $990.00. No questions asked! The no-nonsense man didn't even dicker on price—everyone dickers these days.

Ernest Lee stares at the bank notes stacked in the middle of his desk. *Imagine—the guy does business on a handshake.* He grabs a large deposit envelope and stuffs the bank notes inside. It has been a long time since he penned such a big, round number: $990.00. He's writing the sale up when an odd thought flashes through his mind, *I got the full catalog price for that tractor—Mr. Marshall never expects to get that much. What if I....* He dismisses the thought from his mind and writes down the tractor's full price. Ernest Lee stuffs the receipt in with the bank notes and tosses the envelope into the safe. The metal door bangs shuts and, with a quick swipe of the hand, he emphatically spins the dial locking the money inside. He leans back in his chair, clasps his hands in back of his head and puffs out his proud chest, *Well, won't Mr. Marshall be surprised when he gets back to the office?*

Ernest Lee waits all day for Mr. Marshall to return to the mercantile. Noon comes and goes, and it's quitting time now, but Mr. Marshall is nowhere in sight. Ernest Lee lets everyone out the side door and waits for his boss. The later it gets, the more his thinking shifts, *This is plumb annoying. I made that huge sale, and that fellow doesn't even care to come back and find out. Here I sit in this cold office with a nice hot supper waiting for me at home on the stove.* The more he thinks about it, the more stirred up he gets, *No one pays good money these days, except for this guy that walked in here just now. Good thing I was here to take charge!*

Ernest Lee works up quite a snit waiting for his boss, and he finally decides, *Mr. Marshall isn't coming back tonight. That's for sure! This is the last straw!* He grabs the blank order pad and scratches out a new receipt for the tractor—this one a one hundred dollars less than before. Then he reaches into the safe for the fat deposit envelope, pulls two fifty dollar notes off of the top, and substitutes his new receipt for the first one. A tingling sensation runs along the back of his neck, but, without further thought, he tosses the envelope back in the safe, bangs the door closed, and spins the dial around four or five times.

"Well, that's that," Ernest Lee barks emphatically, whipping on his coat, turning out the office lights, and stepping into the cold night air. He plunges his hand deep into his coat pocket walking home. Yes, they're still there—the nice crisp bills nestle in there with the crumpled up receipt. He slides the bills back and forth, up and down, and around with his fingers, listening to the lovely sound they make rubbing together. He's almost euphoric.

The snow is much deeper than it was this first thing morning, and more flakes start drifting down. A big smile crosses Ernest Lee's face, *Good thing that Norris Gardner bought a new tractor—this snow will cave in the other half of his roof tonight!* He whistles a merry tune all the way home, marveling at his good fortune today.

Ernest Lee walks in the front door, and his whistling is music to Amy's ears. "Had a good day, Ernest Lee?" she asks.

"Yep, sure did."

"What?" she asks.

"Sold a huge tractor and all the attachments."

"Did you get a good price?"

"Sure did—full price," Ernest Lee crows.

"I'm sure Mr. Marshall was tickled pink," Amy grins.

"He was out, and never came back to the office at all. I'll tell him all about it tomorrow."

"When he hears, he'll be mighty pleased—might even give you a big bonus," Amy says hopefully.

"We'll see," Ernest Lee laughs, gloating inside, *Mr. Marshall already gave me a big fat bonus today—only he just doesn't know it!*

Amy tucks into bed that night and drifts off to sleep right away.

Ernest Lee decides to sit up in the front room to read the paper a bit. After turning just a few pages, he dozes off in the chair, but, hours later, he wakes up in a sweat. He can see from the moon that it's way past midnight and he's wide-awake now. His mind wanders and he agonizes, *How could I lower myself to take Mr. Marshall's money? What got into me?"* He runs the scene around in his mind again and again, but there's no way to justify it, *Taking that money was a big, fat, sin. I'll bet Ma is having a fit up there in heaven.*

Remorse replaces the glee Ernest Lee felt walking home, until he finally decides, *I'll make things right first thing in the morning.* He feels better at once.

Just as he's about to get up from his chair, new demons torture, *Should I tell Mr. Marshall and own up to my theft, or just put the notes back so that no one will know?* He decides that replacing the money will be quite enough, but guilt rears up again before he can rise to his feet, *If Mr. Marshall cataches me replacing the money, I'll be caught in the lie and get fired! No, I must to confess my sin to Mr. Marshall and make things right with God.* Satisfied with his decision, at last, Ernest Lee tip-toes up the stairs and slips into bed next to Amy.

Mr. Marshall perches on the stool next to his ailing wife's bed. Elsie stuck by him for forty two years as he built up his business, but now all of his money can't buy her health. He nurses her influenza the best he can by himself, heading over to the mercantile every morning and racing back home by noon. Whereever he is, his mind is only on Elsie. Today she is worse than ever, so he hurried back home almost as soon as he checked in at work. Her fever is up, and now she's half out of her mind, begging to travel—as sick as she is. She's determined to visit their daughter up in Poplar Bluff. He doesn't blame her for wanting to go—their loving daughter will dote on her mother day and night until she is well.

"Maybe you've been right all along, Elsie," her worried husband says. "Maybe it is time for me to retire. What do you think, Elsie my love?"

His wife nods her feverish head, and that's all he needs to know.

"Let's talk to our Lord about it," he says. The couple clasps hands, bows their heads, and he prays, "Lord, I'm asking for your guidance. Please show us if this is the right thing to do." The two of them sit with heads bowed for a very long time before Mr. Marshall bounces up and announces, "I'll tell them tomorrow at work, Elsie. It'll be sad to close the mercantile down, but there's no other way. I know this decision is right!"

Elsie manages a weak smile, and a grateful tear runs down her cheek. She falls asleep at once, dreaming of being with her daughter again before it's too late.

Mr. Marshall pats his wife's sleeping brow, "There, there, Dear. You get a good rest."

Elsie feels better the next morning, and Mr. Marshall is much relieved. "Things are looking up, Elsie, dear," he assures her as she sips warm broth for her breakfast. "I made my decision, and there's no going back on it now." With that he tucks Elsie back into her bed, and heads off to the mercantile, waving, "I'll be back home at noon, my love."

Mr. Marshall breathes in the cold air, and it feels so good and pure. Walking along, he recalls how he started his business so many years ago, peddling pots and brushes door to door, working out of a storefront after awhile, and, before he knew it, having such a fine business. However, his head is clear and his mind is made up, "It's time to put my work aside. God has a plan for Elsie and me." His thoughts turn to sleeping late in the morning, sitting on the porch swing at dusk and playing with his grandchildren up in Poplar Bluff. He smiles, *The Lord sure makes things easy if you just trust in Him.*" He can hardly wait to tell Ernest Lee the news.

Ernest Lee waits at the mercantile to greet his boss bright and early. The minute Mr. Marshall enters, Ernest Lee says, "I have something important to tell you, Sir. May we sit down and talk?" Ernest Lee is so exhausted from worry, that he doesn't notice the smile on his boss's face.

"That's just what I have in mind, too, Ernest Lee. I'll be right along." Mr. Marshall walks down the hall and into his office. He closes the door, and, without hesitation, sits down at his desk, bows his head, and gives thanks to the Lord for his fateful decision.

Ernest Lee worries about what to say when Mr. Marshall walks in though his door. *It wasn't that I stole such a great fortune, but it wasn't my money to take. I must confess my bad deed to Mr. Marshall right away.* However, the longer his boss keeps him waiting, the more Ernest Lee turns things around in his head, *Maybe what I did wasn't that dreadful. After all, I'm returning the money. Why upset Mr. Marshall when I'm righting the wrong?*

The more he thinks about it, the more logical the idea sounds to him, *I'll just return the money and make out a brand new receipt. That way, I won't have to trouble Mr. Marshall at all. I'll just tell him about the sale and nothing more.* That decided, the wait for his boss starts to hang heavy, and Ernest Lee begins to fret, *What is the matter with me? I was going to confess my sin to make things right with God, and that's what I should do!* Then, a brand new perspective develops in Ernest Lee's mind, *What if Mr. Marshall had insisted that I take a bonus for my big sale? Amy said that herself just yesterday! Well, then, that money I took would have been mine anyway. Maybe I'll just keep a little....* Before Ernest can reason his idea out any further, Mr. Marshall appears at his door."

"Well, here I am, son," Mr. Marshall says with a grin.

Ernest Lee starts in, "Mr. Marshall, I've got to tell you...."

"Whatever it is, it can wait, Ernest Lee. Nothing can be more important than what I have to say," Mr. Marshall holds out his hand like he's pushing back the Red Sea.

"But, sir..." Ernest Lee stammers.

"No, no, my turn first," Mr. Marshall chuckles, "After all, I am the boss around here, am I not?"

"Yes, sir," Ernest Lee leans back in his chair.

"Well, son, I haven't mentioned it, but Elsie is down with a bad influenza...."

"I am sorry to hear that, Mr. Marshall. I had no idea...."

"No, no, she's so much better this morning, but that isn't what I was aiming to tell you. Last night Elsie and I talked things over, and I decided that it's time to retire. We'll move in with our daughter up in Missouri like she's been begging for years."

Ernest Lee's sits there stunned, "But, Sir...."

Mr. Marshall grins, "No, no, there's more. I'm coming to the best part right now. I was all set to tell you that I'll be closing the mercantile down, but God gave me another thought just now in my office."

"He did?" Ernest Lee is feeling light headed.

"God surely did, son. I was sitting there thinking what a shame it is, after all these years, to close down my business—what a sad day that will be. Now, if Elsie and I had a son to take over, that would be different. So, I prayed hard to the Lord about it, and he led me to a new way of thinking. I'll go ahead and retire, but fix it so you can buy me out over time—I mean for you to take over Marshall's Mercantile, Ernest Lee. That way, my good name will go on forever, and I'll be helping a fine young man get a good start in life. That seems like the Christian thing to do. What do you think, Ernest Lee?"

"You mean...?"

"I know what you're going to say, Ernest Lee—times are bad now, and I have quite a few personal creditors. You warned me about that many months ago. However, I'm willing to assume that burden myself," Mr. Marshall says proudly.

"That's very generous, sir, but I still could never afford it," Ernest Lee's mind spins.

"I knew you'd say that too, Ernest Lee, but think of it this way: Your salary'll go way up when I leave, and you can put that money toward making the payments—I can let you have as long as you need."

This is the break that Ernest Lee has dreamt about! It would take him years to build up such a business, and he might never be that lucky at all. He's sure that his mother would approve, if she were still alive. He can't believe his good fortune.

"I ...I...I don't know what to say, sir," Ernest Lee stutters.

Mr. Marshall pats his young bookkeeper's arm, "Well, son, why don't you talk it over with your lovely wife, Amy, tonight? You can let me know as soon as you can. How's that sound?"

Ernest Lee gulps, "That sounds mighty fine, sir."

Mr. Marshall leans forward over Ernst Lee's desk, and talks straight from the heart.

"Listen, Ernest Lee. I was thinking in the night how much you've been like a son to me. In fact, I don't think any man's son could work harder than you do. You've *earned* this opportunity, young man."

"You're sure that this is what you want, sir?"

"I'm as sure as I know that our Lord's waiting for me up in heaven," Mr. Marshall throws back his head with a big belly laugh. "Now it's your turn to speak. What was it that you wanted to tell me?"

"Oh, certainly nothing as important as this. Nothing at all. Just about a fine tractor sale that I made yesterday, that's all. I got the usual $890.00."

The babies are put down for their naps, and Amy is ironing when Ernest Lee bounds through the kitchen door. "Home at noon, Ernest Lee? Are you not feeling well?" she asks.

Her husband has a silly look on his face as he shares, "I have some exciting news, so I raced all the way over at lunch time."

"You already told me about your big tractor sale," Amy reminds him.

"This is far better!" he exclaims, setting her flat iron aside and guiding her into a kitchen chair.

"You must be hungry for lunch," Amy insists.

"Food can wait. I could never eat now! God must be smiling on me," Ernest Lee shouts, absolutely radiant with glee.

"What on earth for?" Amy can't imagine.

Ernest Lee leans forward on the table and grabs both of Amy's hands in his own, "What would you say if I…I mean if *we* were to own Marshall's Mercantile? And what if it was someday real soon?"

"How can that be?" Effie exclaims. She can't believe her ears.

"Mr. Marshall has decided to retire, and he wants *me* to buy him out. I'd be a fool not to take him up on his offer, Amy."

"But, I thought that business is terrible trouble on account of the loans he didn't collect?"

"Mr. Marshall says he'll keep that burden himself. I'll get a nice raise in salary—that'll make it a cinch to pay him off over time." Ernest Lee can barely sit still in the chair. "What do you think about this stroke of luck, Amy?'

Amy doesn't know much about finances. In fact, other than the household allowance that her husband gives her on Mondays, she doesn't have any money to call her own. He's the one that knows all about finance. Still, she asks, "Are you sure we can afford this, Ernest Lee?"

"Yes, we can do it. It might mean longer hours at first, but I'll get the job done. Think of our future, Amy! Anyway, it's still wartime, and I might never get another offer like this one again."

Amy hasn't seen Ernest Lee so happy in months, and she starts getting into the spirit herself. She runs over and throws both arms around her husband and praises, "If this is what you want, then we're surely a most fortunate couple."

"That's my sweet Amy," he says. It has been so long since he has seen a smile on Amy's face, and he'd almost forgotten how good she felt in his arms. "I know I haven't been the easiest person to live with these days," he says, and he gives Amy a warm kiss on the lips.

"I haven't been such a blessing, either, Ernest Lee." She gives him back a kiss twice as long. They're standing in front of the kitchen window, and she looks outside, "What will the neighbors say if they see us?" she worries.

He winks at her, "They'll just say, why don't those two kids go upstairs and start acting like grown ups?" With that, he takes his wife's hand and they tippy-toe up the stairs so they don't wake the babies.

Ernest Lee practically skips back to the office, but Mr. Marshall isn't there. Ernest Lee is feeling so happy that he'd like to shout "Hallelujah" from the church roof. He rejoices, *Think of it. This will be my business some day. I better tell Dad!* Ernest Lee walks over to telephone on the wall next to Mr. Marshall's office. He cranks up the operator, and she rings through right away. A man answers the phone, but he doesn't recognize the voice. He's about to hang up and ring the operator again when someone breaks in, "Give me that dang telephone receiver, Homer. Hello, hello, who is it?"

"Hello? Who is this? Is that you Gramps Herald?" Ernest Lee asks.

"You bet it is," he replies, sounding mad at the world.

"Who was that on the phone?"

"It was your Dad, that's who."

"It didn't sound like him. Why's he talking like that, Gramps?"

"Why? You want to know why? 'Cause he's as drunk as a skunk. That's why."

"Say that again, Gramps?"

"Remember I wrote a few weeks ago how nothin' gets done around here, and how the place is run down? Well, I just came up to the house to check on your dad. He's supposed to be getting' chores done, but he's sitting here drinking whisky instead—just like yesterday and the day before that. As drunk as a sailor on leave."

"Dad, he never drinks," Ernest Lee protests.

"Well, he didn't *before*—but he does *now* since your mother went up to heaven, rest her soul. Tell me, Ernest Lee, what did you think of that idea in the letter?"

"Idea, Gramps?" Ernest Lee scratches his head trying to remember.

"Dang. Didn't you read it? I wrote weeks ago. I swear, if you don't come home and take over pretty soon, this place'll fall apart. Last week Aunt Glory packed up and left—she cried like a baby on the way out the door. Now we're in a worse mess than ever. So, what do you think, Ernest Lee? When will you come home?"

"I have a job here in Tuckerman. I just called to tell you that...that...." Ernest Lee stammers.

"Well, Ernest Lee, just think of all the Heralds that lived on this here farm. Generations of work will count for nothin' if you *don't* take charge—those babies of yours won't have no heritage left. But, that's fine 'n dandy with me.

You just stay right there in Tuckerman with your pencils and ledgers."

"Well, I have got to think about…." Ernest Lee stalls.

"Look, Ernest Lee, I'm getting up there in years, if you didn't notice. The ground is slicker than cow snot right now, and we should be getting the land ready for crops in the spring. I can only do so much by myself, and that new guy, Hank, he's no-count to help out. With 'Homer the souse' running the farm, there won't be no planting this year—and there won't be no income."

"Gramps. Listen …".

"Look, I don't have time to yammer with you right now, Ernest Lee. Just let me know what you decide. It's all the same to me. I got my fishing cabin up on that bend in Current River. I can live a peaceful life up there with a few girlie books and none of this aggravation." The phone line goes dead.

CHAPTER 10
WATER RISING

The twins enjoy the wild ride up the steps. Amy swings their bassinet to one side and hops over a wood patch claimed by termites. She catches her breath up on the porch and wonders aloud, "How can a place go down hill this fast?" The rails are peeling and the spindle-wheel screen door hangs loose on its hinges. White wash still clings to the old wooden shingles, but the Herald's little farmhouse has all but lost its charm.

Amy dreaded this move. She'll never forget the night Ernest Lee finally decided that they'd have to leave Tuckerman. It was late at night when she found him sitting next to the lantern downstairs. His mother's last letters were spread out on his lap, and he was bleary eyed from reading them over and over. He almost cried, "Ma was so happy that I got off the farm, but, God help me, I've got to go home."

"But you *are* home, Ernest Lee," Amy pleaded.

"Home to the farm in Success—that's what I mean."

Amy understood her husband's distress, but she didn't want to leave their beautiful new home. She tried reasoning, "Maybe things will get better all by themselves, and then we'd be sorry we moved." Or, "Maybe things will get *worse* and the move will gain nothing at all."

In the end, Ernest Lee was firm, "We have to go. Dad's going over fool's hill, and the least I can do is help after all he's done for us." There was very little discussion after that.

Ernest Lee parks their borrowed truck on a level spot out in the yard and starts unloading a few pieces of furniture and the rope-bound boxes stuffed with everything they own.

"Mind the hole on the step," Amy calls over her shoulder. They left Tuckerman at dawn and her stomach is growling from hunger. "I'm not giving in to your gnarly noise," she scolds. *God grant me the strength to get through this day.* She propels her reluctant legs up and over the threshold and lugs the heavy bassinet inside.

Amy takes a quick look around the front room—it's jumbled up with papers and boxes. She walks straight through to the kitchen and gasps at the sight. Egg shells tangle with coffee grounds in the sink, and half-eaten canned goods sit out on the counter. *No one has lifted a finger around here for weeks since Aunt Glory left.* Amy sets her basket of babies down on the table.

Sally and Timmy gaze all around, their little blue eyes bright as buttons, their rosebud mouths cooing away.

The screen bangs shut and Ernest Lee struggles inside with the crib. Before thinking, Amy starts begging, "Ernest Lee, do we really have to…."

"Yes, Amy. Can't you see that there was no choice?" Ernest Lee has been snapping all day.

"I only wondered…"

"Listen. I know this isn't what we planned on, but what else could I do? Let this place slide down hill?"

"No, but…."

Ernest Lee interrupts, "How could I save Mr. Marshall's business and turn my back on my dad's?" He pauses to look around the kitchen, once his mother's pride and joy, and whistles through his teeth, "What–a–mess!" He stomps back out toward the truck.

Amy wants to call after her husband, but she doesn't. *Best to drop it. No going back now.* Life will be different up here in Success. Down in Tuckerman, most everyone knew your name, but in Success they all know your name, your middle name and all your kinfolk's' names, too. And it's not just privacy that she'll miss. Her spirits were finally lifting in Tuckerman after dear Mary's passing.

Pastor Randolph asked her one Sunday after church, "Amy, will you take over Mary's Sunday school class? I know she'd want you to be the one, so I am asking you first." His eyes looked so hopeful that she accepted right away, her heart leaping with joy.

With the Pastor's help, Amy thought, "*I'll get more involved in the church work and pull out of my blues.* She can't forget the sad look on his face the very next week when she told him they were leaving town.

As Amy ponders her new situation, Homer Herald appears at the kitchen door. His hair is tousled and he's in stocking feet. "Howdy," he yawns. "I heard you folks pull up out front."

Amy is startled. "Good morning, Dad Herald," she tries to smile, hardly recognizing the disheveled, unshaven man that leans against the wall.

"Sorry about the state of the place. I don't know what's gotten into me– just plain lazy I guess."

Amy tries to be cheerful, "Don't pay it any mind, Dad. We'll have things fixed up before long. Looks like you can sure use a hand around here."

"Well, I never would've asked, but Gramps insisted. I bet he pestered the tar out of you two 'til Ernest Lee finally gave in. Right?"

Amy ignores the question. "Have you eaten yet, Dad?"

"Nope," Homer yawns big.

"I'll feed the twins and then whip something up for us grownups."

Homer spots Sally and Timmy in their basket, and a startled look crosses his face.

"Want to hold them?" Amy asks.

"After awhile. It's been a long time since there's been babies 'round here."

Ernest Lee pushes the second crib inside the kitchen door. He looks over at his father and says, "Morning, Dad. Nice of you to roll out of bed today."

Amy raises her eyebrows. "Good gracious! That's not a cheerful greeting for your father."

"Well, it's the truth. Right?" Ernest Lee frowns at his father.

Amy forces a thin smile and shushes her husband, "That talk won't help now." Ernest Lee heads out the door for another load, and Amy looks over at Homer. "Sorry, Dad. It's been a long day and we've hardly eaten since dawn."

Homer nods and disappears back up the stairs.

Ernest Lee soon struggles inside again, this time lugging a large rope-bound box. Amy frowns at him, "What good will sassing your dad do, Ernest Lee?"

"Maybe he'll shape up."

"Punishing him now won't make things better," Amy scolds.

"I'm *not* punishing him," Ernest Lee shoots back.

"Yes, you are. And you've been sniping at me all day, too. Just speak with your dad nice-like and make some sort of a plan."

"Make a plan? What does my dad know about plans? If he had one, we wouldn't be in this mess!" Ernest Lee starts fuming again.

Amy looks at her husband. "Can't you be sweet?"

Ernest Lee straddles a kitchen chair backwards. He softens, resigned, "Not sweet, but I'll talk with him right after lunch. I'll get Gramps in on it too."

That settled, hunger sets in. Ernest Lee pulls the icebox door open and exclaims, "There's one lonely slab of bacon in here." He heaves a sigh, and grabs a bucket off of the counter, "If the chickens cooperate we'll have eggs with that bacon." He heads out the kitchen's back door.

The chickens cluck-cluck around as Ernest Lee enters their yard and greets them, "Good day, ladies." He grabs eggs from their empty nests in the hen house and complains to the poor feathered creatures, "What am I doing here with you dumb chickens? I know what I am *supposed* to be doing—I promised Ma I'd find a good job and make lots of money. *Ha*!" he shouts loudly, kicking the ground and sending frightened chickens flapping about.

Ernest Lee is still haunted by his parting conversation with Mr. Marshall. His boss nearly cried with the disappointment. Ernest Lee planned to confess right then and there about the money he stole. He intended to hand it over and say that he took it in a weak moment when Satan broke through. However, Mr. Marshall was so upset already, that Ernest Lee didn't have the heart to hurt him again. He kept the crisp fifty-dollar bank notes stashed inside his coat pocket, and they remain there today—evidence of his avarice gone wild. The problem still nags — even tortures and awaits resolution.

Ernest Lee returns to the kitchen with his bucket of eggs. His dad is sitting at the table now in a clean shirt, shaved, and with his hair combed in place.

Amy beats the eggs up in an old mixing bowl. They sizzle hot in the pan and then tumble onto the platter alongside the bacon.

Ernest Lee chows down the feast in uneasy silence and turns to his dad, "Look Dad, I'm sorry I sassed you. There's no excuse for it. How about you and me walking down to the mill for a talk with Gramps?" The two men devour the rest of their meal and disappear out the kitchen door.

Amy assesses the kitchen now that it's quiet. The back door swings open, and she calls out, "Ernest Lee?"

"No Ma'am," drawls a tall, lanky man with wavy blonde hair holding a wooden crate filled with small glass jars jiggling around on the bottom. He wears bib overalls, an old denim jacket and muddy work boots. The square-jawed, somber-faced fellow offers no apology for barging right in, "I found this box of preserves out in the shed. I figured Homer could use it."

"My name is Amy Herald, Homer's daughter-in-law. Those are his grandbabies," she says, pointing over to the basket where the babies are snoozing.

"Oh, right," the stranger nods expressionless, "My name is Hank. Hank Conrad. I work on the farm and here around the house. I heard you folks was comin." He sets down the crate by the stove and starts up the stairs, "There's stuff up here I got to clear out."

Though he wasn't asking permission, Amy shrugs and replies, "Sure, go on up, Hank."

Hank comes back down before long toting a sack stuffed to the brim with clothing. Before Amy can bid him goodbye, Hank grabs a jar of bread'n butter pickles out of the cupboard, tosses it into his bag, and disappears out the back door.

That's odd, Amy thinks. *That fellow acts like he lives here.*

The rhythmical sounds of paddles stroking water greet Ernest Lee and his dad as they approach the old mill. Growing up, Ernest Lee imagined ancestors constructing the giant wheel from their rough pencil drawings with their old handmade tools. His father always told the story with pride: "The Heralds pulled up stakes in Tennessee and started all over here on this land." Ernest Lee finds it ironic—he is starting all over here, too.

A loud grinding noise jars Ernest Lee's reflection—he knows the sounds well. It's Gramps Herald inside working the gears, pulling one hard transferring wheel power to the thick grinding stones, and then pulling another releasing grain down the old yellow pine shoot. In a matter of seconds, the hard grain is pulverized into unrecognizable bits. In winter, they grind only one day a week, but come harvest, customers line up every day except Sunday with wagons-full to grind. On a good day they'll take in some cash, but most times they take in grain or meal for their payment.

The grinding noise stops and Gramps Herald emerges from the mill smiling. He wraps his arms around his grandson and slaps him hard on the back, "Lord a' mighty! You're back home at last! 'Bout time."

Ernest Lee self-consciously kicks at the ground. Then, he looks the old man straight in the eye and asks, "This was your idea, Gramps, so let's talk about how things'll work around here."

Gramps Herald has it all planned out. "Well, it's the middle of April, and we got to get that soil ready for seed right away. You can concentrate on the farm, and I'll run the mill. Shouldn't be no problem at all."

Ernest Lee knows that it won't be that simple. Gesturing toward his father, he asks Gramps, "And what will Dad do?"

Homer speaks up emphatically, "I'll work with you on the plowing, of course!"

Ernest Lee squints, "From *first thing* in the morning, Dad?"

His father squirms in his boots, "Yeah, I know. I'll have to get back on that schedule."

Gramps chides, "It'll be easier to teach a cow to milk herself than to get you back on a schedule, Homer!" The old man slaps his knee, amused at the thought.

"You just watch me!" Homer snaps back at his father.

Ernest Lee doesn't intend to referee two grown-up men, "Gramps. Dad. We're starting all over now." The two men eye him sheepishly as he continues, "I'll get things fixed up at the house for Amy today. Then, first thing in the morning, Dad, you and me'll get started plowing with the farm hands." Then he remembers, "By the way, what time do the hands get back in from their chores?"

Gramps Herald shoots back, "You mean Charlie, Striker, and that Hank fella'? They're all sitting around the bunk house right now playing cards, I expect."

Ernest Lee can't believe that their hired hands are lolling about. *Leave it alone—things will change starting now.*

Amy fixes a big breakfast at dawn the next morning. She found a box of grits in the cupboard and flour to make biscuits with the bacon and eggs. Homer rousted out of bed early for the first time in weeks. The men come alive when Amy sets her spread out on the table—the only sound heard is their gobbling grub and slurping down big gulps of coffee.

Ernest Lee breaks the silence, "I found a tin of tobacco under that cot in the spare room last night."

"So?" Homer says.

"So? As far as I know, no one in this family smokes or chews. So, whose is it?" Ernest Lee asks.

Gramps Herald pipes up, "That new guy Hank was staying up there."

"Oh yeah? Why's that?" Ernest Lee asks no one in particular.

"Beats me—you'll have to ask your dad," Gramps Herald shrugs.

Ernest Lee looks over at his father, "Well?"

"No reason—we had the extra room, and it seemed like it shouldn't go to waste. He was new and didn't know anyone good, so...."

Gramps breaks in, "You mean Hank couldn't *get along* with them others down at the bunkhouse."

"He got along just fine down there," Homer defends.

"The *heck* he did," Granpa disputes. "Right away, he called 'ole Charlie a 'bottom-land swamp angel' just to get his goat, and then Charlie called him back a 'hillbilly hick.' They got into quite a scuffle over it, I hear tell. We never had any trouble 'til Hank moved into that bunk house."

Ernest Lee drawls, "I thought the days of bull-headed Arkansas highlanders fighting thick-headed lowlanders were over—generations ago."

Gramps pipes up, "Well, all I know is that Hank's as welcome as a hair on a biscuit down there at the bunk house right now! They were sorry to see him move back in yesterday."

Ernest Lee jumps in, "Hank better understand that there's no more special treatment. He's just one of the boys down at the bunkhouse—and no fighting." He turns to his dad, "Understood?"

"I got no problem with that," Homer nods his head.

"Fine. Now, gobble down those eggs—there's fresh daylight, and we got forty acres to plow." Ernest Lee pushes back from the table, gives Amy a goodbye kiss, and jiggles the babies that are fussing a bit.

The Herald men grab their lunch baskets and march off toward the barnyard. By the time they get down there, the hands are all set to move out into the fields with the plows loaded onto the wagons and the horses hitched up.

Hank stands chewing tobacco next to a wagon with thumbs hooked around his belt. Old-timers Charlie and Striker stand directly across in poses that say, "We're more important than that new-comer is." The tension is thick with everyone waiting to see who will say what.

Ernest Lee quickly climbs into a wagon and shouts, "Hank! You get up here with me." Then, he calls over to his father, "Dad, you and Charlie take the top twenty—we'll take the bottom."

Striker, a short, balding, and solid built fellow, is left standing in the barn yard complaining, "Hey, what about me?"

Ernest Lee calls over, "You work down at the mill with Gramps Herald today."

Gramps protests, "I don't need no help."

Ernest Lee drawls, "You asked me to come back and take charge, Gramps, and *I* say that you do!"

Gramps Herald cups his hands and calls after the wagons rumbling out of the barnyard, "Mind them big rocks out there. They'll ruin a plow quicker than a horny rabbit'll screw a bunny." The old man finds that so funny that he slaps at his knee.

Ernest Lee drives his wagon along the well-worn path behind the barn and past the cluster of beehives that Homer calls his "Bee City." He tries to make conversation. "You work much with bees, Hank?" he asks as they drive past the hives.

Hank replies, "I know all about bees." He stares straight ahead, frowning so hard that his eyebrows almost touch in the center.

Not far down the road, Charlie and Homer split off toward the top twenty acres, but Ernest Lee and Hank head down toward the bottomland—acres so low that they flood at the drop of a hat. Cautious farmers plant rice on their bottomland, a crop that likes to be wet, but Ernest Lee plans to gamble this spring. He explained to his dad, "I know the lower twenty isn't our best land for cotton, but cotton pays highest at the weigh station, so I'll take a chance it won't flood."

His dad had cautioned back, "That's a tricky game, son—half the farmers in Arkansas pray for rain every day and the other half stand knee deep in flood water." But Ernest Lee needs a big crop, and he's in no mood to play safe.

Ernest Lee and Hank reach their field and hitch the horses up to the plows. The sun starts to climb and warms up the spring soil, but it's still frozen down deep—too heavy for the turn-foot plow, so they'll use single-foots, one on each horse.

Ernest Lee calls out to Hank, "First we'll strike out the ground into lands, get it good and dug up, and then we'll drag the harrow around."

"Then what?" Hank asks.

"Then we slice the field up again with the sharp harrow discs. Haven't you ever done this before?" Ernest Lee asks.

"'Course I have," Hank snaps back.

Ernest Lee and Hank head for opposite corners of the huge field. The two men start plowing the reluctant spring soil, coaxing the rich, black dirt up to the top. Soon, black birds are feasting on the juicy red worms that wiggle about and starlings join in. Tomorrow they'll hitch up the bottomland plows and drag harrows again, finishing the field until its pebbly smooth. By the time Ernest Lee gets done, all the root trash will be underground and there won't be one rotten old stalk left standing upright.

Hours later, the sun is high overhead, and it's time for a break. The two men unhitch their horses and find shade under a cluster of oaks on the fence line. It's a crisp spring day, but they're drenched in sweat from their plowing. They lean back against the same tree to chow down bacon and biscuits.

Ernest Lee asks idly, "How's it going, Hank?"

"Fine," Hank answers.

"You enjoy this work?"

"No."

"What work *do* you enjoy, Hank?"

"Horses. I like training horses."

"Where'd you learn that?" Ernest Lee is curious.

"Up in Missouri hill country. On my Grandpappy's farm."

"I'll keep that in mind if we buy any new horses—which we won't." Ernest Lee scoffs.

"Right," Hank replies.

Ernest Lee gives up on conversing with his tight-lipped companion. He downs the last of his lunch and walks across the field to hitch up his plow again. Hank does the same. They'll be at it until suppertime, and then back again until it's too dark to see. Ernest Lee is plowing away when a blood-curdling scream pierces the late afternoon air. He sprints across the field to find Hank lying in the dirt squeezing a bloody gash in his calf. Ernest Lee whips off his shirt and ties it tight above the wound that gapes through Hank's pant leg.

"What on earth happened?" Ernest Lee shouts as Hank rolls back and forth in the dirt, blood dripping down.

Hank grimaces, "…moving a rock out from in front of the plow. The horse spooked and the blade caught me bad."

Ernest Lee pulls the tourniquet tighter, instructing Hank, "Pull on this hard while I bring the wagon around." He dashes across the field, hitches his horse back up to his wagon, and thunders over to where Hank moans on the ground. The two take off down the path toward the barn, leaving Hank's horse and the two plows behind.

The old wagon swipes the tall grasses and grasshoppers jump up like jack-in-the-boxes as they barrel along. "Hold on," Ernest Lee shouts over at Hank who looks about to pass out. They pull up in the barnyard just as Gramps Herald and Striker finish hauling a load of meal bags inside the barn.

Homer and Charlie heard the commotion out in the field, and they pull their wagon up in the barnyard, not too far behind.

"Good gravy. How'd this happen here?" Gramps Herald shouts out, rushing over to pull Hank down from the wagon.

Ernest Lee shouts back, "Doesn't matter now, Gramps. Let's get Hank cleaned up, and then I'll take him into town to see Doc."

Striker stands to one side observing the goings on. He shakes his head side to side—he's not buying the story. He storms off toward the barn muttering, "I bet ya' Hank got his-self gouged on purpose to weasel out of work—he ain't broke a sweat since he got here."

Ernest Lee calls after Striker, "Before you go off in a huff, make yourself useful—bring back the plows and Hank's horse before it expires in the hot sun."

Striker spits back, "Hank's just goldbricking—that's all."

Ernest Lee says nothing, but he can't help wondering the same thing himself. *If Hank is such a good horseman, he'd know to secure the animal well before walking in front of his plow.* He washes out Hank's gaping wound under the pump and binds it again. The two men hobble over to the bunkhouse—a small, one room log structure that sits not too far from the barn. Ernest Lee helps Hank lie down on one of skinny little beds—the only furniture in the room other than a card table and chairs. Then, Ernest Lee heads back up to the house to bring the Model T around.

"You're back already?" Amy runs out to the porch as Ernest Lee approaches.

"Afraid so."

"How's it going?"

"Well, the men are scrapping down in the barnyard like school boys, we're behind on spring planting, and an injured man almost bled to death out in our field. Things won't be any worse come Judgment Day."

CHAPTER 11
JUNE RAIN

Gert shouts from the hall, "You've been staring out at that rain all morning, Pastor. It's not going anywhere."

"You're right, Misses" he calls back. Pastor Blackwell can't keep from looking—he's worried that Current River will flood like it does every June. That's not to say that the Pastor isn't a big fan of the river. He is, and, in fact, he extols its virtues quite often—at each and every baptism. Swatting flies in the summer or dodging ice pads in winter, he stands half-submerged, his voice soaring above treetops, "Over two hundred miles of this mighty river flows south from Missouri. She cascades through the Ozarks, thunders over jagged rocks and flows around steep bluffs into Arkansas. But, right here in Pitman, God sculpted this gentle bend for us to snatch souls from the devil— to baptize our brethren and give them eternal salvation."

It was Current River that drew folks to Pitman in the first place. Pastor Blackwell's ancestors settled along its banks and the river became as familiar as family as it channeled past their fields and irrigated their crops. Running south and then west through town, Current River brought fish so thick they'd jump skyward at dusk and plenty of critters to hunt along shore. And it's no different now—the cold green river still holds a magnetic attraction for townsfolk—the Pastor sees it in the faces of their men returning from war. After bemoaning the horrors they witnessed abroad, they'll wander over to the river and their frown disappears—the familiar old river is the one thing they can count on. But today, even the soldiers admit—Current River is looking for trouble. Some even say it draws strength straight from the devil at flood time.

It has rained three days straight, and it shows no sign of letting up. Pastor Blackwell can't get to his churches in Mud Creek, Poyner, or even up in Missouri because the roads are so thick with muck. Their own brook is so swollen that it gushes into the stream, thundering in to Current River farther down.

The Pastor was at the general store yesterday and Mr. Hamm ranted, "Rain's welcome in Arkansas, but did God have to send so dang much—right after last week's downpour—and the land not yet drained off?" They all have stiff necks from looking up for a clearing.

Gert shouts in to the parlor again, "Why waste your time looking out that window, Pastor? Don't you have tonight's meeting to prepare?"

His wife aggravates Pastor Blackwell to distraction these days. He never minded her taking charge before—it meant more time for him to spend on his church work. The situation is quite different now that he knows how she hid Buck's letters. That terrible night he found out, he asked Gert as they readied for bed, "Buck wrote he was coming back to Pitman for the girls. What ever happened?"

"Nothing," she said.

"Nothing ever happened, or he never came back? Which do you mean?"

Gert answered from behind the wicker screen in their bedroom. "He never came back," she impatiently replied as she forced her night gown down over her belly.

The Pastor brought it up several times more after that, but she kept insisting, "I already told you, Pastor. He never did come back. You would have seen him if he did!"

Still, the Pastor wonders what really *did* happen. His trust in his wife is gone, and he can't get it back. Falling asleep every night, the hazy questions pester, *If Buck didn't plan to come back, then, why did he write he was in that letter? I've got to find out!*

The rain still pelts down on the barn roof. As soon as Gert gets busy in the kitchen, the Pastor closes the parlor door and pulls out Buck's letters. He feels guilty for sneaking around, but he reasons, *I'm not really hiding anything— I'm just trying not to stir up any trouble.* Recalling that the last letter was on letterhead unlike the others, he pulls it out of stack. The blue printing on the old envelope has faded, and he can hardly make out the print, but it looks like the hotel's name was "The St. Louis House." He knows that Brother Charles came from St. Louis, but, after their angry encounters of late, the Pastor wonders if he dares ask the man about the place. Nonetheless, if Brother Charles shows up at the meeting tonight, the Pastor decides to inquire about this St. Louis hotel.

Effie is upstairs preparing for tomorrow's school examination when the Pastor shouts up, "Effie, come over to the church to take minutes tonight."

"All right, Gramps," Effie calls back.

The Pastor and Effie jump puddles walking over to church after supper. They light the sanctuary lanterns and wait for folks to arrive. One wagon pulls up outside and then another. The front door of the church opens and two members of the Current River Baptist Association run in from the downpour and hustle dripping wet up the aisle. The four members wait well past starting time, but no one else appears.

"Brothers," the Pastor says, "looks like no one else can make it out in this rain tonight. We best get started." The small group sings two hymns and prays before Effie begins reading the Current River Baptist Association's last minutes. She has just started when the church door swings open and Brother Charles enters. He is soaked to the skin and slides quietly into a pew behind the others.

Pastor Blackwell asks when Effie concludes, "Any additions or corrections to our minutes?"

Brother Charles stands up, "I had moved that we use only Bible material sanctioned by our State Baptist Convention. I didn't hear that read in the minutes."

"As I recall, you couldn't get a second on that motion," the Pastor says.

"Yes, but I want it on the record just the same. We need that material in our churches because...."

The Pastor cuts him off, "Of course." He turns to Effie who quickly writes it down.

For the rest of the meeting, Brother Charles questions nearly every point that Pastor Blackwell makes. The Pastor has come to expect this, but he's particularly challenged tonight. He decides not to ask the man his questions about St. Louis and Buck. However, after the meeting is over, he looks up and finds Brother Charles standing in front of his pulpit.

"Yes?" the surprised Pastor he asks.

Brother Charles is uncharacteristically agreeable, "I am sorry to trouble you, Pastor Blackwell, but I had wagon trouble traveling over from Maynard–that's why I was so late for our meeting. It's best that I not travel any further tonight. May I lie down on a pew until first light when I can get a good look at that wheel?"

The Pastor is all set to agree when Effie pipes up, "Brother Charles can stay in our spare room upstairs, Gramps. I can get the covers out from the chest."

"Of course, I was just going to say that," the befuddled Pastor chimes in.

By the time Effie, the Pastor and Brother Charles cross the road in the storm, Gert has turned in for the night. Effie lights the lanterns and quietly mounts the stairs to the guestroom, leaving Brother Charles and the Pastor sitting in awkward silence in the parlor.

Pastor Blackwell decides to proceed with his query, "I understand you're from St. Louis originally, Brother Charles."

"Yes, I was raised there, and my parents are still in St. Louis."

"Nice city, St. Louis," the Pastor says.

"Yes, it certainly is."

"Ever hear of a hotel called 'The St. Louis House' by any chance?"

"Yes, but it isn't a hotel," Brother Charles replies.

"Oh?" Pastor Blackwell is surprised.

"It's was a recovery home—mostly for alcoholics and destitutes. I spent time helping out there as a preacher before I answered the call here in Maynard."

The Pastor's heart races. Now he's sorry that he asked. This is the worst news he could have imagined—his son was at a recovery house. He swallows hard, "Ever hear of a fellow named Buck Blackwell up there, about eight or nine years back?"

"No, never did."

The Pastor relaxes a little in his chair. Maybe Buck was just helping out, too. Maybe he was helping bring alcoholics to Christ.

Effie appears at the door with a lantern. "The room is ready for you, Brother Charles," she smiles.

The three walk up the stairs with their lanterns, treading lightly so they won't awaken Gert. Effie leads the way, followed by Brother Charles, and the Pastor is last. Effie opens the guestroom door and shows Brother Charles inside, "This used to be my father's room growing up," she says, "but it makes a real nice guest room now. We don't get much company." The Pastor pulls a dry nightshirt out of the wardrobe and hands it to his guest.

"Much obliged," Brother Charles says. He clears his throat and turns toward his host. "Pastor Blackwell, I know we may differ about Association matters, but I want you to know...."

"I know," the Pastor breaks in and pats his guest's shoulder, "...we're all Christian brothers. It's good to have you stay here, Brother Charles. Truly."

"Thank you kindly," Brother Charles bids his hosts good night and closes the door. It's wet and dank outside, but warm and cozy inside the small bedroom. He sets his lantern down on the night table and stands next to the bed. Brother Charles peels off his damp shirt and pulls the nice dry nightshirt on over his head, and then he peels off his wet pants underneath. He is hanging his clothes over the chair back when he notices a photograph sitting on the night table next to the lantern. It's a picture of a teenage boy standing alongside the Pastor, the kind you pay a penny to have taken at a carnival or such. Brother Charles lifts the picture to the lantern's warm glow to get a better look at the smiling faces. *Gracious,* he thinks. *This young man looks a lot like a fellow that I preached to up in St. Louis. Only his name wasn't Buck like the Preacher asked about—it was Gideon. I never did know his last name. Could there be a connection?* Despite their disagreements, Brother Charles doesn't wish hard luck to anyone, even to cranky old Pastor Blackwell. He decides to say nothing for now, but he'll check on his hunch as soon as he gets home to Maynard.

\

CHAPTER 12
BEE CITY

Ernest Lee has been moody for days. The more that June rains pour down, the grumpier he gets. He stomps into the house and plops down in a chair, paying no attention to Amy or the twins at all.

"Have a hard day?" Amy asks.

"Yep," Ernest Lee grunts.

Amy is tiring of her husband's glum disposition. After supper, when the babies are down, she decides to talk it out in their bedroom. Ernest Lee strips down to put on his pajamas, and Amy admires his strong muscles building— nice lean ridges along his tan forearms and up and down his legs—a nice slim torso. He's not her pale bookkeeper from Tuckerman these days. She wouldn't mind getting friendly right now, but it hasn't been that way lately, and she has important things to discuss.

"Are things that bad, Ernest Lee?" Amy asks.

"Huh?" he looks up and grunts.

"I mean, you've hardly spoken two words all day long," Amy says softly.

He straightens up, "What do you expect? My cotton's about to drown! Do you think I am happy?"

"No, but you don't have to be so cranky. The babies and me didn't make it rain."

"You have to understand. It's different now that we're on the farm," Ernest Lee pulls up his pajama bottoms.

"Oh, I understand just fine—the farm is all you care about now. Nothing's the same." Amy can't help feeling sorry for herself. She's stuck on a farm way out in Success with two little babies and a tired, cranky husband. Tears roll down her cheeks, and she flops face down on the bed.

Ernest Lee is at a loss for words. Amy had seemed cheerful enough after they settled in on the farm, but now he can see what's been buried underneath. He sits down on the bed and pulls Amy up on his shoulder, wiping her tears until she is down to a sniffle.

"Feeling better?" he kisses her wet cheeks.

She said softly, "It's more than just the farm work, Ernest Lee. Something has been wrong since *before* we left Tuckerman. I know that you're troubled, but it's not just the crops."

"Maybe you're right," he says. "First it was Ma's passing, and then Dad's being so low, then our moving from Tuckerman, and now all this rain. It's enough to get a decent man down."

"Most certainly, it is," Amy says gently, but then she digs further, "But what about Mr. Marshall?"

"Huh?" Ernest Lee grunts again.

Amy walks over to the wardrobe and takes out Ernest Lee's brown winter coat. Drawing a deep breath, she begins, "I was putting our winter coats in the attic to make room, and I cleaned out the pockets—I wasn't snooping." Amy reaches in his pocket and pulls out the two crisp fifty dollar bank notes and the crumpled up Marshall's Mercantile receipt. She holds them out, "Where did these come from?"

Ernest Lee looks down at the floor. He had hoped that the problem would disappear, somehow, but it hasn't, and now Amy is asking. "I'm too ashamed to say," he mumbles.

Amy sits back down beside him on the bed, "Tell me where it came from."

Ernest Lee whispers his saga, head hanging low, "I took it from Mr. Marshall's on impulse—from that big tractor sale. At the time, I thought I deserved it, but when I came to my senses, I knew it was wrong. I wanted to give it back but was too ashamed to tell him. It's got to go back. That's all I *do* know."

Amy looks into her husband's shame-filled eyes, "So, that's what it is. I knew there was something more. Now that you've told me the truth, I know for sure what a good man you are, Ernest Lee Herald."

"You don't think any less of me, Amy? I can't stand myself these days—I don't know how you can. What about that Bible commandment that goes...."

Amy finishes, "'Thou shalt not steal?' But, what about those *other* verses? The Bible says over and over that if you repent of your sins, God will forgive. I never saw anyone more torn up with repentance than you are, Ernest Lee. I'm *sure* God forgives you. The Bible says so."

Ernest Lee is overwhelmed. Amy's kind words feel so good, but shame still hangs around his neck like a stone from the mill.

Amy reaches out and puts his hands in hers, "Don't you see? You could have taken over Mr. Marshall's mercantile, but you were a good son instead and came here to help your dad out. And, you could have *spent* that money you took from Mr. Marshall, but it's right over there in your coat pocket, and you intend to give it back. God must be proud of you for that—I know that I am." She leans over and gives him a kiss on the cheek. "You had one bad moment, and you're going to make it right. You're a wonderful person, that's what you are."

Amy's words wrap around him like a warm blanket on a freezing cold day. He licks her lips, and they lie back on the bed and melt red-hot together. Nothing more has to be said. He'll tell Mr. Marshall the truth and return every cent of the money—they'll do it together. He lifts strands of her hair up and watches them sparkle in the lamplight. He never felt such closeness in the depths of his soul. They talk on into the night, and he whispers, "Why did you consent to marry me, Amy? I knew we'd be perfect right off, but you barely knew me at all. What made you say yes?"

Amy whispers back, "I knew right off, too, that I loved you." The young couple falls asleep truly contented for the first time on the farm.

Amy creeps downstairs at dawn the next morning to start coffee and biscuits for breakfast. Then, she strolls out onto the porch to survey the land. Three days of rain have finally subsided, but new cotton sprouts up through the water and their barnyard is mired in muck. She leans on the porch rail and whispers, "Dear Lord, please bake all this water away." Moments later, a warm breeze ruffles her hair and she laughs, "Thank you, Lord." She saunters back inside and sinks into the only soft chair in the front room.

Everything revolves around the weather these days. It's all they talk about morning, noon, and night. Amy is weary from worry, so she decides not to think about the weather this morning. Her eyes wander around the sparkling clean front room. The couple worked hard getting things back into order. Amy scrubbed and polished by day, and Ernest Lee painted, patched and plastered by lantern glow after farm work. Now the room is tidy, the walls washed, and the windows gleam from a vinegar rinse. She even sand-scrubbed the white oak floors, wiping them shiny with oil—a process Mrs. Isay shared with her way back. For a final touch, Amy hung dear departed Martha's embroidery samplers up on new golden cords, and she freshly starched Martha's tatted doilies that now grace every chair—the very room she where she and Ernest Lee married.

There's still no movement in the house, so Amy starts listing the week's chores in her head—she has a different routine for every day of the week: Monday is wash day, Tuesday is for cooking and canning, Wednesday she cleans, Thursday is for mending and sewing, and Friday is for whatever comes up. Saturday morning they run into town for supplies, and Sunday, of course, is strictly for prayer. Amy frets, *I could get even more done except for all this rain.*

Amy can hear the babies fussing upstairs in their crib, so she rushes to pull the biscuits out of the oven and then runs up the stairs. She bumps into Ernest Lee on the top step and grins, "You ready to start a new day?"

"You bet," Ernest Lee winks, flashing the endearing smile that she hasn't seen in weeks. A knowing look passes between them as they remember last night. He starts down the stairs and Amy calls after, "Hot coffee's on the stove, and most everything's put out for breakfast. I'll be right down to start eggs." She walks past the next room and sings out, "Morning Gramps, Dad, coffee's ready."

Gramps is sitting on his bed pulling up his boots, and Homer is in front of a mirror smoothing down his sparse strands of hair. Thankfully, as far as they know, he has turned over a new leaf.

Amy totes Timmy and Sally carefully down the stairs. Ernest Lee has the eggs and potatoes sizzling in the skillet, and Homer and Gramps are gobbling down Amy's biscuits. As usual, baby Timmy complains when Amy props him up in his chair, but he'll have to wait his turn while she nurses Sally.

"Looks like the sun's trying to come out," Amy smiles up at Ernest Lee bringing the platter over to the table.

Ernest Lee ruffles her hair and teases, "Yes, a new day dawns on the Herald farm. Hallelujah!" Then he takes a seat and turns serious, "Well, it's too wet to work in the fields much today, but I can widen the channels to help drain off the cotton."

Gramps licks jam off two fingers, "That precious cotton of yours probably floated downstream last night. You shouldn't've planted it on bottom land like you did, Ernest Lee."

Ernest Lee is unfazed by Gramp Herald's remark. He passes the platter heaping with bacon, eggs and potatoes and explains, "It's a chance I took. Anyway, only part of the lower land got flooded." Between chomps of bacon, he lays out his plan for their day, "Dad, you and Charlie can work in the barn. Gramps, you take Striker to work in the mill."

Gramps protests, "I don't need Striker's help."

Ernest Lee says matter-of-factly, "Striker'll help you move grain bags higher up in the loft, just to be safe, Gramps."

Gramps shrugs, and then he remembers to ask, "What about Hank?"

"Hank will work at Bee City today," Ernest Lee answers.

"Bee City, what for?" Homer calls out. The hives are his pride and joy, and he doesn't like any one messing with them.

"We need to see how our bees made out in the rain. Anyway, isn't it about time we inspect the hives for queen eggs?" Ernest Lee asks.

"I can do that!" Homer is indignant.

Ernest Lee gulps down his coffee, "I know you can, Dad, but I'm looking for work that Hank can do on his gimpy leg. To tell the truth, this'll be his last chance to shape up before he's tossed out on his ear."

The group finishes breakfast in silence and heads down to the barn where Ernest Lee assigns the hands' work.

"Bee City? I'd rather work in the barn," Hank complains, mouth stuffed with a fresh plug of tobacco.

"Fine, you can work in the barn—after you finish checking out the hives," Ernest Lee answers, adding skeptically, "You said you worked with bees before, didn't you?"

"Yes, but…." Hank stammers, running his hands through his blonde wavy hair, but excuses elude him.

"Look, Hank, I'll show you what to do this first time, but from now on, you're on your own." Ernest Lee says, grabbing the bag of bee keeping gear off of a peg in the barn. He walks with Hank along the path to Bee City after the others split up from their chores.

"Don't do me any favors," Hank spits a juicy chaw of tobacco at the ground.

Ernest Lee has had enough of Hank's surly attitude. He halts in his tracks and grabs Hank by a shoulder. "Look, I wasn't going to say it, but this bee keeping is a test to see if you can do *anything* around here."

"Yeah, well this bee keeping stuff ain't what I do." Hank spits again, this time hitting Ernest Lee's boot with a brown mushy plug.

Ernest Lee's face reddens all the way out to his ears. He clenches his teeth. "I've been as patient as I care to be, you ornery cuss. You don't get to *choose* jobs around here. As far as I'm concerned, you can go back to the bunk house and clear out." Ernest Lee storms off toward the barn.

"All right," Hank mumbles.

"What's that you say?" Ernest Lee asks, stopping short in his tracks.

"I said…alright, I'm sorry," Hank says a little louder, clearing his throat.

Ernest Lee walks back to where Hank stands and snarls in his face, "Well, I'm thinking it's too *late* for that, Hank. I'm already glad at the thought of getting *rid* of you."

Hank clears his throat again, "It's just that…well, I like this here farm. Everything was fine 'n dandy—'til you got here."

Leaning forward, Ernest Lee growls, "Till I got here? I was *born* here, fella', and that's just the way it is. Tough timber!"

Ernest Lee's words stump Hank. After all, how do you reply to "tough timber"? He finally ekes out, "All right. I want to stay on. I'll work with the bees like you want." Now, it strikes Hank how ridiculous this is—a twerpy accountant acting so tough, and, him, a tough hand, acting like a pussycat. It strikes Hank so funny that he belches up a guffaw that he can't hold back.

Hank's disrespect makes Ernest Lee frown, but then gets tickled at the situation himself. He tries to hold back his own grin, but it breaks out on his face, so he turns to the side. The two men struggle trying to get serious again. Finally, they walk down the path toward Bee City like nothing happened at all.

Ernest Lee continues where he left off, "You know how tricky bees are, Hank. They don't need attention from fall 'til about March. But, then you've got to get busy if you want any honey. It's June and we're way behind schedule." He looks over and Hank is nodding his head in agreement, so Ernest Lee goes on instructing, "So, now is a good time to get honey and check for queen bee cells."

"Queen bees?" Hank asks.

"You know about queen bees, right? Everything is fine as long as there's only one queen in a hive. But, if a new queen egg hatches, well, then, you've got trouble."

"Trouble?" Hank's eyes widen.

"That's right. When a new queen bee hatches, the first queen gets her nose out of joint, and she'll swarm off with half of your hive. The worst of it is—nothing says the *new* queen will make honey as good as the old one— some bees are just plain lazy. That's why we keep checking for queen eggs. We want to get rid of them before they can hatch. That way, our good queen won't get mad and buzz off."

"Sure," Hank says like he knew that all along.

Ernest Lee continues, "Now, if the bees do swarm out of the hive and land in a tree, a clever person can smoke them back into an empty hive, but that doesn't always work out. Some swarms turn real mean, and you can get stung bad."

"That's right—I seen it happen," Hank nods.

The men finally arrive at Bee City. "We've got about twenty five hives in all," Ernest Lee explains. "There used to be more—we had over a hundred one time back, but, with Ma being sick, Dad sold a lot off." Ernest Lee opens up his bag and pulls out the bee keeping gear. He has a funnel-topped smoker with bellows attached, and two sets of hoods, veils, coveralls, and gloves. "Some old timers don't use any of this stuff," Ernest Lee shakes his head. "But I never figured out how they keep from getting stung."

"Maybe they *do* get stung." Hank looks scared to death.

"You never *really* did this work before, did you Hank?" Ernest Lee asks.

"Naw," Hank admits. "I seen my Grandpappy do it plenty of times, but he never did need no help. So, I just held the bowl for his slinging out the honey."

Ernest Lee knew it was something like that, so he goes on with explaining, "Our hives are these rectangular wooden ones that dad made himself," he says, walking over to the first one. "They have a hive body on the bottom and supers on top where bees store the honey. Got that?"

Hank nods, "Yep, That's the kind my Grandpappy had."

Ernest Lee looks over at one hive that sits away from the others. "Oh, here's this hive in back. It's made from a hollowed out black gum tree like they used years ago." Ernest Lee brags, "This ole' log hive has been here on this farm for close to fifty years that I heard of—maybe a hundred. As long as we keep the comb cut out, the bees keep right on making new comb and honey year after year." He turns dead serious, "Don't mess with this hive, Hank. It's gone queenless and the bees have turned mean. Don't mess with this one at all."

The men pull their coveralls on and zip their veils down the front. Ernest Lee walks over to a bale of hay, pulls out a handful, and lights it up with a match. He stuffs the smoldering hay into the smoker and blows on it for a good burn. "Now let's look for those queen eggs, like I told you, Hank," he says.

The men put on their gloves and Ernest Lee hands the smoker to Hank, "Swing this smoker back and forth where there's bees on the hive. The smoke'll distract them and make them real calm—most of the time."

"Most of the time?" Hank raises his eyebrows.

Ernest Lee laughs, "Just remember—never bump into a hive or make a loud noise, and never wear your Saturday night cologne around bees—that riles them up worse than anything. Oh yeah, and if a swarm ever chases you, just run like mad—they don't chase very far from their hive. Works every time."

None of these assurances sit well with Hank, nonetheless, he agrees, "Right. Got it."

Ernest Lee pulls out a small brush and a pry bar from his bag. He pries the lid off of the first hive and whisks bees away with the soft bristled brush. "No queen eggs here in this chamber," Ernest Lee says and takes a deep breath. "Now it's time to get us some honey."

Bees buzz around his head and his gloves, so Ernest Lee whispers to Hank, "Wave that smoker around over here. It'll drive the bees down bottom." Ernest Lee pulls out the frame capped with bee wax and says, "This comb is sealed over good, so it's fine to sling out the honey. If you ever find one not sealed with wax, don't eat the stuff or you'll have the runs for a week!" He chuckles slinging the honey into the bowl that Hank holds out. The men proceed, hive by hive, examining for queen eggs and then robbing the honey. By noon they're only half finished.

"See, Hank, look at all the honey we got and not one sting all morning. Nothing to it," Ernest Lee says. "You can finish up the rest of the hives this afternoon."

"By myself?" Hanks is surprised.

"Yep," Ernest Lee replies. "All by yourself."

Hank pulls off his veil and flings it to the ground. An angry bee buzzes over at once and stings him hard on the neck. Hank swats it and shouts, "Ouch. Dang thing."

Ernest Lee chides, "One more thing, Hank. Always keep your veil and hood on till you're far away from the hives. Bees'll get you like that sometimes for stealing their honey!"

Hank scrapes off the stinger and drawls, "Got any more of them bee keeping secrets?"

Brother Charles can't leave the questions unanswered: *Is "Buck Blackwell" the same as that "Gideon" kid that I knew in St. Louis? And was either one the boy standing with Pastor Blackwell in that photo?* He telephones the director of the St. Louis House and asks, "Remember back years ago, a fellow who lived there that called himself Gideon?" The director says that he does, so the next question is, "Do you recall what ever happened to him?"

The Director replies, "He took off one day to visit some relatives, as I recall. He never came back. Don't remember his last name."

Brother Charles asks, "Do you know any more?"

The director answers, "No, never heard from him again. You know how unreliable alcoholics can be."

Brother Charles is just about to hang up when the director remembers, "Oh, something else. I think the fellow left a suitcase and some stuff up in his room. After awhile, I stuck it out in the storeroom. Do you want me to go hunt it up?"

About an hour later the director calls back, "I have the suitcase right here, Brother Charles. There's something more, though. I opened up the fella's Bible and it has 'Gideon Blackwell' written inside. Should I put the suitcase back in the storeroom?"

Brother Charles heaves a deep sigh, "No, just put it on a wagon headed down here to Maynard."

The suitcase arrives the next week and Brother Charles can't decide what to do next. Last week he asked a church Deacon about Pastor Blackwell's son, and the answer was rather sad—something about Buck losing his wife to pneumonia, moving back home to Pitman, and then taking off and leaving his two girls behind with the Pastor. Brother Charles realizes, *One of those girls must be Effie—and to think, her father abandoned her and her sister.*

Brother Charles has had differences with Holloway Blackwell, but he'd never wish anyone discord with a son. He hitches up his horse and heaves the old suitcase into the back of his wagon. The roads are still wet from the June rain, so the horse trots slowly to Pitman, and Brother Charles wonders all the way, *I wonder where Buck Blackwell is now?*

CHAPTER 13
ONE DAY IN JULY

The three days of June rain have finally let up, and Mrs. Isay hopes Effie will pay her a visit today. She waits in her cabin all morning, but by noon there's still no sign of Effie, so Mrs. Isay shuffles out onto the porch. The wind is picking up and the elm leaves blow over backwards—a sure sign of more rain. Mrs. Isay sighs, "If rain starts up again, I might not see Effie for days." That simply won't do, so Mrs. Isay decides to hunt up Effie herself.

It has been ages since Mrs. Isay ventured across to the other side of the brook. She stays mostly up on her hill, except for filling her bucket with water, but she hardly ever crosses over, and she almost *never* walks up the hill toward the Pastor's house. However, the urge to find Effie is powerful today, like the time she found her face down in the brook. The ground is still soft from the rain, so Mrs. Isay pulls on her tall boots and wraps a shawl around her shoulders. She edges down the steep slope, by-passing the soft spots, holding onto a tree where it's rough, and stepping on a flat rock when she finds one. Slowly, she zig zags her way down the hill.

When Mrs. Isay reaches bottom at last, she finds the brook flooded up over its bank. *My gracious*, she thinks, *if it's this bad back here in the woods, imagine the torrent by the time it reaches Current River*. The babbling brook has become Mrs. Isay's barometer for conditions up and down stream. One day she told Effie, "Watch out for the water—it will smile and twinkle but turn mean in a minute. Water's just like people that pass rage along." She

179

carefully tiptoes across, balancing on rocktops above the swift-moving water, reaching the other side at last.

The perilous crossing has her heart is racing, so Mrs. Isay sits down to rest on a huge rock before starting up the next hill. She closes her eyes to relax for awhile, but the urge to get going takes over, so she hops up and starts climbing the hill toward the Pastor's house. She loves Effie like a daughter now, and she can't wait to find her.

Mrs. Isay is winded when she reaches the hilltop, so she leans against the Blackwell's red wooden barn. She takes a long look around, *My, everything's so different from what I remembered. The house is so much smaller and the trees are much taller.* As she rests against the side of the barn, she notices a wagon turn off of Military Road and onto the farm road leading up to the Pastor's house. *I better stay put and see who it is before I go visitin'*, she tells herself.

The one-horse wagon draws nearer until it finally pulls up in front of the house. Her eyes can't see faces too well this far away, but she can make out a tall man with very good posture climbing down from the wagon and reaching in back for some sort of a box. *No, it's a suitcase*, she thinks. He strides quickly up the porch steps, knocks on the door, and enters quickly when someone—Pastor Blackwell, no doubt—greets him.

Oh, my heavens, Mrs. Isay thinks. *A man with a suitcase knocking on the Preacher's door? Who else could it be? This must be Effie's father. He's come back!* Mrs. Isay is overjoyed. Still, she waits in the shade of the barn to see what happens next. She can't find a dry spot to sit on the ground, so she walks over to the fence and sits on the wide middle rail, wrapping her arm around the post and leaning her head up against it. She sighs, *The warmth feels so good on my skin. I don't get much sun up there in the trees on my hill.* Before Mrs. Isay knows it, she dozes off with her head leaning up against the fence post.

The old woman doesn't know how long she's been napping when she snaps awake. She still sits on the fence rail and groggily looks over toward the house. She makes out Effie standing on the porch, so she shakes her head to wake up a bit more and starts sloshing across the mucky barnyard. When she's half way there, she notices the tall stranger rush back out onto the porch and wrap his arms around Effie. Mrs. Isay keeps trudging along, and, finally, when she is only a stone's throw from the porch, Effie spots her and calls out.

"Oh, Mrs. Isay, thank goodness you're here!" Effie yells.

Mrs. Isay rushes up onto the porch. She can see that Effie has been crying—tears of joy, she imagines, over her father's return. The old woman smiles up at the tall man she hasn't seen since he wandered outside her cabin that time. He doesn't quite look the same, but, that was so many years ago; maybe her memory fails. She asks, "Are you Effie's father?"

The stranger's face is somber as he replies, "No, I'm Brother Charles."

Effie holds out her arms to her old friend and wails, "Oh, Mrs. Isay, my Daddy is dead."

Mrs. Isay doesn't think she heard Effie right. She's about to ask more when the screen door flies open, and Grandma Gert storms out onto the porch.

"What's that foolish old woman doin' here?" Gert snorts, turning to Effie, "Don't you go tellin' that old witch anything stupid about your father."

The other three on the porch are stunned, and Effie starts waling all over again.

Pastor Blackwell rushes out to the porch and pleads with his wife, "No one is accusing you of anything, Misses. But, that suitcase Brother Charles just brought belonged to our Buck—and a receipt for his train ticket this way was tucked in a page. Why don't you tell us what happened that day?"

Gert shifts her mood now, and seems delighted to expound, "Well, putting it that way, Pastor, I can tell you that it wasn't my fault. I just dealt with the circumstances as best I could. That's all."

"What do you mean it wasn't your fault?" the Pastor asks. "*What* wasn't?"

Gert now lapses into her sing-songy voice that she uses trying to gain favor, "Well, it was a hot morning in September. Effie and Amy had just left for school, and you were already left to teach your own classroom, Pastor, so, I went out back to work in my lily patch."

You could hear a pin drop as Gert begins her tale that sounds like a garden club story so far. "Go on, Misses" the Pastor encourages, hoping his wife will be more enlightening than she has been so far.

"Well, like I said, I was out in my lily patch, and when I looked up I saw Buck standing there on the back porch with his hat in his hand. He'd been away for over two years, but I knew right away it was him. I could see he was perspiring up there in the sun, but I was about to divide the lilies up, so I kept right on goin'." Gert pauses, her hands clasped in front.

"And?" the Pastor encourages again.

"Oh...well, then I heard Buck call out to me, 'Mama Gert.' (That's what he always called me.) 'Can you come up to the house so we can talk?'"

I called right back, 'No, I'm too busy now, Buck. Pour yourself some ice water to cool off, and I'll be up directly.' You see, I knew he would come visit sooner or later because of that letter he wrote, so I didn't see anything to be in such a rush about, and I took my sweet time with my lilies."

The Pastor is exasperated, "Go on, Misses. Get to the end of the story."

She smiles, "Why certainly. Sorry I digress." She curtseys to the group and continues, "I worked in the garden 'til I got to a good quitting place. When I finally came up on the porch, well, that's when I had quite a scare."

"Yes?" Pastor Blackwell insists. All ears are trained as Gert stands wide-eyed and picks up the pace of her story.

"Well, there was Buck, lying flat on his back on the porch; writhing and twitching he was. I ran to fill up a bucket with pump water—I thought that a good splash would revive him, but, by the time I got back, he'd stopped twitching. Yes. He was dead as a doornail," she nods, chest puffed out for the important announcement.

Effie cries hysterically holding onto Mrs. Isay's shoulder, and Brother Charles guides them down onto the porch swing.

Gert stands there smiling and says, "So there. Now you all know." She claps her hands together as if her story has made everything crystal clear.

The Pastor's voice quivers, "For heaven sakes, Misses! You don't say what happened to our Buck! Tell us right now!"

"Well, as best I can gather, it was because of the icebox," she says.

"The icebox?" The pastor is incredulous.

"Yes. Well, it was the *ice* in the icebox, to be exact." Gert nods, clears her throat and continues, "You see, Mr. Hamm delivered a fresh block of ice that very mornin'—like he does every Monday—but first, he always lifts our food up off the old block and sets the stuff on the shelf right above. But, this time, when he put our food back down on his new block of ice—Mr. Hamm always puts things back just like they were—he must have grabbed, by mistake, that big Mason jar that I keep stored up there."

"What jar?" the Pastor voice is still shaking.

"Well, good heavens! You know, Pastor! The one I keep filled up with kerosene! Remember? I soak the corncobs in it for kindling, and, oh yes, I always throw in a big pinch of roach powder, just in case, to kill any bugs. Anyway, Mr. Hamm must have grabbed that jar by mistake and set it there on the ice block along with our food." Gert gets no response from the stunned group on the porch, so she continues explaining. "Well, I figure that Buck must have gone for ice water, just like I told him to do. I'm sure he was plenty hot from the trip—Lord knows how he got here—he had no horse or suitcase or anything with him. Maybe he walked in from the train station miles away...or maybe...."

"Get to the point!" The Pastor is about to have a conniption.

Gert continues, "Anyway, Buck must've grabbed that quart jar of kerosene sitting on the ice instead of the water jug and chugged it down before he knew what it was—well, he had kerosene on his breath, so that's what I figured."

Pastor Blackwell is too upset to continue. He can't even muster a squeak, so Brother Charles takes over, "And then, Mrs. Blackwell?"

"I knew you'd ask, and, when you hear the rest, you'll all be perfectly satisfied that what I done was right. Well, I already had those deep holes dug up along side the smokehouse for my lilies, so I just dug them all together into a deep trench. This next part wasn't easy—I pulled poor Buck down off the porch by his ankles, dragged him all the way down the hill, and then I rolled him into that trench. Thanks be to God I am a good'n healthy woman and had the strength to do it. A lesser woman couldn't of." She turns to her husband, who is a white as a sheet now, "Well, don't you see, Pastor? That way, the girls weren't all upset seeing their father in that sorry state when they got home from school. Anyway, they already knew he was gone, so it did them no harm. And, none of us had to suffer through a sad funeral either. I gave Buck a perfectly nice service. I sung him, 'Nearer My God to Thee' and I said him a nice long prayer after I buried him and planted my lilies on top."

Effie sobs louder on the porch swing holding on to Mrs. Isay.

Pastor Blackwell walks silently off of the porch into the house.

Grandma Gert shrugs wondering what the fuss is all about. She thinks, *After all, it was just one of my willins'.* She walks back into the kitchen humming, takes out the meat cleaver, wields it high over her head, and begins chopping up beef for a stew.

Brother Charles hears the back screen door bang shut, and he follows the sound. He finds Pastor Blackwell in the backyard kneeling down in the mud by the lilies.

The heartbroken Pastor looks up at Brother Charles and says, "How could this be?"

Brother Charles kneels down next the Pastor and lays his hand on the shaking man's shoulder. He says, "Let us pray."

The Pastor looks up at him in a daze, "His name wasn't really Buck, you know. His name was really Gideon."

"Yes I know," Brother Charles whispers.

"He got the name Buck—oh, he was such a precocious child," the Pastor smiles, "but he…he loved rodeo horses. He'd turn anything into a bronco just to hear us grown ups cheer, 'Buck 'em, Gideon!' A porch railing, banister, wagon rail, or anything flat enough for would do for a ride. Well, pretty soon, with all the bucking about, folks nicknamed him 'Bucky,' and then they shortened it to 'Buck.'" The Pastor chuckles, "I remember one time ole' Deacon Fitzgerald lingered too long in the porch rocker, and little Buck hopped up on his knee. You should have heard his 'Yahoos' galore. Well, ole' Fitz was too polite to complain, so I put a stop to it, but the minute I left the proch, Buck was at it again on ole' Fitz's knee. That boy—he sure had a will of his own." The Pastor looks somberly at Brother Charles, "I should have insisted folks use his biblical name, Gideon. Maybe he would have stayed closer to God. Maybe…" the Pastor chokes off in sobs.

"You must know that Gert's not in her right mind, don't you Pastor Blackwell?" Brother Charles rasps.

"I know it now," the Pastor nods sadly. No more needs to be said between the two men. They gather Effie off of the front porch, climb into the wagon, and Brother Charles' takes the reins.

Gert hears the commotion and runs out on the porch all excited, "Where are you folks going? Should I go get my hat?"

Pastor Blackwell replies stoically, "No. You stay here Gert. We'll talk more when I return. It might be a few days." The roads are still wet and muddy, and it's starting to rain again, but that doesn't matter—the Pastor has to tell Amy the bad news so they can all grieve together and plan a proper burial for Buck. The forlorn group takes off up the road toward Success.

Gert waves goodbye to the group, and, when she turns around, Mrs. Isay is still standing there on the porch. "Are you still here, you old witch?" Gert snorts.

Mrs. Isay snorts back, "I'm not an old witch—I'm a Baptist, same as you!"

"You *can't* be a Baptist 'cause we don't commune with dead spirits like you do, old woman."

"Good Baptist folks don't make *willins'* either'" Mrs. Isay says smugly.

Gert's grabs hold of the porch rail to steady herself and asks, "What do *you* know of my 'willin's?'"

"Oh, I know all about your 'willins'—'cause your Mama's spirit told me some years ago."

"That's absurd," Gert is indignant.

Mrs. Isay replies, "Suit yourself, but just in case you're curious— your

Mama said your pecan pie is no match for hers."

Gert's mouth flies open.

Mrs. Isay adds, "She also said you're a 'dang fool' for laying claim to those willins'— 'cause those things would've all happened anyway. She asked me to tell you back then, but I'm just now getting around to it." The old woman smiles triumphantly and heads back toward the peace of her cabin,

Ernest Lee leaves Hank to his beekeeping. He's thankful that, for once, it wasn't *him* that got stung. He's walking down to the bottom land when Charlie shouts from across the field in the barnyard, "Ernest Lee! The bridge went out!"

"What?" Ernest Lee cups his hand to his ear and calls back.

Charlie shouts again, "The dang bridge went out!" He waves his arms about madly, motioning for Ernest Lee to come over.

"Calm down, Charlie! I can't make heads nor tails of what you're hollering!" Ernest Lee runs across the field to the barnyard,

Charlie begins his story, "First thing this morning, I headed up to the ridge to check on them cattle," Charlie sputters. "I rode my mule over the ditch bridge, and, just as I made it across, the dang thing gave way—the whole thing slid plumb into the water!"

Ernest Lee knows the old wooden bridge well. His father built it many years ago, and it's the only path up to their grazing ridge when it floods.

Charlie goes on, "Now what'll we do? Them cows been stranded up there two days already—now they'll have to swim back across, and that won't do 'em no good."

Ernest Lee has seen cows cross water lots of times, but, never once has he seen a cow swim. In fact, he didn't know that cows could swim real good. He questions Charlie, "But that ditch water is up to more than ten feet in some places. Won't the cows sink like a stone to the bottom?"

"Naw, we'll find the shallowest place and they'll just float across."

"Are you joshing me, Charlie?" Ernest Lee is amazed.

"You never seen a cow swim? Sometimes a calf gets into trouble, but mostly a cow'll swim across like a horse—they stay afloat from all that alfalfa gas in their belly."

The idea of gassy cows floating across the Herald's flooded ditch sounds silly to Ernest Lee, but Charlie usually knows what he's talking about. Still, Ernest Lee asks, "Won't it be safer for them to stay put until the water goes down or until we build the bridge back?"

"Well, that could take days. I'd hate to think of those cows stuck up on the ridge looking for grub all that time," Charlie drawls. "They'll scatter or starve to death, one or t'other. Swimming 'em back isn't the best way, but it'll get 'em back down again."

Ernest Lee nods, and then thinks to ask, "By the way, Charlie, how'd you get back over the ditch after the bridge went out this morning?"

"Me and my mule swum back across, of course. It was all I could do to stay upright on my mule's back. I liked to've drowned in that ditch current—felt more like Current River!" Charlie brags.

Ernest Lee laughs, "I'm glad it was *you* that got stuck over there, Charlie. I can't swim at all!"

Charlie fails to find humor in Ernest Lee's comment, "That's *so* funny!" he squints, "So, what're *you* gonna do about them cattle stranded up there?"

Ernest Lee rubs the back of his neck, "Well, let's see what happens. Sometimes the ditch drains off if it opens up down stream. If it isn't drained down by supper, we'll have the cows swim back across, like you said."

Charlie nods and walks off into the barn mumbling, "What else can go wrong today?"

Ernest Lee wants to check out the bottom land, so he saddles up old Blackie, their biggest but most gentle horse. Half way down, he finds the path flooded and huge carp swimming past. *They've swum up from the overflowed river,* he thinks, amazed. *I don't know much about cows, but I sure can gig a fish on the end of a pole. Amy'll have fresh fish for supper!"* He rides back to the barn and grabs his long-shaft gig, pulls on his rubber waders, and heads back down the path. Ernest Lee wades in until he's knee deep, but he doesn't have to wait long. Pretty soon, he gigs three carp and two catfish and strings them onto his line. Just as he drops his gear off at the barn, the sky turns dark as night, so, he hustles up to the house with his fish. He finds Amy in the kitchen, and he walks over boasting, "Look what I caught for you, Sweet Amy. They were swimming right down there in the flooded path."

Amy's face lights up. She grabs the string of fish, fills up a bucket, and plunks in his catch. She gives Ernest Lee a big hug but backs off, "Phew, you smell like ole' fish."

Ernest Lee dutifully washes his hands off under pump water, and then bends down to play with his babies crawling around in the playpen. He picks up little Timmy and Sally in his arms and kisses them on their big apple cheeks.

The rain starts pelting sideways against the kitchen windows, and the sky turns blacker still. Ernest sets his babies back down, and complains, "Well, that's Arkansas weather for you!"

"Where are you going now?" Amy asks, hoping he'll stay home now that it's raining again.

"Well, we've got cows stranded on the ridge. Charlie and I are going up—Striker too."

"Can't Dad and or Hank go with them instead?"

"No, Hank's working Bee City, and Dad's best off in the barn. I'll have to go up with them."

"But, it doesn't make good sense with the sky so black like it is. It could start lightning," Amy argues.

"Right, but, if we don't go get them, it'd be Christmas until we round up the cows—if we found them at all. No, we'll be up and right back before it gets any worse, I promise," he says holding his hand over his heart. "I'll be back long before that fish dinner is ready." He gives Amy a kiss on the cheek and promises, "And I haven't forgotten—next week we'll take that trip down to Tuckerman. I'll make things right with Mr. Marshall before he closes up the Mercantile."

Amy crinkles up her nose and whispers, "I'm so proud of you, Ernest Lee." She looks into his eyes and something moves her to say, "You won't believe this, Ernest Lee, but I'm actually glad we came here to the farm. You look more like your old happy self all the time."

"Take another look at harvest time," Ernest Lee laughs. He gives her a lingering kiss on the lips, and heads out into the rain ranting, "Dang cows!" When he reaches the barn, he finds Charlie mucking out a stall and his dad pitching hay. "It's time," he says to Charlie.

"With the sky black-as-night?" Charlie raises his eyebrows.

"This was *your* idea in the first place. Remember?" Ernest Lee says, climbing atop Blackie.

"I'll saddle up, too," Homer says.

"No, Striker can go with us—no need of everyone getting drenched on the ridge," Ernest Lee replies.

The men reach the swollen ditch bank, and Ernest Lee shouts above thunder, "You two go on across, and I'll follow behind."

Charlie swims his mule across first. Striker follows, and the two men head up to the ridge.

Ernest Lee takes a big gulp, wishing he didn't have to ride into the ugly black water, but he's the boss now. How would that look?

Hank is all suited up and ready to tackle Bee City alone. *Let's see, I think this is how Ernest Lee did it,"* he says grabbing a big hank of hay from the bale, lighting one end and then stuffing it into the smoker. He blows until the hay smokes, pulls on his gloves, and slowly opens up a hive just like Ernest Lee showed him. After all the trouble he's caused, Hank feels like a new day is dawning. *Ernest Lee's not such a bad fellow—a lot like his dad.*

There aren't any queen eggs in the first three hives, so Hank only slings out their honey. However, when he opens up the fourth hive and pulls out the brood chamber, he gasps, *Doggone it! Here's one of them ole' queen egg cells!* He remembers, *Ernest Lee said I'd know one for sure— it would be so much bigger with that queen egg floating around in some kind of jelly.* Hank is positive this is it. He considers skipping this hive and fetching Ernest Lee later, but he's bound to finish alone. *It can't be all that hard. I bet I can cut out that cell without upsetting them bees.* Hank looks up at the black sky and a raindrop splashes on his head. He's determined, *I'll get this over with before rain puts out the smoker.*

Hank figures his pocketknife is as good as anything to cut out the cell, but he can't grasp the knife or the frame good with bulky gloves on. He shakes his gloves off on to the ground, grabs the smoker with one hand and the frame with the other. However, he can't get a good angle with the knife, so he moves the frame even closer.

The bees have been passive so far, but, now, they start wiggling about on the frame. Hank puts down the knife and grabs the smoker to wave about, but it doesn't calm the bees this time. All at once, dozens of them descend on his bare hands, stinging one after the other, falling dead to the ground with their mission complete, new bees reinforcing fallen brothers.

In a matter of seconds, Hank's hands blow up like two red balloons. He cries out in pain, dropping the knife and the frame, too. More furious bees empty into the air, stinging hard through his hood and his jumpsuit. Hank bats his hands up and down and twirls around and around, but the bees aren't dissuaded. In his panic, he knocks over the old black gum hive, jarring even more angry bees into the thick buzzing air.

Hank recalls that bees don't chase far from their hive, so, he ignores his bum leg and races all-out toward the barn, but the nasty swarm follows behind. His hood and veil fly off, but he can't stop running and wildly swinging his arms about, screaming out in terror. The bees keep on chasing. Then, he remembers his Grandpappy once said, "Bees'll leave you alone if you dive under water," so, Hanks runs on past the barn and heads straight for the drainage ditch.

Ernest Lee calls out again to Striker and Charlie, "Don't wait for me. Go on ahead." He never forded the swollen ditch before, and he pats Blackie's neck and sooths, "Steady now, girl." He rides the huge horse into the flow up to her belly. Muddy water spills over his boot tops, but he isn't daunted. He whispers to himself, "It's no matter, as long as I can stay atop Blackie." The rain pelts down stinging his face, and the ugly brown water swirls about his legs. Ernest Lee can hear someone shouting behind and wonders who it could be, but he can't stop now, so he rides Blackie deeper and deeper into the flooded channel.

Hank runs all-out toward the ditch, arms flailing, head tossed back and yelling a blood-curdling cry. When he reaches the ditch he springs up into the air and lands a huge belly flop right next to Blackie. The flat thud sends sheets of dirty drainage splashing high into the air and all over Ernest Lee and his mighty black horse.

Ernest Lee swipes at his drenched face with one hand, and, then, out of nowhere, the bees commence stinging. He flaps his hand furiously to shoo them away, but the effort is futile—irate bees sting every spot they can find. Ernest Lee frantically pulls tight on the reins, but it's the wrong thing to do. Blackie's huge body rears up in response, boosting Ernest Lee high into the air. He hangs onto tight to the saddle screaming, "Help! Help! Jesus save me."

The bees are relentless. They fly up into poor Blackie's nostrils, dive deep down into her ears, and strike at her huge glassy eyes. The anguished horse rears up once again, this time rising up on her haunches until she's vertical in the air, like on a rodeo poster.

A terrified Ernest Lee careens down the horse's slick back like a carnival slide. Gasping for breath, he frantically grabs for Blackie's leather saddle, but a flailing stirrup strikes him hard in the head, and he sinks like a stone into the bubbling brew.

Blackie whinnies louder and, snorting bees from her nostrils, she smacks down on her side where Ernest Lee disappears.

The blow on his head makes Ernest Lee groggy. He kicks toward the surface as hard as he can, but his water-filled boots pull him down toward the bottom. Groggy as he is, he knows for sure what has happened. It's a hot summer day and he's cooling off at Current River. He had grabbed hold of the thick braided rope that hangs high in the oak tree and pushed off hard with both legs against the rough bark, swinging out in a giant arc over the middle of the river. It was such fun when he dropped into the swiftly moving current, laughing and yelling "Geronimo" all the way down. Now he'll paddle back to the shore for more fun on the rope swing. Trixie is waiting on shore, nodding her head up and down approving his antics.

Ernest Lee cups his hands and pulls hard against the current, praying, *If I can only get up top for a breath of fresh air.* This has happened before to him, and just when he thinks can't hold his breath any longer, his head always pops above water. Trixie is always standing on the grassy bank next to his neatly folded overalls and knapsack stuffed with Horatio Alger books and a jelly sandwich inside.

Seconds tick away and Ernest Lee frantically kicks at the inky black water. His arms swing up and down, but he's not up on top yet. Now he's in a panic, *Which way is up?* He feels his body moving along with the torrent no matter how hard he paddles. Sometimes he scrapes along on his back, sometimes on his side, but he never stops or comes up to the surface. Finally, he feels his body flow by a bush and grabs hold of it with all of his might. *God sent me this bush for safety at last. I'll just hold on and rest for awhile.* At last, Ernest Lee relaxes and rises to the surface, just like he knew he would all along. His mother waits on shore next to Trixie. Her radiant smile beckons him out of the water.

Amy's skillet sizzles as she pushes the fat fish chunks around in the hot bubbling grease. *Ernest Lee likes them nice and crispy. He'll be hungry after working so hard all day.* Little Timmy and Sally play in their playpen swatting shiny colored paper balls that Amy strung across to amuse. Amy sings to them as she tosses sliced onions into the fat the way Ernest Lee likes. She looks out the window and thinks, *It's raining pretty good out there now. The men will be running in here hungry as bears any minute.* But now she makes out Homer and Striker running up the knoll toward the house in the rain. They're hollering something, so Amy sets her pan of frying fish aside, and rushes out onto the porch.

Homer calls out again, "Ernest Lee's fell into the ditch." Homer runs hard toward the yard with the rain pelting down, but Amy still can't make out what he's saying.

"What?" she calls back, but the two men disappear behind the house, racing back around moments later with the rowboat held over their heads, moving as fast as they can.

Charlie shouts up to Amy as they pass by the house, "Call the Sheriff right away! Ernest Lee's gone into the ditch!"

Amy can't believe her ears, *Why on earth would they need Sheriff Carter? All they have to do is pull Ernest Lee into the boat.* Amy decides that she should be on the safe side, so she does as Charlie asks and rings up the operator. The Sheriff is out on a call, but operator promises to pass the message along. Amy sighs, *There's nothing to do but wait until Ernest Lee returns fhome or his dinner.* She finishes frying the fish, then trots up to their bedroom to lay out dry clothes for her husband. Then she nurses Timmy and Sally, and, before she knows it, almost an hour has passed. Amy is still nursing when there's a knock at the door.

Sheriff Carter stands on the porch with two of his men, all dripping wet in the rain. Amy explains, "Ernest Lee took Striker and Charlie up to the ridge, and the next thing I know, Homer and Charlie came back for the rowboat saying Ernest Lee fell into the ditch."

The Sheriff Carter nods and says, "We'll go down and check. Don't you worry none."

Amy calls nervously after the Sheriff and his men, "I'm sure everything's fixed up by now. Ernest Lee just got busy."

"Probably so," the Sheriff Carter calls back. He and his stone-faced men take off in the direction Amy pointed down past the barn.

Amy sets the dinner table and straightens up the kitchen. She takes another quick glance out of the window. Sheriff Carter and his men are marching back up the hill, and she runs out on the porch, relieved they're returning so soon. She calls out to invite them for dinner, but they don't answer. Hank limps up the hill alongside the Sheriff. Striker, Homer, and Charlie slowly trudge behind, arms locked, carrying Ernest Lee's limp body.

Gramps lags behind bawling like a baby.

Amy cries out, "No, no, Ernest Lee." She runs down off the porch and falls to the ground just as the wagon from Pitman pulls up in the yard.

Homer, Striker and Charlie carry Ernest Lee's body in to the house, walking past Amy sobbing flat on the ground.

Grandpa Blackwell runs over and pulls her up from the muck, but she's hysterical, yelling after the men, "How could you all let this happen? You're the ones who know what to do!" By the time they pull her up onto her feet, Amy's gasping for breath.

The men lay Earnest Lee's body down on the cloth-covered table in the front room. Charlie and Striker back away as Homer cradles his son's lifeless, wet body. A sobbing Amy gently unfolds Ernest Lee's tightly clenched fist and finds a sprig of evergreen pressed into his palm. She tenderly kisses his hand holding the bright evergreen cross.

The group keeps vigil long into the night—everyone deep in their own thoughts as they comprehend the tragedy. Brother Charles comforts, "Ernest Lee is up in heaven with our Lord—he has a plan for the faithful—it's written clearly in the Bible."

Such words may comfort *other* mourning families, but they don't soothe the Heralds today. Ernest Lee's dead body lies out on the table, and nothing anyone says will make that all right.

Homer lashes out, "What kind of God lets such horrible things happen?"

Amy refuses to leave Ernest Lee's side. Effie stays with her sister every second, stumbling through the night, nodding and agreeing over and over, "How could God let this happen?"

The next morning neighbors start travelling up the muddy roads on foot, on horseback or by wagon—anyway they can get there to comfort the grieving family as the word spreads. Ernest Lee Harold was a beloved son, husband and father, a citizen of Success and a friend to countless others he touched.

Late in the morning, a crest-fallen Hank limps up the porch stairs. He's covered with baking soda paste that the men smeared all over his bee stings, and both hands bound up in bandages.

Gramps Herald walks out onto the porch right away.

Hank says somberly, "I come by to pay my respects, Mr. Harold, and then I'll be leaving."

Gramps Herald said, "Why is that?

Hank's head hangs low. He is crying. "This was all my fault," he whimpers. "If I didn't dive in the ditch next to Blackie, Ernest Lee would still be alive."

Gramps looks up at the heavens and chokes back his own tears, "You have it wrong, Hank. It was all *my* fault for insisting that Ernest Lee come back home to Success, and Homer thinks it's all *his* fault because of his drinking, and Charlie and Striker think it's all *their* fault for riding on ahead up to the ridge. We can't *all* be at fault and leave the farm. Can we, Hank?"

Hank whispers, "No, I guess we can't all take off now. But, I still feel like it was my fault the most."

Gramps speaks slowly, "Ernest Lee told me that morning how you asked to stay on. He wouldn't want you to pack up and go because of this. Neither do I." Gramps holds open the screen door.

Hank nods, walks inside, and right over to Amy.

Amy chokes out the words, "I know, Hank. It's all right. No one meant for this to happen." She speaks loud enough so that Charlie and Striker can hear as they hover nearby.

Those traveling the farthest arrive the next day. Aunt Glory returns from her sister's in Delephan packed to stay on. Mr. Marshall and Doctor Wallace come up from Tuckerman, and so does Pastor Randolph, who doesn't intrude, but Amy knows that he's there.

It's not until nightfall that Amy asks the Pastor, "Grandpa, how did you, Brother Charles and Effie know to come yesterday?"

He replies, "We *didn't* know."

Even in the haze of her grief, Amy knows that such extraordinary timing can't be a coincidence. She sighs contentedly, "The Lord must have sent you to be with us in our sorrow."

"Yes, I believe He did send us," the Pastor answers, deciding that the news of her father can wait until tomorrow. Amy never asks at all about Grandma Gert.

CHAPTER 14
MOVING ON

Amy's not sure she heard right, "What did you say, Grandpa? I don't understand."

He repeats, "I wish I didn't have to bear the news, but your father is with our Lord up in heaven."

"That can't be!" Amy collapses into a chair in the front room.

Her grandfather details the events of that warm fall day years ago, and how Grandma Gert's secrecy compounded the tragedy. He omits the part about Buck foaming at the mouth, but he spares little else.

When Amy's anger and tears subside, she hisses, "The wretched, ungodly woman."

The Pastor doesn't contradict one word Amy says, but he adds, "I don't understand what possessed the Misses to hide it, accidental or not, but I know one thing for certain—we must give Buck a proper burial along with poor Ernest Lee." Distraught as he is, the Pastor begins planning with Amy two funerals at his beloved Pleasant Hill church.

The sad morning dawns. Amy settles the twins with Aunt Glory, and prepares for her journey. Homer pulls the Model T around, and Gramps Herald climbs up in front. Pastor Blackwell and Amy ride in the back, and she asks him as they drive off for Pitman, "Will Grandma Gert be at the service today?"

"No," the Pastor answers stoically, "…and she won't be over at the house either."

Amy is grateful not to face the woman today. Still, she wonders and asks, "Where has she gone, Grandpa?"

"She's with her sister Minnie Mae over in Mountain Home. Minnie's only too glad to be the sister in charge now and to keep a close eye on Gert—just like she did their on mother who turned the same way," the Pastor says somberly.

"What will happen to her?" Amy rasps.

The Pastor repeats by heart, "The Lord has a plan." Then, he thumbs open his old family Bible to Psalms and reads in trance-like reflection all the way to his beloved church in Pitman

Two caskets rest alongside the pulpit—one for Ernest Lee's body and one for Buck's bones. Mourners from all over Randolph County cram into the pews and spill out onto the lawn, crying oceans of tears for two young men lost so young. Amy summons up her long-forgotten shroud and watches the unreal scene play out like a silent picture show. She remains in her tearless, blank state all through the funeral and afterwards as friends gather across the street at the house.

Mr. Marshall is the last one to leave. Amy finds strength to speak with him on the front porch, "I'm not sure when I'll see you again, so I must share something Ernest Lee intended to tell you himself. We spoke about it the very morning he died."

"You mean, about the money?" Mr. Marshall smiles kindly.

"You knew?" Amy exclaims.

Mr. Marshall explains, "You see, the farmer that Ernest Lee sold that tractor to was my wife's second cousin—Norris forgot to mention that fact. The next day, when I saw how proud Ernest Lee was of his sale, I never said anything about it. Well, Cousin Norris is given to bragging, and he couldn't resist telling us what he laid out for the tractor. I'll admit, I was mighty surprised to hear how much it was."

Amy gasps, "Oh my goodness; if Ernest Lee had known. He was going to return it when…."

Mr. Marshall says, "I know, my dear. I knew he'd return it one day. I never doubted it, but now I want you to keep the money for the twins." Mr. Marshall hugs Amy and then takes off for Tuckerman, his heart broken over losing Ernest Lee who had been like a son.

196

Bleak days and sleepless nights turn into a full week in Pitman. Amy stays to herself in her old bedroom upstairs, gathering courage to begin life alone with the twins. One hot afternoon, Effie clamors up the stairs, just like old times, and plops down on her bed, "Amy, why don't you move back home to Pitman?" she asks hopefully.

Amy has given the idea some thought herself. It would be so nice to be with Effie again and raise the twins in the house she grew up in. Still, she says, "What about Grandpa?"

Effie replies, "Golly, now that you've been through so much together, I feel sure that he'll soften. He's been so much easier to live with lately—at least, he was before all this happened. Will you, at least, speak to him, Amy?"

Amy shrugs, figuring there is no harm in talking.

Effie springs off of the bed, "I'll go get dinner fixed now. Tonight'll be the perfect time to bring it up." She rushes over and hugs her sister, "Oh, Amy! It'll be so wonderful to have you back home again!" Effie runs downstairs and gets busy in the kitchen that she inherited from her Grandma Gert.

The fragrant vegetable soup boils away in the pot, and Effie's biscuits bake in the oven. She puts the bowls around on the table and calls her sister and Grandpa in for their dinner.

The Pastor barely finishes saying his blessing when Effie blurts out, "Grandpa, Amy is thinking about coming to live with us here in Pitman."

"Well, of course! She'll need to give these babies get a good Baptist upbringing," the Pastor says, matter-of-factly.

A chill runs down Amy's back. Why would he think she'd do anything less, but why *only* in Pitman?

As if reading her mind, the Pastor turns to Amy and says, "You'll stay closer to the faith here in Pitman than out there on that farm."

Amy feels her grandfather's religious net drawing tighter already. She wrings her hands together tightly under the table and struggles to breathe, just like old times.

The Pastor spots her uneasy look, and he says firmly, "At a time like this, you should *want* to be right near our church, Amy."

Amy continues staring down at her soup bowl.

The Pastor furrows his brow. "Why is there any contemplating on this matter at all?" he says, breaking into his full pulpit voice, "You should *want* come back to Pitman and raise those babies right here, Amy. You're a Pleasant Hill Baptist—I baptized you myself!"

The words explode like a holiday firecracker inside Amy's head. Before she gets under control, she blazes down a path that she vowed to never take, snapping back at once, "Well, maybe you baptized me, Grandpa, but it was for all the *wrong* reasons!" Amy glares over at her grandfather sitting rigid in his chair. She notices that his once angel-white hair looks mangy gray now, and he seems less imposing, somehow.

"What do you *mean* I baptized you for all the 'wrong reasons'?" he glares back.

Amy draws in a deep breath, "I knew that you'd never quit preaching until I gave in and got baptized right then." She points her finger directly at him, "I could tell by that pious, self-righteous look—like the one plastered on your face right now!"

Effie gasps and the Pastor looks furious, but Amy doesn't stop ranting. Rolling her eyes up to the ceiling, she exclaims, "The way you used to shame me, Grandpa—no matter who was standing there listening! Remember? You'd say, 'Why can't you believe like everyone else—it's the devil that's holding you back!'"

The Pastor slaps his napkin down on the table, shouting at Amy, "What was wrong about that?"

"Wrong? Saying that I was possessed by the devil? The simple truth was—I just couldn't accept the faith then. I still had my questions."

The Pastor sneers, "Then, why *did* you ask for the baptism?"

Amy quivers with the force of her venom, "Don't you understand, Grandpa? Because it was better than suffering that awful guilt day after day!" She tries to calm down. She pauses to think, finally whispering, *What's gotten hold of me? Two wrongs don't make a right. What's to be gained?* Nonetheless, out it pours anyway as her grandfather's grip fades, and her own strength comes alive.

Holloway Blackwell leans back in his chair, the wind knocked out of his sails, "You never said so," he says, knowing that he had never asked, either. Then, he looks up indignantly, gathering his resolve, "You mean that you don't believe in our Lord?"

"Of course, I do, Grandpa! I'm every bit the Baptist that you are. But, like Ernest Lee always said, 'God gave us a brain to think things through for our selves.' I have my own way to look at the teachings."

The Pastor ignores his granddaughter's logic, just like he has for years. He rises up from his chair and storms over to where she is sitting, determined to reach her, "I have only one mind about the Bible, Amy. It's all I ever knew—

and you should believe like that, too, just like I taught you!" The Pastor looks down, and adds one final blast, "You shouldn't have any doubts. It's un-Christian!"

Amy grins, knowing that she has him at last. She jumps up from her chair and blasts him right back, "It's un-Christian, Grandpa? What are you going to do—lock me down in the root cellar now? You think *that's* Christian?"

Effie is frozen to her chair and the Pastor stands in stunned silence.

Amy keeps on grinning at her Grandpa, almost nose to nose, anxious to tell him what she knows now is the truth—she's never been more certain. "I always wondered if God saved me that baptisim day, Grandpa—on account of disgracing myself and having doubts in my heart. It troubled me for years, but now I know for sure that he did."

"God spoke to you?" the Pastor gasps.

"He did better than that—he sent me beautiful twins as a sign. I just didn't see it 'til now." The bitter floodgates are open, and Amy keeps on talking, "For years, your narrow-minded ideas drove me away, just like they drove out my Daddy! But, I'm not afraid of you now, Grandpa." Amy knows at this very moment that she'll never move back to this house in Pitman.

Pastor Blackwell feels the stab in his heart. He figured all along that he drove Buck away, but no one *else* ever said it before. He slumps back down into a chair as the light dawns, *I lost Buck with my preaching, I almost lost Effie, and now I'm pushing Amy out, too.* However, pride prevents him from resolving the situation with his oldest granddaughter this day, so he simply asks, "What will you do?"

"I'll make a life of my own," Amy says. After putting up dinner she goes up to the bedroom and eagerly packs to leave for the Herald's farm in Success. Nothing Effie reasons or says can change her mind.

The next day, the Pastor bids her goodbye without further debating the matter. Effie tries to hold back her tears as Homer arrives and drives Amy away.

One day in August, not long after Amy moved back to the Herald's farm in Success, the postman trudges up the knoll to the farmhouse. He knocks at the screen door and calls in, "I usually leave 'em out there in the box, Mrs. Herald, but this un' looked mighty important with them official-looking stamps stuck all over."

Amy rushes out onto the porch with a cool glass of water for the postman who is perspiring profusely. She bids him, "Good day," and then takes her letter into the front room to read. She scours every word, two and three times, staring wide-eyed at the check enclosed for thousands of dollars. *I didn't know anything about this insurance,* she marvels, *Ernest Lee must have signed up.* The letter says, " It's 'double indemnity,' twice what was due because of "the circumstances of drowning." Amy chokes up. Her poor Ernest Lee worked so hard to provide—she just doesn't want it this way. She tosses the letter and check into a desk drawer and returns to her chores in the kitchen.

Amy and Aunt Glory diligently run the household for Homer and Gramps, and Effie visits quite often. In what seems like an eternity to Amy, one year finally elapses since the day Ernest Lee died. Despite her great loss, she tells herself there's a lot to be thankful for—the twins are healthy and, in four months, they'll be two. Last November, "the war to end all wars" was over, and, those that made it through, have come home. Town spirits are high, and the summer crops flourish. Still, Amy struggles to smile and get through time that drags on the farm.

One afternoon, as the sisters sit minding the twins on the porch, Pastor Rob Randolph pays an unexpected call from Tuckerman. Amy eagerly invites him inside and they sit in the front room talking on about his little white church and news from Amy's former neighbors and friends. Before she realizes it, she is telling him about her lonely life on the farm. "I can't bare it here in Success—the memories are simply too painful," she says, not looking to Rob Randolph for a solution—it's enough just to have his sympathetic ear.

"I know how it must be," Rob says, "It's been that way for me, too, since I lost my Mary. I wish I could say that it will get easier some, but I don't think it will, ever." Time flies by quickly. On the way out the door, Rob says, "In case you have any interest, my Great Aunt Ila is selling her house over in Maynard—well, it's partly a boarding house, because she rents her extra bedrooms out to school teachers. It would provide you an income if you ever leave the farm—and there's a swing on the porch for the twins," he smiles.

Amy laughs, "I know nothing about running a boarding house."

Effie overhears the conversation from out in the kitchen, and asks after Rob Randolph leaves, "Why aren't you interested in that house that he mentioned? Maynard is a real nice place to live, and it's right down the road from our house in Pitman."

Amy shakes her head and says emphatically, "No." It seems out of the question.

Much to Amy's surprise, Rob Randolph stops by the following month and, then, the month after that. Soon, she starts looking forward to his wagon pulling up in front of the Herald's farmhouse.

"I think Rob Randolph is sweet on you," Effie teases during one of her visits. The sisters sit and rock on the porch.

"Where ever did you get a thought like that?" Amy laughs, remembering back when they were young girls, adding, "You silly goose!"

Effie grows serious, "Can't you see it, Amy? He's got feelings for you. And anyway, what's wrong about it?"

"Nothing, except, it's not like that. Anyway, we're both still grieving. It wouldn't be right."

"Even widows get second chances. Especially pretty ones like you," Effie smiles.

"Me? Pretty?" Amy scoffs. "You just say that because you're my sister."

"Well, you *are* pretty. And you've been in mourning well over a year—a proper length of time," Effie nods. The two sit rocking the babies in silence until supper.

On Rob Randolph's very next visit, he mentions his Aunt Ila's house that's for sale once again. This time, Amy asks more about it. The following week, the sisters drive over to take a look at the house, riding in the Model T that Amy has finally mastered.

It's a two story, pretty white wooden house with lots of "gingerbread" trim. It sits on a corner with a church on one side and a school on the other. The rooms and windows are large, and it has front and back porches where the twins can play in bad weather and stay cool in the summer.

Riding back to Success, Effie insists, "Why don't you buy it, Amy?" You have money from the insurance. Ernest Lee would want that."

Amy mulls it over in her mind riding along, before finally asking, "Would you move in with me, Effie?"

Effie replies, "I'm sorry, Amy. I'd like to say "yes" but I can't. With all of his faults, Grandpa really needs me now—he does lots of good for his Pleasant Hill flock, and I take comfort in helping. Maybe I'll be Pitman's first woman pastor one day," she chuckles.

Amy is surprised, "But surely Grandpa can get on alone—he won't be that far away. You said that yourself."

"Maybe so, but I'm all that he has now." Then, she adds with a grin,

"And, believe it or not, Amy, I couldn't leave Mrs. Isay behind. In truth, when she gets too old to live alone in the woods, I plan to ask her to move into our spare room—maybe soon."

Amy smiles at the thought, but, still, she is disappointed. "Oh, I see."

Effie quickly adds, "But I *know* you can manage that house in Maynard alone. Look at all that you got done out on the farm! I promise, I'll help you get set up and help out with Sally and Timmy, too. Like you just said, I'll be right down the road."

Right then and there, Amy decides to move out to Maynard and be that much closer to Effie.

Homer maneuvers the Model T out of the yard and down the dirt road. Amy perches on the front seat beside him, juggling the twins on her lap and bidding a tearful goodbye to Gramps Herald and Aunt Gory standing out on the porch. All of her belongings are stuffed in the back—she's leaving the farm for who knows how long. She gazes across the Herald's rolling fields and then down at old Blackie tossing his tail in the barnyard. She closes her eyes tight trying to block out the memories, but they flood back just the same. How could they not? Horror of horrors. The funerals were over one year ago on that sorrowful day last July.

Homer turns to Amy driving along. They're half way to Maynard. "You can still change your mind, Amy. I really wish you and the twins would stay on at the farm, well, forever."

"I know you do, Dad Herald," Amy says, trying to keep her resolve. This decision has taken her months, and she won't break down now, even though the farm and its memories tug at her heart.

The nearer they get to Amy's new house in Maynard, the more Amy's excitement builds. They drive up in front and Effie stands there waving with a big smile on her face.

Homer helps them unload, set up, and check that everything is in good working order. At the end of the day he asks, "Do you need me to stay on tonight?"

Amy shakes her head, surprised that she doesn't feel afraid like she dreaded. In fact, she feels incredibly happy. Homer drives off, and Amy stands with Effie admiring the house as Sally and Timmy toddle about in the yard.

Amy sighs, "It sure was nice of Rob Randolph to set this sale up with his aunt."

Effie asks hesitantly, "Amy, you don't suppose that you and Brother Randolph—down the road.... Would you two get together one day?"

Effie had asked the very same question last week, and Amy laughingly replied at the time, "Oh, I don't think it's anything like that between us." This time Amy isn't so quick to answer her sister. She spots Rob Randolph's wagon rolling up in front, and her face lights up instantly. Hurrying over to greet him, she calls out to Effie, "Whatever happens, Eff, I can already tell—coming to Maynard was a *very* good move."

THE END

Printed in the United States
21771LVS00003B/139-342